– Book 1 –

SHADOWED SPACE

# SHADOW BEHIND THE STARS

LUCINDA PEBRE

A K DUBOFF

Published by Dawnrunner Press
Cover Copyright © 2020 A.K. DuBoff

ISBN-10: 1954344082
ISBN-13: 978-1954344082

0 9 8 7 6 5 4 3 2

Produced in the United States of America

# TABLE OF CONTENTS

# THE CADICLE UNIVERSE

Tarans are the predominant race in the Cadicle Universe; humans are a Taran sub-race. Most of the Taran sphere falls within the purview of the Taran Empire, governed from the planet Tararia by a council of High Dynasties. Earth is one of several rogue colonies on the outskirts of the Empire, separated so long ago that they have forgotten their Taran ancestry.

The Tararian Guard is the primary military force for the Taran Empire. Its counterpart, the Tararian Selective Service, includes a specialty branch with Agents gifted in telekinetic and telepathic abilities. The TSS is headquartered in Earth's moon, and its iconic Agents are known in Earth lore as the mysterious 'men in black'.

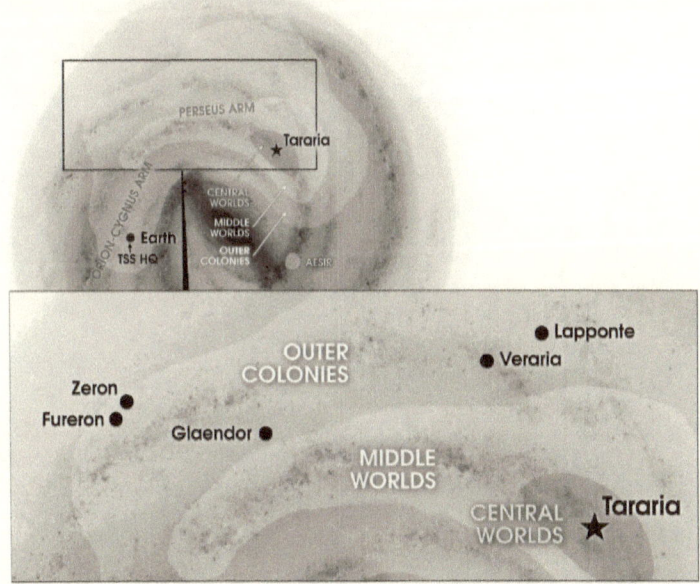

# CHAPTER 1

KALI TRUDGED AFTER Tanya, hardly noticing her surroundings until they arrived in the middle of the Primus Junior Agent lounge. Other trainees had already banded together in small friendship groups, too excited for the upcoming announcement to sit on the upholstered benches or chairs.

Of course, Tanya headed straight for the loudest circle. "Come on. Let's see what the fuss is about."

Kali rolled her eyes and dragged her feet, far from eager to engage in forced social interaction. She peered through the strands of her deep brunette hair.

Like the rest of Tararian Selective Service's Headquarters, the room was comfortable and utilitarian— not that Kali would be able to stomach bold stylings, such as her mother's over-the-top floral prints, after being away for so long. Before being kidnapped by the corrupt Priesthood when she was sixteen years old, she'd thought deep pile carpets and white furniture that stained if you looked at it wrong was how everyone lived. By contrast, she'd grown fond of the simple comforts in TSS Headquarters, particularly the trainee lounge where she liked to sit in the far corner with a cup of hot chocolate. If she ever made it to Agent, she intended to get someone to take a photo of her in that exact spot.

Kali absently began chewing on the ruined nail of her left index finger. *This has to be it.* Everyone must have received the same cryptic message to convene, which would explain why the room contained enough nervous energy to feed her anxiety to a steaming point.

Internships were coming up, and Kali knew she wasn't ready to take on her final test as a Junior Agent before graduation. A few months ago, she would have been eager for the challenge. But that was before the nightmares had started again. Before she was reminded about the dark evil that could overpower her.

She'd thought she'd put the trauma from her teenage years behind her, but memories of her time as a captive always seemed to resurface at the most inopportune times. Now, the emotional baggage might threaten her chance to become an Agent—the only future Kali could imagine.

Tanya grabbed Kali's arm with a telekinetic force and yanked her fingers away from her mouth, jarring her focus back to the present. Kali wished, not for the first time, that she hadn't asked her friend to help break her of the habit of biting her nails when she got anxious.

Kali narrowed her eyes at her tall friend, but the effort was wasted. Tanya was too busy scanning faces.

Spotting Ben, a gangly guy with pale lips and a hint of facial hair, Tanya sidled close. "What's going on?"

Kali sighed. Nobody would know anything, and they were both capable of enough wild speculation. Despite her irritation, Kali kept her mouth shut. Tanya couldn't resist flirting with any male within shouting distance. Perhaps it was caused by a deficiency in her DNA; it was only one of the reasons why their friendship was so unlikely.

Ben's eyes slid to Kali with a calculated glean, and he smiled, revealing teeth too perfect to be real. It was scary that there'd been a time when she would have been attracted to his tall frame and clean-cut image. Perhaps she should be more worried that she couldn't imagine wanting anything to do with him now.

Before he could open his mouth, she said, "Don't bother."

"I was going to—"

"I said, don't bother."

Tanya interrupted, "Seriously, Ben, she's right, you are wasting your time. You have to have heard about her reputation. Kali doesn't date, full stop. She has an allergy to having a good time and, apparently, there's no cure."

Ben's smile faded, either due to Tanya's serious expression or because he'd never been turned down before. She half wanted to reassure him that nobody had said anything bad about him and the problem was her. It wasn't the sort of conversation she was about to get into with anybody, never mind someone she didn't really know.

The door slid open, saving Kali from the effort of punching Tanya on the arm. The whole group turned toward two figures entering the room, a woman Kali instantly recognized as Saera Alexri, the Lead Agent, and a man she didn't know, also dressed in Agent black. All conversation and nervous laughter trailed away.

Agent Alexri surveyed the room, poised and annoyingly beautiful, as always. "Thank you for joining us."

Next to her, the man beamed, inviting a camaraderie that would be snapped up by the more outgoing individuals in Primus. Kali had seen him a few times in the corridors and the mess hall. He had the same ageless look of most Agents in their middle years—a youthfulness coupled with a measured demeanor tempered by life experience.

His smile was less than perfect, with a hint of something feral that made Kali think he'd tasted some of the horrors that lay outside their protected environment. It should have made her back away. Instead, she was curious.

He appeared relaxed but, like every other TSS Agent she'd ever met, his bioluminescent eyes took in every detail. It must be her imagination, but they appeared to linger longer on her.

"I'm sure Agent Alexri needs no introduction. Since many of us haven't met, I'm Andy Renteria." His voice carried out into the corridor with ease. "Anyone want to guess why you've been called here?" There was no response. Everyone waited, not wanting to be singled out as a fool.

"I'm sure most of you have already guessed," the Lead Agent added.

People looked at each other as if expecting to find an answer there. Tanya dug an elbow into Kali's ribs, causing her to let out a pained gasp. Kali dropped the offending hand from her mouth to hang limp and out of place at her side. Then without thinking, she grabbed a piece of flesh from under Tanya's arm and twisted.

Tanya let out a squeak and pulled away, rubbing the injured spot. She covered her mouth as Agent Renteria's full attention snapped to her. Shaking her head, she stepped back, and his eyes slid to Kali.

*Oh no!*

Fortunately, Ben raised a tentative hand, as if in class, but then seemed to realize it might be inappropriate and blurted, "Is it about the internship assignments?"

Kali let out a breath as Agent Renteria looked at him. She returned Tanya's glare with an apologetic shrug. Best to merge into the background, even if it was something she tried and failed to do frequently.

"That's right," Agent Alexri confirmed. "This is the moment you've all been waiting for but, a word of warning: some of you will be starting sooner than you thought. Others will have more time to prepare and become acquainted with the specifics of your assignment. Likewise, some of these assignments may take a week to complete while others may have you in the field for months. As you can appreciate, coordinating these many internships is a huge task, and this is the largest Junior Agent cohort we've ever had. So, the timing is dependent on what is available and when. I've asked Agent Renteria to assist with the coordination this year, since Agent Andres is otherwise occupied."

Kali's heart sank. She should be excited at the prospect of getting away from the confines of the base, but the thought of venturing into the outside world made her skin prickle and her head pound. The intensity of their training had allowed Kali to avoid leaving the only place she felt safe. Even then, she couldn't hide from the nightmares. Worst was the guilt, which was never far away.

She knew that she couldn't stay locked within TSS Headquarters forever. Not unless they could find her a job training the new recruits, or perhaps an administrative role. Of course, first, she had to complete the dreaded internship assignment.

Kali had scored well on tests but her aptitude had never been the problem. Though she tried to tell herself that the internship was just another routine test before graduation, she couldn't delude herself. Every internship assignment was personalized to give each trainee a chance to overcome their weaknesses. Kali could only imagine what challenges hers would present—she had so many faults.

To make matters worse, if she was going away for any length of time, she owed it to her family to let them know. Unfortunately, there was no way of doing that without actually speaking to them. She'd tried sending messages before, but her mother refused anything other than direct contact.

It still hurt that they wouldn't support her decision to join the TSS and didn't understand that she could never slip back into her old life. Why was it so difficult to understand that she couldn't think about marrying and having a family? Instead of acknowledging what she'd been through, her parents seemed keen to pretend it never happened. But it *did*, and Kali carried the memory with her every day. Just like she'd carried the child implanted in her womb against her will, genetically engineered by the Priesthood as part of their perverse experimentations. She'd been liberated from the Priesthood's holding cells, but she still found herself there in her mind in her dark moments.

Most days, she was barely holding it together in the artificially protective environment of the TSS; she would combust if she was forced into the constraints of so-called civilized society.

Agent Renteria was speaking, and Kali forced her attention back to what he was saying. "To find out about your individual assignment, look at your handheld in... three, two, one, now."

Everyone's eyes instantly dropped to their personal devices. Except for Kali, who was not so eager to see her future, which was why she caught the glance that Agent Renteria gave her before he left with the Lead Agent.

*I wasn't imagining his interest in me.*

Tanya was unusually quiet while reading the small screen, biting her bottom lip. After several moments, she lifted her head, grinning. "Lapponte, to help secure the prison and make it safe for both guards and prisoners." A thoughtful expression crossed her face. "Sounds difficult." Her smile returned. "Just think, me amongst all those half-naked men."

Despite the stress, Kali couldn't help a burst of laughter at the twinkle in Tanya's eyes. "Where are their clothes?" When Tanya continued to grin, Kali shook her head.

Finally, unable to put it off any longer, she looked at her own handheld and scrolled through the data to the critical information.

Tanya leaned over Kali's shoulder, using her height to pry. "Come on, let's see."

Kali read and then re-read the words. *No, it can't be. They want me to investigate a band. They wouldn't do that, would they? Don't they think I'm capable of something more challenging? Do they feel sorry for me?* All thoughts of staying in Headquarters for the rest of her life evaporated.

"They want you to join a traveling band?" Tanya's eyes were wide. "That is *so* my type of assignment. Are you sure they haven't got us mixed up? We do spend too much time together, it's possible..." Tanya's voice faded as a surge of adrenaline made Kali's head spin.

"This isn't fair." Kali spun on her heel and stormed out of Primus lounge, leaving a speechless Tanya behind.

A voice screamed at the back of her mind as she headed for the command wing on Level 1. *Stop!*

She ignored the inner warning. There was no way she would let them do this. Not after everything she'd been through. She'd had a few problems, but she'd worked hard, scored well on tests, had done everything they'd asked.

They'd given her a joke internship—a softball assignment, going through the motions without any of the rigor. It was too much. They needed to forget her past and stop giving her special treatment like she was helpless. If only she could go somewhere nobody knew about her past. Somewhere they didn't see her as a victim.

She let out a bitter laugh. Where would that be? Her family pretended that nothing had happened. How could she pick up where she'd left off as a sixteen-year-old? A girl who had only cared about clothes and boys and getting good grades.

Kali had joined the TSS desperate to give her life some meaning. To make up for what she'd done by refusing to become a single mother to the child she was forced to bear. The Priesthood had made her a surrogate to one of their illegal clones while she was held as their prisoner, and she'd struggled to reconcile her lack of connection to the innocent life she'd carried to term. She couldn't look at him without thinking about how his life came into being—how her own innocence had been robbed in the process.

In the years since, she'd been trying to find a way to feel secure. She wanted to be as strong as she could be, so no one could take advantage of her again. In time, she hoped she could use that strength to protect others, too. Though the Priesthood had been destroyed after Kali's time as a captive, there would always be new enemies to face.

The truth was that the TSS was the only place where she could learn to master her telekinetic and telepathic abilities. They were her greatest asset in protecting herself, even though that had been what drew the Priesthood to her as a target for their program.

As far as Kali could see, she had two choices: deny who she was and spend the rest of her life running, or embrace it and use her abilities for the good of the Taran race. *Doesn't that sound selfless?* Yet, she couldn't deny that the altruism was secondary to the fact that TSS Headquarters was safer than the outside world.

But how did the TSS repay her for dedicating her life to their cause? By giving her an internship assignment to babysit a foking *band*. A wave of bitterness washed over her, morphing into resentment and then anger. She charged toward the Administrative wing.

*It's professional suicide. You'll never work in the TSS if you march in there like this.*

The voice sounded remarkably like her mother's, and it got louder the nearer she got to Lead Agent Alexri's office. She had to ignore her own warning. If she let them treat her like this, it was the same as saying she deserved it. Then she would never get a chance to do anything. Never be able to make her life matter.

Tanya was off to a prison, for fok's sake. She would have to use everything she'd learned in training, while Kali would be at risk of... a hangover.

Kali had intended to burst into the Lead Agent's office and give her a piece of her mind, but she faltered at the door. *No, I won't let anyone take advantage of me.* She pressed the buzzer.

All dreams of making a dramatic entrance evaporated when the frosted glass door slid open to reveal Agent Alexri sitting at her desk behind a holoprojection of a mission report. "Can I help you?"

The Agent's expression remained neutral as Kali rode her tide of righteousness to stand before the desk. "Did you let me into the TSS because you felt sorry for me?"

Agent Alexri frowned, clearly confused.

"My internship, it's—"

The Lead Agent's face cleared. "Ah, yes. An important assignment."

"It sounds like a joke!" Kali blurted out.

"Have you read the details?"

The Agent's level tone caught Kali off-guard. "Well, I mean, the summary says it all. You want me to follow a band across the star system because you don't think I can manage a real challenge."

Agent Alexri rose from her seat with a sigh. "If that's how you took it, I can understand why you stormed into my office—not that I'll accept that as an excuse. At this stage of your training, you need to have better control over your actions and emotions."

Kali's head swam, but her gaze managed to meet the Agent's bioluminescent green eyes. "How else was I supposed to take it? Other people are getting sent off on diplomatic or security missions, but I'm supposed to just be a groupie for a few months. How is that a test?"

The Agent came around her desk and leaned against the front. "Kali, you show a great deal of promise, but that only counts for anything if you embrace your own worth. You're the only one here who's not taking you seriously."

Kali wanted to argue, but she didn't dare open her mouth. She was afraid of saying something she would regret.

"I want to see you graduate and flourish," Agent Alexri continued after a pause. "I know firsthand what it's like to have demons from your past coloring your perceptions. The TSS can help you move on, but it has to be something you want for yourself. If you aren't ready, then this isn't the place for you."

Kali looked down, faintly nauseated now the anger was

draining away. Talk of leaving the TSS was too real and cut through her anger more effectively than anything else could. She swallowed. "I know, I'm sorry. You're right. It's just... I don't know how to explain it. Sometimes things set me off and I can't think."

Agent Alexri nodded, her eyes softening. "I understand more than you think, but I have to make sure you're up to the job, because people's lives are on the line. You can't be the weak link." She returned to the seat behind her desk, gesturing for Kali to take one of the two chairs across from her.

Kali collapsed to sit as the strength seeped from her legs, the enormity of the situation starting to sink in. She shoved her hands under her thighs so she couldn't bite her nails.

"Why did you stop counseling sessions after your first year?" Agent Alexri asked.

Kali blanched. "I didn't find them useful."

"That may have been shortsighted. I'm sorry we didn't pay closer attention to your needs sooner."

Over the years, Kali had talked regularly with Agent Alexri as part of her Primus trainee check-ins. Agent Alexri had told Kali that only her supervising Agent would know her history.

It hadn't worked out that way. A couple of women who'd been held captive with Kali had told their stories, and everyone involved had become instantly famous. The few, including Kali, who refused interviews were considered the most mysterious.

Kali had been grateful for the protective bubble of the TSS, but it hadn't taken long for her fellow trainees to find out the truth. Their less than compassionate reactions had reminded her about why it was better to keep people at a distance. How could she possibly know who to trust? Tanya had slithered under her barrier somehow, probably because she was relentless. No one else could be considered more than a casual acquaintance.

"I didn't exactly let on," Kali eventually replied.

"I should have known better." Agent Alexri looked at her for a long moment before pressing the comm link on her desktop.

A familiar male voice answered, "Hello, Saera."

"Can you join us in my office, please?"

"Be right there."

Agent Alexri returned her attention to Kali. "I'm going to ignore your outburst for now, but don't think this is the end of the matter."

The door slid open and Agent Renteria entered. He smiled at Kali as if he expected to find her in the Lead Agent's office. As he took the second chair, the two Agents looked at each other, the telltale electrical hum of a telepathic exchange rippling through the air.

Kali sat on her hands again and waited, focusing her entire energy on staying calm.

"Kali came to me before I could send for her, so we might as well do this now," Agent Alexri stated.

Agent Renteria nodded. "The sooner, the better as far as I'm concerned." He looked at Kali. "Call me Andy. I'm not much for hierarchy."

Agent Alexri continued, "She was concerned about being sent on a meaningless mission." Kali opened her mouth to apologize again, but Agent Alexri waved it off. "You couldn't be further from the truth."

# CHAPTER 2

KALI TRIED TO sink deeper into her seat. *Was I really that wrong about my internship assignment?*

She had known it was in poor form to protest, but she'd been swept up in the emotion. Now that the initial wave of bitter disappointment had passed, she found herself curious about what might be going on.

Agent Alexri looked at Andy. "Do you want to start, and I'll jump in?"

Andy nodded. "We have reports that a woman was abducted from Glaendor. It's a planet in the middle worlds that relies heavily on tourism."

"The abduction coincided with the arrival of the band that you were so upset about," Agent Alexri interjected.

Kali mouthed, "Sorry."

Andy looked from one to the other before shaking his head slightly and continuing, "The band played three nights before leaving without a flight plan. In fact, there was no record of the ship's arrival or departure."

Kali forgot to be embarrassed as she listened. While unusual, the lack of a flight plan didn't mean anything. Not everyone liked to leave a visible trail and that might be a legitimate concern for famous artists. Kali guessed that Andy wasn't saying something.

"Is that significant?" she asked.

Andy looked at her. "I'm not sure. The local authorities appear to be policing the planet but not bothering with their airspace, and that's a concern."

Agent Alexri frowned. "While the absence of data is likely due to a lack of vigilance by the authorities on Glaendor, it needs investigating in light of the missing woman."

"The planetary authorities believe that Darlia Ferrangi was a groupie who left of her own accord," Andy continued. "That would be plausible if there wasn't a witness who claimed to have seen her following the band's departure."

"So, why suspect the band at all?" Kali asked, chewing on a particularly satisfying piece of thumb skin before pulling her hand away. "Their presence could just be a coincidence."

"Let me get to that," Andy said, "I have located four planets where they visited for a few nights. On three there were reports of similar disappearances, but we cannot be sure that they are related. I have requested more details."

Agent Alexri poured a glass of water from a carafe and held it up. Both Andy and Kali shook their heads.

She took a sip. "Those are the women we know about after investigating. The weird thing is that in two cases, the women were seen after the band departed.

"When the information was put together, it seems like too much of a coincidence. Could the band have come back for them?"

Kali pursed her lips. "If we don't know where they've been, there are probably other places that they've visited that we don't know about."

Andy nodded and glanced at his handheld. "That's right. Looking at their publicity information, The Higgs Boson Bruisers, or The Bruisers for short, formed two years ago."

Agent Alexri laughed. "They're named after Earth's particle physics theory? I suppose if they emulate Earth's music, it makes a twisted sort of sense."

Kali glanced at Andy to see that he shared her blank expression. Then, she remembered that Agent Alexri had lived on Earth while her children grew up.

"Never mind." Agent Alexri shook her head, still chuckling to herself.

Andy resumed reading, "Critics say they are loud, brash, tasteless, and play some primitive Earth music called the blues. Their lyrics are emotionally charged with tales of sex, violence, glamour, and retribution. I could go on."

"Sounds awful," Kali said.

Andy laughed. "I was just thinking about how much I'd like to go to one of their gigs." Agent Alexri cleared her throat, and Andy sobered. "I will send the details to your handheld."

"I think that's enough for Kali to get her head around for now." Agent Alexri met Kali's eyes. "Go and say your goodbyes. The obvious time-sensitivity of this mission means that you will leave with your assigned supervisor in two days. Remember, this proctor will only be there to monitor your progress and will not be able to help in any way unless your life is at risk."

"Thank you." Kali stood, eager to read the information that Andy had sent and start packing. It wouldn't take long to say goodbye to the few people who mattered. Although, she dreaded calling her family and wondered if there was a way around it.

Agent Alexri nodded. "Kali, don't forget that the purpose of the internship is to help you come to terms with any weakness. I expect you to do your best."

"I won't let you down."

— — —

Andy's eyes remained fixed on the door after Kali had gone. "She's a handful. Her proctor is going to be in for quite a ride."

"About that," Saera folded her hands on the desktop, "I think that person should be you."

"Me?" Andy let out an uncomfortable chuckle. "I've never overseen an internship before. I thought I was just helping out with the planning and oversight for this cohort's assignments."

"Your coordination of the missions has given you more insight into this particular case than anyone else. Michael's time should be freed up soon, so he can resume normal administrative duties while you're in the field."

"Still, shouldn't I have some sort of training on how to proctor an internship?"

"Yes, but we don't have the time or resources for that. Follow your gut. In the end, what you're looking for is if she's someone you'd trust with your life. That should be well within your existing skillset to evaluate."

Andy looked down and sighed. "My first time proctoring an internship and you don't feel the need to go easy on me?"

Saera let out a little laugh. "What do you really think?"

Until that moment, he hadn't given much thought to the responsibilities involved for proctors. The internship planning had been a good opportunity to catch up with Wil and Saera and to relive his best days. Still, when he'd agreed to Saera's request to help out with administration, it had felt too much like getting ready for retirement. To now have that flipped around to being out in the field, especially with someone volatile like Kali, he'd be back in the thick of it.

"She certainly has brains, and there's that obvious temper you've noted." He shook his head slightly. "But, there's also a very real chance that she might not make the grade."

"That's why I'd like to assign her to you, and you're right about her aptitude. If she graduates, she could be top of her class based on current test scores and grades." Saera paused as if unsure whether to continue. "Not many people know this, but her elevated skills may be a result of exposure to the Priesthood during her time in confinement."

Andy frowned. *What is Saera thinking?* He didn't have enough experience in this field to take on such a complicated situation. "I don't have a crystal ball."

"No, but you've put your life on the line and lost people. You know what trauma does to a person."

"It's not the same."

"Are you sure?"

"No, but..."

"You *are* the right person. Trust me, I'm good at this."

Andy smiled. "She certainly has a temper if she was willing to tackle you from the position of a trainee. Have you considered what she might be like once she graduates?"

"You have no idea. If you'd seen the way she stormed into my office, unhappy because she thought we were going *easy* on her."

Andy chuckled. "I'm sorry to have missed that." He became more serious. "I noticed that she wasn't as eager as everyone else to read the details of her assignment."

Saera leaned back in her chair. "Have you read her file?"

"Yes. Good scores, she focuses on the task and gets the job done. Oh, and argues a lot." Andy glanced at his handheld. "She rarely leaves the base and seems more anxious than she should about this assignment. Together, those two things ring alarm bells."

Saera thought for a moment. "She clearly has more unresolved issues than most."

"It's no surprise, given what she went through. Still, I don't see her temper as the root of the problem." Andy leaned forward. "I've done my homework. Do me a favor and pull up her flight record."

Saera frowned but did as he asked. They studied the figures displayed on the holoprojection.

Saera put both hands on the desk. "Stars, I can't believe

I didn't notice."

Andy nodded. "It was just a hunch, but it fits."

Saera switched off the display. "What made you suspect?"

"That kind of uncontrolled anger is almost always based in fear."

She sank into her chair, staring at the wall over Andy's shoulder. "She can't go."

"I think she has to. If not, you'll lose a promising Agent, but she stands to lose much more."

Her attention snapped to him. "What are you proposing?"

They couldn't risk Kali losing control in the outside world, not armed and in a position of power. "I don't think she's realized, so tomorrow I'll make sure she understands. Then we take it from there."

"Sink or swim?" Saera sounded distracted.

"Yep, but she's not a coward, so we'll see how she handles tomorrow." Andy touched her arm. "I'll be there to supervise."

"You think she can get over it?" She let out a small laugh. "We started this conversation with me trying to convince you that you could do it, and now it's the other way around."

"I hope she can. If not, I'm going to be the one needing counseling."

"Training in Primus is a challenge, and she's done all right so far. I guess that's what the internship is about—it'll either make or break her."

"Indeed. We need to be sure either way because it would be a shame to lose someone so talented. Besides," he smiled, "it's about time life gave her a break."

"See, I told you that you were the right person."

"I'm also quite capable of failing her if that is what's needed. The fallout of letting an unstable TSS Agent with ability out into the universe doesn't bear thinking about."

Saera got a smug expression, and he realized he was

again proving her point. He shook his head in exasperation.

"Treat her like everybody else," she said. "You know we don't play favorites based on who someone is outside the TSS."

"I've had a lot of practice with your family, no worries there."

Saera smiled. "Anyway, that's enough about business. Are you going to join Wil and me for dinner this evening, say at 19:00? Don't worry, we'll let you get an early night."

Andy laughed. "When you put it like that, how could I refuse?" He got to his feet. "If it's okay with you, I'm going to spend the next couple of hours planning out a test flight to give Kali some much-needed practice before we set off."

"Poor Kali, she won't get away with anything."

Andy had a lot to accomplish in the next few hours, and he couldn't afford for his plan to fail. One way or another, he needed Kali to realize the truth about herself before they left Headquarters and went into unknown territories.

—  —  —

Kali raced back to her quarters. She hadn't forgotten her promise to Tanya, although she would have liked to; things had just taken over, as they tended to do when she lost her temper.

She fell through the door to find Tanya waiting with her handheld on the table next to her—a sure sign she was stressed. Kali wasn't used to seeing her friend with such a serious expression and was immediately sorry.

Tanya surged to her feet. "I thought you'd forgotten! It's okay, I wouldn't blame you if you've changed your mind. I know you don't like Rabin."

"It's not that. I had to follow up on my assignment." She sighed. "A promise is a promise, even if I don't know how you got me to agree in the first place."

Tanya's eyes were wide. "You went storming in there, didn't you? Did you get thrown out? Kali—"

"It's fine. The assignment's fine. Come on, let's go see Rabin before I change my mind." Kali really needed to get it over with.

Tanya didn't need telling twice, already out of the door and leading the way before Kali could blink.

She hurried to catch up. "We're going to his quarters?"

"Chill, everyone will think we're going there for sex."

"Exactly!"

They had reached their destination down the hall in the Primus Junior Agent wing. Tanya pressed the buzzer. As soon as the door slid open, Tanya and Rabin embraced, kissing noisily as if they had been separated for a month, not a couple of hours. Kali was uncomfortable with the display of affection and hung back until she had no choice but to follow them inside.

Tanya and Rabin sat together in the middle of the sofa, both looking at her as if she held the answers. Stars, how had she become an expert in trauma?

She looked at Tanya. "Are you staying?"

Tanya frowned. "Of course."

"Are you happy for her to stay?" Kali asked Rabin ignoring Tanya's glare. Truth was, Kali wasn't happy with having Tanya witness something so personal.

Rabin and Tanya looked at each other, their answer obvious. Kali rolled her eyes and flicked a shoe off the chair behind so she could sit. The smell of stale body odor permeated the air and Kali was glad not to have to suffer living in mixed-gender accommodation.

Silence stretched until Kali was sure that Rabin was practicing an interview technique to get her to talk. She looked at Tanya, who had never been quiet for so long. It was unnerving.

Kali gave in. "I'm not sure how I can help."

Rabin looked past her at the blank viewscreen on the wall. "Tatiana wanted me to talk to you."

*Tatiana—oh for stars' sake!*

"There are people qualified in grief counseling. I think

you would find it more useful to talk to one of those."

"I was offered all that straight after Jude died, but it didn't feel real then."

"There isn't a time limit on accessing support." Now, Kali sounded like one of their instructors.

She wondered if this was as weird for him as it was for her. Tanya—or Tatiana, as Rabin called her—stared at Kali with pleading eyes, like she somehow held the answers.

It was only because Tanya had told her that Rabin wasn't sleeping that she noticed the smudges under his eyes. Trouble was, she hated having anyone in her head, and Tanya was asking her to lay herself open to someone she didn't really know and didn't like. The only reason she was considering it at all was that Tanya mattered, and she didn't like to see her unhappy.

Kali took a deep breath. "I didn't lose someone in the same way as you." She had lost a child, but that wasn't something she could talk about, not even to Tanya. "I do understand what you're going through, and it's normal, but I can't fix it. Nobody can."

Rabin met her eyes with a hollowness that she knew intimately. "But you can help?"

"I could try."

His voice was soft. "Will you? Please?"

Kali felt her head nod of its own accord and had to ignore the tightness in her throat. Before she could think of reasons not to, she allowed her telepathic shield to drop and invited Rabin into her mind.

The whole process lasted for under a minute. The intensity of the experience made offering any longer impossible. If she'd had to describe what happened, Kali would say that they shared a deep mental connection.

After they separated, there was silence. Kali's face felt wet and an intense emptiness lingered, as if she had given away part of herself.

Rabin's smile was shaky. "Thank you."

Tanya was staring at them both. "It's incredible isn't

it?" When nobody spoke, she went on, "I don't know what I would have done without Kali when my mom died."

"I don't know what it is." Rabin hurried on when Tanya poked him. "It's like being understood or knowing I'm not alone with these feelings."

Kali found her voice. "I can't do this often. It takes too much."

"I won't tell anyone." He said quickly.

Kali wasn't worried about that. She had no intention of being sucked dry by everyone suffering bereavement. They couldn't make her do it.

"You *can't* tell anyone," Tanya insisted. "I know she doesn't look like it, but Kali is too soft-hearted to turn away someone in need."

Kali spoke over the top of her, "And, you still need to get professional help." It wasn't lost on her that she was giving advice when she hadn't stuck with her own counseling—*hypocrite*.

"I will." Rabin's smile was genuine now. "Kali, thank you. I know that you didn't have to do this and you're leaving for your internship in a few days."

"That's okay. I'll have time to recover."

Tanya jumped up and gave Kali a hug. "I owe you."

Kali patted her back. "I'll see you tomorrow." It took more effort than it should to get to her feet, and she offered a feeble wave as she left.

Before the door closed, Tanya shouted, "Sleep well."

Kali sighed, there was no chance of that tonight. She would be plagued by images, dreams and nightmares of her past.

# CHAPTER 3

MIKA SIPPED WARM beer from a cracked glass and grimaced. This planet was no tourist destination.

A few days ago, they'd been sitting in a jetted hot tub, sipping 'sparkly', as Caryanne called it, from fluted crystal. *That* had been more like the so-called 'rock-and-roll lifestyle' he'd been sold on when he took on management of the band. Unfortunately, planets like Glaendor were few and far between.

The decision to stop at this dust-hole of Zeron had been unanimous, despite the likelihood that any profit would be tiny. At the first sign of protest, Luca pointed out that real artists received rewards higher than money.

Mika snorted, remembering the conversation. Those rewards must include alcohol and whatever sexual pleasures were on offer. Nobody in the band had a clue when it came to financial matters. Mika could guarantee that their collective eyes would glaze over at the mention of payment.

*How did I get to be so old at twenty-five?* He was the same age as Owen, and yet, there was a universe between them. Hardly surprising, since none of the band members had Mika's worries.

Mika couldn't help smiling as the Bruisers launched

into their fourth song—Dark Matter. The crowd shoved each other, leaping in time to the music. Their colored jumpsuits made a strange sight packed together.

He suspected that the audience didn't care what song was played, they just wanted a good time. Would the band have given up their luxurious surroundings and indifferent audience for this craziness if they'd known the truth? It didn't matter to Mika; he would still have to listen to them moan about the lack of a pool and the quality of the breakfast rations.

Zeron reminded him of home, full of rough-speaking people who were quick to laugh, just like those he'd grown up amongst. That led to thoughts of his mother. He had to believe that he'd see her again.

The crowd was smaller than last night, but they were still a rowdy bunch considering the workday started soon. Mika's attention was caught by a couple at the bar. To the untrained eye, they didn't stand out from the others queuing for warm beer. Except, Mika could see their brighter auras.

The effect was possibly due to the position of the bar lights, but Mika didn't think so. His ability was finely honed to the point where he didn't doubt his senses, even across distance.

His heart sank. He'd not expected to find anyone with a spark of promise amongst the manual workers of Zeron. It had been one of the attractions of the planet.

With a deep breath, he moved through the crowd while keeping the couple in view. A clear image of his mother in his head helped him remember why he was destroying other people's lives.

As he got closer, it became apparent that he'd not been mistaken. It was strange, though, that the woman's companion had a similar tell-tale brightness around him, as if the two had been drawn to one another because of it. Mika wondered if they were aware that they were different from their colleagues and friends. No, the Priesthood had done too good a job of repressing the potential for ability. If these people had any awareness of their abilities, it was most likely that it was only on a subconscious level.

Mika weaved his way to the bar until he was next to the woman. The bar system was inconvenient, but it allowed Mika to get close without creating suspicion. He would normally order drinks on a holo interface located at the empty tables even though it was poorly serviced. People didn't come here for a civilized chat. They came to party.

He telepathically skimmed their minds while checking on the band. Nobody was looking in his direction, if they could even spot him in the dim lighting through the crowd, but it was best to make sure. He didn't want to have to answer difficult questions later.

The couple argued in hushed voices, which was good since they were less likely to notice Mika. Their private thoughts were similar to each other, and he caught phrases, *"she couldn't have spent any time there,"* and, *"what does he want to know that for?"* Despite not looking alike, it became clear that the pair were brother and sister.

The large number of people surrounding them was a blessing and a curse. It allowed Mika to blend in easily, but any number of eyes could spot what he did and report him to the authorities. As a stranger, no doubt, he would have to prove his innocence if accused, and it wouldn't help his case that he was guilty.

He fished for the vial of liquid at the bottom of his pocket. The glass was cold and smooth as he manipulated it in his hand. Unable to get the rubber stopper off with his thumbnail, he used telekinesis. The fear of being caught and the precision of the task made sweat bead on his forehead—sweat that would stand out under the bar's spotlight.

Mika hid the vial in the palm of his hand while holding onto it with his mind. Sometimes it was more dangerous to use telekinesis to spike a drink. The sight of an object floating across a room was unusual anywhere, but on the outer planets, any glimpse would draw hysterical screams. Better to rely on alternative skills. Two drops of sweat rolled into Mika's eye and he blinked to clear his vision.

*There's always a choice.* His mother had always told him that. Strange, how he remembered a lot of the things she said, now she was gone. There was no way she'd have approved of what he was doing, but he hoped to ask her forgiveness one day.

A drunk stumbled into Mika's left side, shouting above the music, "Are you their manager?" When Mika didn't answer, the man went on, "It's just that they could do great things."

Mika grunted. *Go away. I have work to do.*

The target woman was wisely keeping her drink close, preventing Mika from carrying out his task for a couple of minutes. No matter, he had a contingency plan.

"I heard—" the drunk began again.

Mika took the opening. Turning quickly, he intentionally knocked into the target woman, jostling her arm with the drink. A spike of guilt struck him as the liquid sloshed onto her brother, who stepped back, almost bumping into somebody else and setting off a chain reaction.

The annoying drunk was still talking while Mika apologized to the woman. "So sorry. Please, here, let me help. I'll get you both a drink."

The woman was staring at her glass as if she didn't know what had happened to the alcohol. Mika suspected that the last thing she needed was another drink, but that wasn't his problem.

He spoke to the bartender, who had stepped close, anticipating trouble. "Another drink for the lady, and one for her br... friend, please." He caught himself before carelessly identifying the man as her brother—information no stranger should have. He tried to focus, but it was difficult to think clearly with the annoying man prattling in his ear.

The bartender nodded and glanced at what they were drinking, able to identify the content from the different glasses. Mika prepared for action. The drunken man was his biggest problem, but if Mika was too rude, it might draw more attention. Instead, Mika smiled and nodded, no longer making any attempt to take in what he was saying.

The bartender returned with similarly shaped glasses, one large and one small; that made it easier. The bartender took Mika's thumbprint for payment and turned away.

Mika quickly used his body to block the view of the room enough to allow him to slip the content of the vial into the small glass, then he lifted the drinks and passed them to the couple.

Both had identical smiles, showing their shared lineage for the first time. Another pang of guilt struck Mika as he saw their desire to communicate that there were no hard feelings.

The brother said something, but Mika couldn't hear him above the sound of the music, so he just nodded and smiled. To Mika's relief, the woman took a sip of her drink. That's all that was needed for the chemical to work. Now, he could safely leave.

The band would have to forgive him for not watching the entire set. It wasn't like he didn't see them every night. He sighed, knowing how they liked to analyze every detail afterward.

Mika nodded to the duo to bid them farewell and started toward the back exit. He was almost there when he remembered the annoying drunk. He'd disappeared. To Mika's frustration, he couldn't recall what the man looked like. *Come on, focus.* He shook his head to clear it. The stress was getting to him.

"Hey!"

Mika froze. He shouldn't have been able to hear the shout above the music. Perhaps the words had sounded in his head. Had he finally been caught? Did the bartender see him spike the drink?

Mika slowly turned back to face the sibling duo, cringing on the inside. They were both staring at him. Mika concentrated on the man's lips since he had no hope of hearing anything.

He mouthed, "You forgot your drink."

It took longer than it should for relief to sink in. Mika managed a wobbly smile and dismissive wave of his hand before he practically ran for the exit. Only when he was in the corridor did he let out the air that had paralyzed his lungs. He leaned against the cold wall and took four slow, steadying breaths before straightening and heading to the rooms assigned to the band during their stay.

Mika palmed open the door to his private room, which automatically re-locked behind him. He needed to compose himself before he brought up the communication interface on the viewscreen. Heart racing and hands shaking, he started the manual contact protocol.

An image of a figure robed in black appeared on the screen. Tregaren's wrinkled face, straight from his nightmares, made Mika want to step back.

"Thank you for answering so quickly," Mika said in Old Taran. It had been the only language Mika had ever heard Tregaren use, even though it would draw attention publicly. Most people spoke galactic common New Taran, whereas Mika had learned as a child to speak both.

Tregaren scanned the room behind Mika. "What can I do for you?"

Mika swallowed. He wasn't fooled by Tregaren's civility. The man could change in an instant, and he never raised his voice before violence.

"Sorry, I don't have long and will get straight to the point." Mika would not have dared lied so blatantly if Tregaren had been closer. He actually had another forty-five minutes until the band finished their set.

Tregaren's piercing sorrel eyes narrowed. "It's *my* time that is valuable, boy."

"I only wanted to tell you that I have someone for you.

She swallowed the tracking solution a few minutes ago."

"Where are you?"

They both knew that Tregaren could locate him no matter the distance. It was an unspoken threat that hung over Mika. At any moment, Tregaren could tighten his cage.

"Zeron." He paused, uncertain about the next words, but they slipped out in a rush. "It's not right to rip her from her life. Why do you want her with the Priesthood gone?" He daren't go so far as to ask whether Tregaren had taken his mother to the same place as he took the other women.

Tregaren was silent, allowing the tension to grow before his face relaxed into a smile. It sent a shiver down Mika's spine. What terrified him more than anything was the way Tregaren could hide behind a mask so completely that even knowing what he was capable of; Mika could almost believe him to be compassionate.

"It's necessary," Tregaren's eyes softened, "because the Priesthood was so effective at outlawing the use of telepathy and telekinesis. It's essential to the future of the Taran race to help to develop these women's talents."

Everyone knew that the Priesthood had suppressed the use of abilities, so what Tregaren said was plausible enough, but there were too many unanswered questions. Why did he only want women, and why not recruit people rather than kidnap them? Still, Mika knew how far he could push, and right now he'd gone far enough.

Instead of asking the question at the forefront of his mind, Mika said, "There was a man—"

"Not yet." Tregaren's voice sharpened even though his eyes remained soft. "The program is only suitable for women for now. How long until you leave?"

Mika straightened. *How did he know what I was going to say?* "Four, possibly five days." They had planned to stay three at the most. It was a tiny rebellion and would buy the unknown woman a few more days of freedom.

Tregaren's face had lost any trace of softness. "This is not a holiday. If I feel that you need more supervision, you will come to help me on my ship."

"No." Mika couldn't help the reaction, despite knowing that it was what Tregaren wanted.

*What would happen to his band if he was forced to leave the Sepiantia?*

Tregaren smiled. "Oh, I've always had a back-up plan to deal with them, so don't worry about that."

Mika tried to force down a wave of nausea; he had not spoken aloud. "The band is a brilliant cover. We get on and off of planets without rousing any suspicion. I wouldn't want to lose it." Despite the risk, Tregaren's satisfied smile prompted Mika to ask, "Who else is involved in this program?"

"You do as I tell you and hope that I don't change my mind."

The screen flickered to black, and Mika let out a long breath before folding into the large chair at the desk. He felt a husk of his former self, as if the essence had been sucked out of him. It was the same every single time, and he had to forget how bad it was to do it all over again.

*Is anything Tregaren tells me real?* He couldn't imagine why else the old man would want women. It turned Mika's stomach to know he helped to abduct them.

*What choice do I have?* If he tried to run, Tregaren would find him. There was no choice for now but to carry on selling his soul and lying to his friends. Once he found his mother, everything would change.

# CHAPTER 4

"KALI, ARE YOU listening?" Andy's voice cut into her thoughts as she stared out the window of the TSS spaceport.

"Yes, sorry," she half-lied and picked at her nails.

Andy's flight briefing didn't include anything she hadn't heard dozens of times, even though she'd now have to put more of that information into practice. *They were bound to notice eventually. Time's up.*

"You seem distracted. You need experience flying a shuttle since I'll only be with you in an observational capacity on this assignment."

"I know. I'm ready."

Truthfully, she didn't feel prepared at all. But, when she thought about trying to explain her hesitation, there wasn't anything she could say that wouldn't convince him that she wasn't suitable for *any* assignment. Best keep her mouth shut. She'd gotten away with pretending to be competent so far.

Andy stared at her. "Come on, let's get on with it. This is a straightforward practice flight. There's nothing to be nervous about."

Kali's hands shook. *What's wrong with me?* She hadn't flown much in the black, but she had done her fair share of hours in the simulator without any problems. She'd scored very well on every single flight test.

With the recent influx of TSS trainees, there hadn't been as many opportunities to get in real flight hours, but she'd made a bad habit of passing on practice slots. Being out there in the void, only a thin barrier separating her from nothingness, traveling to strange planets with unknown dangers... She hated the idea. Of course, it had been stupid to make excuses before, since there was no choice but to face her fears now—and with an Agent she didn't know watching, rather than her familiar instructor.

The voice that sounded like her mother whispered at the back of her mind, *It's more than that.* She shut it down with the same ruthlessness that she gave to Tanya when she was trying to set up a date.

Kali's heart thudded against her rib cage. Part of the problem was that she hadn't been able to shake off the last nightmare. After not having one for six months, she couldn't remember most of it. Only a crying baby and endless corridors, searching for something.

It felt as though she'd been thrown into a tank full of predators that were circling her, and all she could think about was getting out. Except, she had to pretend that everything was okay while they took chunks out of her.

Andy's voice parted the mental fog. "So, are you going to board the shuttle?"

"Right, yeah." Kali's cheeks flushed when she realized she'd completely ignored Andy's cue to begin. She reluctantly stepped aboard the practice craft, a sleek shuttle fifteen meters long with a passenger area up front and a small storage area in the aft. *He must know I don't have many actual flight hours. Why else would he make me do this the day before we leave?*

"Don't worry, I just need to know that you are competent," Andy said, seemingly reading her mind.

To be fair, she wasn't sure that he hadn't, and if he said that one more time, she wouldn't be responsible for her actions. Kali checked her ever-present mental guards to make sure they hadn't lapsed. Everything felt normal. The topic must have been a coincidence, which was a relief.

She settled into the pilot's chair and began the preparations for departure. It helped to do something.

Andy's explanation for the test flight was reasonable, but Kali suspected that it was about something more than what he told her. During her time as a captive, Kali had learned to trust her instincts. Unfortunately, knowing there might be hidden motivations didn't do much to help her prepare for whatever was coming.

"Pre-flight checks finished." She was surprised that her voice didn't shake. In fact, she sounded confident. Now, as long as Andy didn't see the tremor that had moved from her hand up her arm, she would be fine.

Andy grinned. "Let's go."

She secured her flight harness. *Concentrate, Kali. You can do this. It's nothing compared with everything else you've been through.*

Kali initiated the departure sequence. There was a slight thud when the docking clamps released, but it wasn't as pronounced as in the simulator. She checked the console to make sure that the ship had actually been fully released before she accelerated away from the station using manual inputs rather than the standard automated protocol.

They moved steadily through the transit lane between two arms of the station, with docked ships on either side. It was definitely narrower than in the simulator, even though it should be the same. Kali checked the controls and tried not to notice how it reminded her of a birth canal. She'd hear that crying baby next if she didn't get a grip.

Kali directed the ship to the training course, which was a short way from the port. Like TSS Headquarters, it was on the far side of the moon, hiding it from Earth. As the planet's space program gained sophistication, it was becoming increasingly difficult to keep the structures hidden. Advanced shields accomplished the task for now, but the time would no doubt come to bring the inhabitants of the planet back into the fold of the Taran Empire so they could rejoin their forgotten brethren. Now knowing that there were Taran bands imitating Earth music, Kali couldn't help but wonder if that reunion was on the horizon.

As she navigated the practice course, she slowly started to get a feel for the controls. They were so similar to the simulator and yet, the reaction of the ship to her commands was just different enough to make her hesitate. After fifteen minutes, she'd figured out how to compensate for the variance.

"That's good." Andy was smiling at her. "Switch to automatic pilot if you want."

"That's okay. I'm here to practice, right?" She risked a glance at Andy, disconcerted to find him watching her when he could have been checking the readings.

"What?" she blurted out when she could still feel his intense gaze on her. He'd better not stare at her for the entire trip, or she might end up rocking in a corner after a month. The thought made her want to laugh, but a bout of maniacal laughter probably wouldn't help convince Andy of her sanity.

"Just doing my job," he replied.

She felt like he doubled the intensity of his focus on her. He wanted a reaction, and the response that came as far as her throat was entirely inappropriate. For once, she stopped it from spewing out.

Kali forced herself to concentrate on flying. Even though everything appeared to be going smoothly, she hadn't flown enough to become blasé. He was right about her needing to gain experience, even if she wasn't planning on doing any fancy flying. There was nothing to worry about. She could do this.

Still, part of her couldn't escape the nightmare. She didn't need a psychiatrist to tell her what it meant. She was terrified about leaving the protected environment of the base. She knew firsthand how dangerous it was outside.

*I'm frightened.* Kali acknowledged the fear because the counselor had said that would make it go away. She was surprised to remember any of the mumbo jumbo the woman had spouted and hated to admit she'd gained anything from the sessions. Each one had taken her back to the worst time of her life.

The once-omnipotent Priesthood might be gone, wiped out by the TSS and the Sietinen family, but that didn't mean there wasn't any danger out here.

Kali took a calming breath. She was part of the TSS now. In a position to help others, not in need of rescue. She tried to relax while pressing her right thumb against her leg to hide where she'd bitten it until it bled.

Andy leaned against the console between the two seats at the front of the shuttle. "You've trained in navigation, correct?"

"Of course." She had a nasty feeling about where he was going.

"Good, because we are going to take a short jump to these coordinates." Rather than input them directly into the nav system, he displayed the information on his handheld. "A tiny jump, but the principles are the same."

With a glance at the coordinates, she started to input them. They would travel to the other side of Earth—far enough away to avoid routine satellite detection, but only just. A straightforward verification of her skills, that was all.

*Come on, Kali. You have to do this, because the alternative is living in a box for the rest of your life. Don't let the Priesthood take your future as well as your past.*

Andy rubbed the stubble on his chin. "You do realize there's a risk of us dropping out of subspace in the middle of Earth if you get the inputs wrong?"

*He is just trying to make me nervous. It's another test.* She feigned an assured smile. "All I have to do is program the nav console with the coordinates. It's not that difficult." She wouldn't allow herself to lose her temper and would never give her anger free reign ever again.

"It's good practice to always double-check calculations." He was right, particularly as her brain felt like mush. Before she could ask for assistance, Andy said, "Your internship hasn't officially started yet, so I can do it this time."

The assignment might not have started, but she sure felt as if she was under observation. "Is it true that some of the fighters have a direct neural link for the independent jump drives?" she asked, bringing up the graphical interface. Anything to take her mind off all the things that could go wrong.

The console lit up with a three-dimensional image that showed where they were expected to exit subspace. Andy shifted into a better position to see. Kali instinctively half-turned to keep him in her peripheral vision. She didn't realize what she'd done until she caught the flicker of his eyes in her direction—he'd noticed.

"The short answer is yes," he replied. "Jump when you're ready."

Kali focused on the console and initiated the jump sequence as she'd done a hundred times in the simulator. The floor vibrated and a low hum traveled through the ship as the jump drive powered up.

Outside the front viewport, the scene changed to a stunning blue-green as the ship slipped into subspace.

Kali gripped the controls, her knuckles white. She forced herself to let go and swallowed down the bile at the back of her throat. The simulator was supposed to be as accurate as real life. Now that she had something to compare it with, she noticed the differences.

Seconds later, the blue-green of subspace began to fade as they re-entered normal space after the short hop. Kali let out a relieved breath. She'd done it and they were still in one piece—easy really.

A shadow darkened the flight deck. Kali's head snapped up to look out the front viewport, horrified to see an enormous ship almost filling the window.

A proximity alarm blared out a late warning and Kali froze. It shouldn't be that close. The anti-collision safeguards for the jump exit must have failed. Blind panic stopped her cold.

*We're going to die.*

Andy was speaking, but she couldn't hear him.

Kali's skin was clammy as she filled her lungs and desperately tried to focus. The emptiness of space stretched out in all directions. She was falling into endless black.

The smell of stale sweat filled her nostrils and her left foot scuffed against the concrete floor. The sound was absorbed by a press of bodies, both reassuring and claustrophobic. The dim artificial light never changed, hiding her greasy hair and dirty nails. Her right arm hurt from where she'd banged it over and over against the composite glass wall caging her, wanting to see which would give first. The flesh was tender and sore, and she could make out the darker patch where the bruise was forming.

A baby's high-pitched cry echoed through the cells, jarring and real. If she was free, Kali didn't know whether she would run toward or away from the sound.

Andy's voice was sharp. "Kali!"

Sweat beaded her scalp and ran down the back of her neck, but he was real and solid. Andy was sitting within touching distance. Stars, she'd forgotten about the ship about to knock them into another solar system.

"Y-yes," she stammered, hardly able to get out the word.

She had to get her emotions under control or else they were going to die. She needed to live and make sure her life mattered.

She grabbed the yoke of the manual controls and pulled to port. The ship responded, but it was too slow. They wouldn't make it.

Helpless to change course, she watched as the hull of the other ship rushed toward them. She thought about grabbing Andy and running from the imminent collision, but there was no time to move. She braced against the front console, gripping it so hard it hurt.

A shudder ran through the shuttle as the two ships grazed each other, their shields and specialized hulls absorbing the impact.

It took her brain a few seconds to accept that they were going to be okay. "How did it drop us out next to another ship? That shouldn't happen!" Kali exclaimed, her hands still shaking.

"Things don't always go right in the real world." Andy was unperturbed, way too calm. "It isn't a case of switching the engine on and off. That's why we're all trained to fly."

*He knows that I've spent the last six-and-a-half years hiding. The dream last night was a warning that it wasn't going to be a good day.* Her suspicion turned to certainty. "You set that up."

When he didn't answer, she stared out the front viewport at the space that had been filled by the other ship. There was nothing now, only distant planets and far away stars. Kali couldn't see the beauty as she struggled to draw even breaths and keep from hyperventilating.

*We're safe. The emergency is over.*

Adrenaline continued to flood her system as if they were in imminent danger. This was bad. Andy had set it up to see how she would react.

She couldn't look at him. She daren't look at him. *It couldn't have gone any worse.*

Kali clenched her jaw and took a slow deep breath. "We could have been killed."

"No, the shuttle would have redirected to avoid a fatal impact regardless of what you'd done."

A familiar heat coursed through her body, and she glared at him. "There was no need to do that." Her hands curled into fists. "You lied to me! This was supposed to be about checking that I knew the basics, not seeing if I could handle emergency situations. If you had told me, I could have been prepared." She paused, realizing how ridiculous that was. "Not that I expect to be prepared for emergency situations out there, but this is different—"

This was the worst thing that could happen. Denied the chance to graduate after all the years she'd dedicated to the TSS. What else could she do? There was nothing that she wanted to do with her life.

*Get it together. He's done this to provoke you into an outburst. Don't let him win.*

She forced her hands to uncurl. There was no way that she was going to make it easy for them to get rid of her.

"You can put those daggers away." His expression was hard. "Are you aware that you've been suffering from post-traumatic stress disorder?"

*PTSD! After all this time?*

Perhaps it was what she'd done for Rabin that had brought it on, but she knew that wasn't right. The lack of sleep wouldn't have helped, but it hadn't caused this to happen.

"If you want any chance of graduating, I need you to talk to me."

"I'm sorry... it's just..." Kali trailed off, unable to find the words and not knowing what she wanted to say anyway.

"What?" Andy's shoulders lost a little tension. "Talk to me, Kali. Does Agent Alexri know how bad it is? Did you?"

She shook her head. She'd made a point of trying to blend in and pretend everything was fine since she joined the TSS, keeping her mind guarded from anyone who might see the turmoil inside. How could others know what she was feeling if she didn't show any signs? She hadn't even admitted it to herself.

"No, I knew that I avoided things," she said at last. If he wanted to fail her, there was nothing she could say that would change his mind. "I have nightmares, but that's only to be expected."

"After almost seven years?" His voice was incredulous, and she winced because when he said it out loud, it sounded stupid. "And, I bet you didn't talk to anyone about these nightmares."

She didn't answer, because what could she say? That there was only Tanya and they never talked about stuff like that.

"Tell me what happened."

She couldn't talk about it now.

"If you don't, we can't proceed with sending you into the field. I have to be sure that you're going to be safe out there. What you say next will determine whether you continue in the TSS."

Kali was incredibly tired. Whether it was the post-adrenaline crash or the years of trying to hold it together alone, she wasn't sure.

She fought to form the first few words. "When I was taken, it took too long for me to recognize what was happening." She looked down at the grey deck. "I couldn't accept that what the Priesthood was doing was wrong. That seems idiotic now." She dared to glance at him, afraid to see judgment on his face but needing to know.

Andy nodded encouragement but didn't interrupt, not letting her off the hook.

"It wasn't what they did to me that woke me up. It was what happened to the other women. Witnessing their pain and struggle." *Like Jamine, who never returned after miscarrying.* "I thought I must be dead and in hell because nothing made any sense."

A minute passed while Kali stared at her feet. The only sound was the constant mechanical hum of the ship as they drifted.

"What are you going to do about it?" Andy's voice was quieter. Too quiet, because it was the tone someone used to deliver bad news.

Her head came up. "Face it." Her response was immediate.

"Get better. I'm okay." She saw his expression and added, "I'm *not* okay, but I want to be. *Will* be. I should have faced it a long time ago."

"You hid it well. There are a dozen people who should have picked up on the signs, but your evals were all fine, so everyone thought you were resilient."

Kali let out a bitter scoff. "Nope, just an expert in denial."

Andy leaned back in his chair. "You've put us in a tough position. Resolving these kinds of issues isn't something that can happen overnight, but that's exactly the timeline we're working with."

Kali's heart skipped a beat. "You mean that I can still go on the internship?"

"That depends on Agent Alexri." He paused. "When it comes down to it, you've made it this far, which means you've already proven your capabilities. Internships are designed to test your weakness, so my recommendation will be to allow the experience to do just that. That's why it's a part of our process. It doesn't matter what's going on inside, you need to show you can hold it together under pressure."

Kali was so numb. She didn't know how she felt. Everything seemed impossibly difficult.

"This could have been avoided if you'd been honest with yourself and stuck with the counseling."

She nodded. There was no point arguing because he was right. She'd used her training to block out the pain rather than dealing with it and moving forward. Not a mistake she intended to make again.

"Can I give you some advice before the assessment starts?" Andy asked.

Kali knew that she should just nod, but a part of her rebelled against receiving any more well-meaning advice. She'd had a lot from trainers and from other trainees, most of it worthless.

Before she had the chance to cover up her reluctance

with a hasty agreement, Andy chuckled. "I know how it sounds, but it's valuable, I promise."

The worst sort of advice, but, now that she had herself under control, she smiled.

Andy's eyes twinkled as if he knew what she was thinking. "Whenever anything makes you react with rage, stop and check your body, then your mind. Ask, what could be going on that is worthy of such an intense reaction. Do that before you act, and you might find that you don't need to do anything at all."

"Okay." She meant it and would give it a try.

Andy stared at her as if trying to work out if she was sincere. She met his gaze.

He sighed. "Okay, I'll let it go for now, but we will need to revisit this conversation. Let's head back to Headquarters. I'll let you know Agent Alexri's decision. If she says you can go, make sure you rest tonight; we'll be leaving early."

Kali nodded. *Another chance.* Andy didn't have to tell her that it would be her last.

# CHAPTER 5

DARLIA'S WORLD WAS black. She blinked, unsure for a few seconds if she was awake or still in a haze and dreaming. The smell confirmed it must be the real world; no dream would smell of recycled air.

She hovered on an edge, unsure whether to be grateful or distressed that this was her reality. The air and background mechanical hum indicated that she was on a ship, but she couldn't make out any other clues in the dark.

She was in deep trouble—the sort of trouble her mother called, 'no way back woe'. She'd spent her childhood resisting that no-nonsense wisdom. What she wouldn't give for more of it right now.

The muscle of her left calf cramped. Unable to move enough to relieve the pain due to the confinement of her prison, it became more intense. A cry caught in her throat. She swallowed it down, not wanting that creepy old man in the black robe to return. Who knew what he'd do to her if she annoyed him?

He hadn't hurt her yet, but she didn't have any faith he wouldn't. Though she'd only seen him for a few minutes, there'd been nothing in his demeanor to demonstrate care or compassion for other people—cold and calculating. She had no idea what he wanted, but that didn't stop her imagination from coming up with the worst scenarios.

She'd only seen one robed man. Was he alone or were there more of the robed fanatics elsewhere on the ship? Her heart dropped. *It doesn't matter how many.* One or a hundred, she wasn't strong enough to escape unaided.

Darlia tried to remember more of what he'd said or done. It might be useful. There could have been something in his ramblings that indicated what he intended to do with her. She had a flash of him mumbling about children. Thank the stars, her own children had been with her mother when he'd got hold of her.

*My children... I need to get back to them.*

She struggled to stand, trying to lever herself up against cool metal walls. Her throat was raw from holding back tears. A strangled sob escaped as she collapsed back down.

Her daughters' faces floated before her eyes. They were both smiling—something that probably happened more than she realized.

*Please let them be safe. Don't let them find out what happened to me.*

Silent tears wet her cheeks. She was unable to keep them at bay. She didn't want to cry but knowing that her children would never know what had happened to her was too much. Would they worry? Or worse, think she'd left because she didn't love them? It didn't matter that she'd never given them a reason to believe that.

They would no doubt remember the little stuff. The things that didn't matter—like when she was mad because they wouldn't get out of bed, or go to bed, or eat their meal. Would they know that her long work hours at the casino had only been for them, so, they didn't have to go without? Or would they think it was to get away from them?

Her heart ached with regret for all the lost moments due to work and the times when she'd raised her voice. Would she ever have a chance to make new memories with them? There was so much she had been looking forward to.

Alma had her first play in two days. She'd already planned Samantha's fifth birthday party—got her the juggler she'd been talking about since she saw him at Stevie's party.

Darlia tried again to stand, feeling she would suffocate if she couldn't get more air. The walls were too close. She fought the claustrophobia that wanted to take over.

Both hands had gone numb from where she pressed them against the door; at least, she thought it was the door. It was the same as the other three sides so, who knew for sure. Whoever the robed man was, he wasn't taking any chances that she'd get away.

He had recorded her on some primitive handheld device. What was that for? A ransom? He was crazy if he thought that anybody could afford to pay anything to make it worth his while. Perhaps he thought she was someone else.

Was he recording her now? Her mind conjured more images and scenarios that made her stomach roil.

Darlia tried to steady her breathing, to make it slow and even. She managed three breaths before the urge to shout and scream almost overwhelmed her.

*Calm down Darlia. Focus on the next thing.*

There was no point in feeling sorry for herself. She had to survive for her children.

The first thing she needed to do was work out where she was. Her memory was hazy, but her body had betrayed her. She shuddered, remembering her legs moving even though she'd willed them to stop.

The surroundings had passed in a blur. Images flashed through her head, and she knew that if only she could concentrate, she would remember everything. She didn't know if she was strong enough for that. It was clearly a ship of some sort, but was she in the cargo hold or somewhere else? Where were they going?

Darlia relaxed her hands and, ignoring the cramp in her fingers, began to breathe with purpose. She filled her lungs, allowing her mind to wander like she'd done as a child.

The words came as whispers that she couldn't make out at first. There weren't many, just the occasional phrase or group of words. They didn't make much sense, but she collected them anyway: *"Zeron is a day's travel." "Time is running out." "The woman with the ability might be able to tell me." "Where is he going? He should be doing more by now." "Perhaps, perhaps, perhaps..."*

She didn't know what to make of the snippets yet, but Darlia was patient; she had to be with two small children and nobody to help.

*I'll come back to you.* They had to be okay—to believe that she would come home. She had never let them down, and she wouldn't start now.

# CHAPTER 6

ANDY RACED TO Saera's office. The consequences for Kali, whatever decision they made, were far-reaching. He was already outside Saera's door when it occurred to him that he didn't know what Kali would choose to do, if given the option. Thankfully, it wasn't his decision to make.

Saera smiled as he entered her office, although she looked as tired as he felt. "You seem stressed," she said. "How'd it go?"

He sat opposite Saera. "Why wasn't she diagnosed with PTSD when she was a new recruit? She must have been screened, given her history."

Saera pushed her chair back from her desk and sighed. "After our last conversation, I looked into it. The short answer is that she hid it well."

Andy crossed his arms. "She said as much when I pressed the issue."

"She was in mandatory counseling for a year, and it was her choice not to continue beyond. Maybe we shouldn't have taken her at her word, but she had passed every evaluation since then. The counselor did flag her lack of engagement, but that's hardly unusual with young adults. Her instructors have always passed off her temper as...

misdirected enthusiasm. I'm mostly upset I didn't spot it myself during our check-ins."

"I can't begin to imagine what she went through. She was held captive by the Priesthood for, what, eighteen months?"

Saera slowly shook her head. "If I could turn back time... Stars, she was taken by the Priesthood after we knew what they were doing to women on that island. We wanted so badly to take them down the moment we found out, but we had to wait until we had the political leverage. I can't help but feel responsible for her ever being there in the first place."

"They were sick bastards. That's not on you."

"But maybe there was another way. I don't know." Saera sighed. "Regardless, Kali fell through the cracks, and we need to do right by her now. That means giving her a good future."

Andy saw where this was going. "Proceed with the internship, as planned?"

"That very well may be the best treatment for her."

"She needs therapy. Badly. I thought she was about to lose it multiple times during our short time together."

"Did she?" Saera asked.

"Not exactly. She froze once, but she didn't lose control."

The Lead Agent sat for several seconds in quiet contemplation. "While we can't have our Agents less than a hundred percent, Kali has never shown any symptoms within the confines of the base. Your report indicated that her fear response was only triggered by a genuinely stressful situation. As part of her treatment, she would have to confront such situations anyway—albeit in a more controlled manner than if she's away on an internship. The only way for us to know if she can function as an Agent in the real world is to give her a chance to prove herself."

"It should be her decision," Andy said immediately.

Saera frowned. "Why? Of course, she would want to go."

"I'm not so sure. She knows the risks of going into a

situation where we don't have control." He took a breath. "It'll take a great deal of courage to go ahead, especially when she knows that we will have to keep a close eye on her."

Saera studied his face. "Despite treatment, some people never recover fully from that sort of trauma." She stared absently at the touchscreen desktop. "We shouldn't underestimate her determination. Stars, she gave up a cloned baby after being forced to give birth to him, and she survived to join the TSS. She has courage."

Andy met her stare. "I hope you're right, but I still think she should get to choose. She needs to feel as if she has some control over her future."

"You're right. If she doesn't want this badly enough to accept the challenge, she shouldn't be out there anyway."

Andy stood. "I'll go talk with her now."

— — —

Kali was still reeling from the day's earlier events. Did it matter that she had a diagnosis for what was wrong with her? She'd known that something wasn't right. Having a name for the disorder didn't really change anything.

Her heart lurched at the sound of the door buzzer. Since Tanya was with Rabin and their two other roommates were out studying, it was probably Andy coming by to deliver the decision regarding her internship.

She marched across the common room to open the door before she could change her mind. Sure enough, Andy stood outside, looking serious.

"Hi," he greeted.

It was only one word, but she didn't like his soft tone, suddenly sure that he was going to destroy her world.

"Come in. Everyone's out."

Andy's presence shrank the space somehow, and Kali became a little self-conscious about her sloppy dress. After a long shower, she'd only wanted to be comfortable in lounge clothes; now she wished she'd made more of an effort.

"Sorry about..." She waved a hand down to indicate her appearance.

"This isn't a formal meeting, no worries."

Kali gestured to the sofa. Andy perched on the edge, clearly not wanting to sink into the cushions and get too comfortable. She sat in the chair opposite, drawing her knees up since there was no point pretending that she was anywhere but home.

"I've spoken to Agent Alexri and we've agreed on two options." He paused. "Stop biting your nails, you'll have no fingers left."

Kali hadn't even known she was doing it. She tucked her hands between her knees and stared until he continued.

"Option one is that you begin formal treatment for your PTSD, which means staying at Headquarters for therapy and monitoring. There's a good chance that you'll be able to get rid of all of your symptoms with medication and counseling. That way, you'll have a fresh start—"

"What about graduating?" Kali interrupted.

"You wouldn't be able to graduate, although the TSS might find you a support job."

"Like admin?"

"Something like that."

She wanted to laugh; only yesterday she had fantasized about staying at the base. That was before she knew that it might be possible to fix her.

Andy raised his eyebrows. "The other course is more uncertain and dangerous because we can't control what you will come up against."

Kali wanted to scream at him to tell her. She pressed her lips together, confident that an outburst wouldn't further her cause and might make him reconsider an alternative to intensive treatment.

He met her gaze. "Option two is to continue with the

mission."

She looked down. There, he'd said the words she'd been both desperate for and afraid to hear. Now, it was real. She would have to control her reactions, and her life might be at risk. Even if it wasn't, it would feel dangerous.

*How will I react to a real threat? Will I freeze like I did today?* Kali wouldn't ever be sure unless she tried. Yet, it was one thing risking her own life, but she was going to be responsible for the lives of others. *Can I do it?*

If she didn't pass her internship, she'd be marked as a failure, even if only in her own mind. Conversely, there was no shame in accepting treatment and a new start. Even if Kali would never be an Agent, she could work toward being whole again.

In the first option, though, she would likely end up working with Agents who knew that she'd given up her chance to be one of them. First, she'd put her baby up for adoption and then she'd given up her career. She would never know if she could have done it.

Kali met Andy's gaze. "I accept the mission."

She saw by the set of his jaw that he wanted to check she was sure and had considered all the ramifications. When she didn't falter, he smiled and nodded. "Okay, you'd better get some sleep."

He got up to go, pausing at the door. "Remember what I said about checking your anger." Without waiting for a response, he slipped out.

Kali was left alone, and the last thing she felt like doing was going to sleep. She groaned, realizing that there was one thing she had been putting off. If Agent Alexri had refused to let her go, she wouldn't have to call her parents, but now, there was no more time. She couldn't put it off any longer.

She went to the corner desk in her private bedroom and initiated the call before she could change her mind. It didn't take long before the screen cleared to show the grinning face of her baby brother.

"Sam, what are you up to? Doing your homework?"

"No school tomorrow, silly." Before she could say anything, he plowed on, "Are you coming home? I miss you, K."

She shook her head. When his face fell, she felt it in her chest. "I'm going on a secret mission tomorrow."

He brightened. "Where?"

"It wouldn't be secret if I told you."

Her mother's voice drifted from behind him. "Who are you talking to?"

Sam turned his head for a moment. "K."

His eye roll was exceptionally dramatic as he turned back, and she grinned. He'd be lucky if their mother hadn't caught that. Sam was so like her at that age, it made her both happy and sad. She would do her bit to make the world a better place, so he never had to experience the sort of trauma she'd been through.

"Get your homework done," their mother's voice was loud enough to be in the same room.

He turned away again. "No, mom. I want to talk to K."

"I'm sure you do, but if you're going to roll your eyes and disrespect your mother like that, you can go while I talk to your sister." She became louder as she moved closer.

Kali couldn't help smiling at the typical banter. After running from that family life for a few years, this was the first time she'd realized what she was missing.

Sam turned back one last time with a look of desperation in his eyes. "You'll come visit after the mission, right?"

She opened her mouth to say that she might not be able to but couldn't get the words out. Instead, she smiled and nodded. She could always tell him that she had been called away unless forced to return for good. That wasn't a happy thought.

"Love you, K."

"Love you too, Sammy."

He disappeared to be replaced with her mother's face.

Kali was startled to see that she looked older. *It hasn't been that long since we've spoken, has it?*

"Your dad is still at the office. Otherwise, I'd fetch him." She touched the ends of her hair as if self-conscious. Kali didn't know why; her hair and make-up were as pristine as ever. "You're not coming home, are you?" Kali tried to ignore the pleading tone.

"No, mom. You know I can't."

Her mother snorted. "That's what you tell us, but I think you're avoiding us for some reason." She lowered her voice. "Is it because you blame us?"

*No, it's because I don't want to be reminded every five minutes about what happened.* Kali couldn't say that, so she told the same lie as she had said to Sam. "I'll come home after this mission." If she failed her final exam, she'd be going home, anyway.

Her mother stared at her for a long moment. She really did look older.

"Is dad okay?"

"Working too hard, but he won't be told. You know how he is—stubborn like someone else." She gave Kali a meaningful look.

"I am going on my internship assignment tomorrow, so you won't be able to contact me for a while." She saw her mother begin to compile a list of questions. "I can't tell you anything. No, it isn't dangerous. I'll have a supervisor with me, and we have no idea how long it will take. I'll contact you as soon as we are back. Does that cover everything?"

Her mother narrowed her eyes. "Sometimes, you're too clever for your own good, madam. Just make sure to stay safe, else I'll be coming after you. Understood?"

Kali smiled. "Yeah, and I love you too, Mom."

# CHAPTER 7

KALI STEPPED OFF the glass-sided gangway onto the standard grey carpet of a TSS transport ship. She had a single bag slung over one shoulder, containing everything she would need for the entire six months—or year, or however long it would take—until her internship assignment was complete.

At sixty meters long, the aptly named *Journey IV* was small compared to some of the TSS ships. Its lustrous hull and smooth lines made her think of an amoeba, and while it was a working vessel, it had enough comforts to make long journeys tolerable. Designed to carry up to eight passengers but small enough not to require a crew, it was ideal for this mission. With just her and Andy, there would be space to breathe even for an extended duration on board.

Kali had been so sure that her recurring nightmare would be back after the stress of the previous day that she'd been desperate enough to go to the infirmary for something to help her sleep. It was the first time, and it might have been a mistake—not that she minded taking drugs, but she didn't want it noted on her record alongside the long list of other colorful notes about her issues.

She noticed her free hand was at her lips and that she

was about to start on her nails. Now, she couldn't. Each finger was encased in a small piece of transparent silicone thanks to the infirmary, and she couldn't tell that she had them on. She sighed. It was probably the only way she would keep her skin intact.

The morning's goodbyes had left her in a funk. Tanya had acted like Kali was off on holiday, rather than an assignment that would test her fitness to graduate. Kali had barely escaped a party. She would have been happier to slip off quietly.

Kali shook her head to clear it. She couldn't quite believe she had another chance after yesterday and she was determined not to mess it up.

*What if I fail?*

Just the thought of returning to her family and their cloying concern made her feel ill. She needed to show everyone that she was not irreparably damaged, and the best way to do that was by graduating to Agent. What would happen after that, she didn't know.

The five cabins were identical, each containing two bunks. Kali didn't waste time checking them all. Cabin one was locked, and so she dropped her bag on the bottom bunk of the second and headed to the flight deck.

Andy leaned against the nav console in the center. She would have to stand close to him and didn't like the way proximity affected her brain. It was hard enough to think without the added pressure of him watching every move she made.

She bit her tongue to stop from saying anything. It was difficult to forgive the stunt he pulled, even though she accepted the reason for it. For now, she didn't trust him.

Her head was swimming. *Please don't let today be as bad as yesterday.*

Kali did her best to ignore Andy as she concentrated on plotting a course to the designated coordinates in the nav computer. The system verified the navigation beacon sequence and flashed with approval for the lock.

"Lead the way," Andy told her, taking the co-pilot's seat.

Kali settled into the pilot's chair, doing her best to suppress her nerves. *I can do this. It's just like I've done hundreds of times in the simulator.*

She initiated the jump sequence. A low rumble vibrated throughout the ship, and the stars became masked by blue-green light as the vessel slipped into subspace. They were on their way.

"Well done," Andy said.

She pushed down a wave of irritation as he leaned close to touch the front control console. Immediately, music thundered through the flight deck and she covered her ears with both hands.

"Turn it off."

Andy chuckled. "You have to listen to this. It's homework." His head bobbed with the beat. "It's the band."

"The Bof band?"

His head stilled. "The what?"

She laughed, letting out some of her nerves. "My nickname for them."

"I'm sure they'd be thrilled." He glanced at the screen. "You've got everything covered here, so I'm going to take the opportunity to relax with a little game." With that, he disappeared out the door, and Kali watched on camera as he made his way to the lounge and sprawled out.

Kali wondered if he knew how much she needed the breathing space as she turned down the music and checked the readout. Five hours to Glaendor.

Surprised to find she was feeling okay, she realized she'd been more afraid of the panic than of any evil lurking outside Headquarters ready to enslave her. *I do an excellent job of suppressing my own freedom.*

It felt like no time at all until the ship dropped out of subspace. Stars reappeared as the swirling blue-green light faded. In the distance, Kali glimpsed Glaendor encased in an orange haze. Two of its three moons could be seen orbiting close to the planet. The slightly elongated moons were smaller than Earth's moon, more reminiscent of asteroids.

*"Good job."*

Kali jumped at the sound of Andy's voice in her head and realized that it was the first time he had spoken to her telepathically—something she generally avoided. Another one of her issues? She supposed telepathy would be useful on the mission.

*"Thank you. I hope you enjoyed the flight."* She didn't manage to erase the sarcasm that came naturally.

Andy strolled onto the flight deck to stand next to Kali, too close as usual, and stare out of the expansive front viewport. They were approaching the most enormous space dock that Kali had ever seen. Andy whistled, just as the comm link sounded an alert.

Kali accepted the call, and a pre-recorded female voice said, "Welcome to Glaendor, the planet that caters for every need. From thrills and excitement to total relaxation, we have it all." Kali rolled her eyes. "Please accept our automatic docking request. We regret that for the safety of everyone, we are unable to allow ships to dock without assistance."

A warning tone accompanied a request for override. Kali glanced at Andy, who ignored her. Right, she was on her own. She couldn't imagine the TSS regularly gave over control of their ships, but there didn't appear to be another option. The warning sounded again and she reluctantly accepted.

"Thank you for your cooperation. Please sit back and relax, you will soon be on the largest leisure planet in the sector."

Kali chewed on her thumb, tasted silicone and spat it out. There wasn't anything to do but look out at the view and plan while they glided smoothly into position.

Lights reflected off leisure crafts of all sizes lining the space dock as far as Kali could see. Her jaw dropped when she saw their neighbor—it was the size of a small space station.

Andy whistled. "There's serious money on this planet."

"No kidding."

As soon as they docked, Andy escorted Kali down the gangway extending from the port to the ship. He stopped at the end. "This is as far as I go."

Kali's heart kicked up a degree at his words. She hadn't liked feeling watched and judged, but it was better than being on her own.

Andy saw her face drop and added, "I'll keep an eye on things from the ship. You're not truly alone, and don't forget that you represent the TSS and all the authority that conveys."

Instinctively, Kali smoothed her dark blue Junior Agent uniform, consisting of fitted pants, boots, and a sleek overcoat that hung to her knees. She managed a small smile as Andy headed back up the gangway. There was no time for worry because she'd spotted a lone figure headed in her direction.

Andy's voice sounded in her head. *This must be the welcome party. Be careful.*

As the man got near, she tried to make out what he was wearing—an intricate crimson jacket, complete with gold epaulets. It wasn't a practical uniform, but he was big enough that it didn't look like it was just for show. Her initial impression had him almost as wide as he was tall—not fat, more compact. He had chosen not to correct a receding hairline and yet had a carefully trimmed beard. There was a slight furrow between his bright blue eyes as he regarded her.

He stared over her shoulder at Andy's retreating back. "Is he—"

Kali straightened her shoulders. "He will be staying on the ship." She cleared her throat. "I'm with the TSS," she said, even though it was evident from their ship and her uniform. If he needed further proof, she had elected to not wear her contact lenses so the natural bioluminescence of her hazel eyes glowed brightly—an unmistakable indication of her advanced telepathic and telekinetic abilities. "I am here to investigate what happened that led to a woman going missing." She held out her hand, as was customary on the world. "Junior Agent Wietris."

Formality felt right for this situation. The security officer needed to respect her position, and she was aware of how young she must appear to him. It was best to be clear about expectations from the start.

He took her hand without any of the reluctance she'd been warned might happen. Apparently, it was best not to reassure people that she didn't need to touch them to read their minds. This man either hadn't thought about the possibility or didn't care. She gave him a slow shake and didn't get so much as a spark from him. No trace of ability.

"Jon Del-Awai, security guard for Avon Security on Glaendor. I've been assigned to assist you in your investigation." He paused, before continuing, "Although, I must make you aware that it is very likely that the woman you are investigating went off of her own accord."

Kali recognized Jon Del-Awai's name from the official report about Darlia Ferrangi's disappearance. She kept her face neutral. "Can we go somewhere more private?"

"Call me Jon." Despite the friendly gesture, his voice was cold and she decided that she wouldn't. He turned back the way he'd come. "We can go to the local office to discuss the… incident."

Kali wanted to ask about his choice of words but resisted. She knew the authorities on the planet didn't accept that a woman had been kidnapped, and from everything she had learned, she didn't anticipate that they were going to be helpful. Her trainer's voice came into her head, reminding her that diplomacy is essential when values are not aligned. *Look at me, putting all these lessons to use in the real world.*

Del-Awai's long legs carried him at a quick pace down the walkway, and she had to hurry so that she didn't fall behind. Unlike the minimalistic design of the TSS port, this one had giant screens advertising what Kali presumed were local venues and bars. Bright and too loud, the metal floor was coated to look like stone. Structural beams appeared alive with colored light flowing upwards over a glass ceiling where it merged with the stars.

When researching their destination, Kali had noted that there was no galactic police presence from the Guard Enforcers. Business tax paid directly for a private planetary security service. It raised a question as to how much she could trust their investigation, given that their priority would be protecting profit margins. It also explained the terrible uniform.

Kali didn't get much emotion from Del-Awai and couldn't think of him as a Jon. His face was stern. The man hiding behind a professional facade. If she hadn't been at the end of her training, she would have been tempted to scan his mind. Since she knew better, she resisted breaking the rules. If there was any indication that he was covering up a crime, she'd be able to justify the use of telepathy given his position, but so far, she had nothing.

Del-Awai didn't make small talk as they negotiated the busy terminal. Perhaps he was stuck with a severe face, which might not reflect his personality. Inside, she smiled at an image of him in a bright shirt, drunk and dancing in a club.

An Agent should never judge too quickly, she recalled from another one of her classes. Although, Tanya had added, "Except when there's a weapon pointed at your heart. Then you'd better judge foking quickly."

Where were these memories coming from? Perhaps she had absorbed everything she needed to know, after all. Kali was glad Del-Awai was slightly ahead so he couldn't see her smirk at the ridiculous thought.

The port appeared to be connected to the planet by a network of shuttle links, going to distant destinations. It was huge, much bigger than anything she had seen on

Tararia. Despite the size, there were only a handful of people moving under the giant dome. The colored lights cast a strange glow over the faces of those they encountered on the moving walkway.

Del-Awai must have guessed part of what she was thinking. "It gets busy when there are huge events or festivals, or when nearby planets have their holidays. You're visiting during our quiet time."

Kali was surprised when they didn't board any of the shuttles but instead took the powered walkway. Long shadows made it difficult to see far, and Kali felt the familiar sensation of adrenaline starting to build in her system. She spun three-hundred-sixty degrees to make sure they weren't being followed. There was no sign of danger, and yet, she couldn't shake the feeling of being watched. She hoped it was unfounded paranoia.

With one last visual sweep, she reached out with her mind—something she'd rarely needed to do before. Nothing. She reached for Andy, but he was too far to find without having established a telepathic link ahead of time. She felt better when she ascertained that there were no Gifted close to them.

She *was* paranoid. With a deep breath, she let go of the fear and thought about the information she wanted from Del-Awai. Unable to ask sensitive questions until they were in a secure environment, she could still plan. They needed to follow the band as soon as possible to rule them out.

Not everything was sensitive, so she started with a warm-up topic. "I couldn't find out anything about the planet beyond Glaendor City."

"There isn't anything beyond the artificial environment of the city, except for some primitive plant-life. Most people stick to the hotel complex and shopping areas."

"What about the workers? Surely they don't live there."

"Some do, but we're housed in a separate area." He must have realized how that sounded and added, "Basic but safe."

"So, you don't have much crime?" Kali wondered what disincentives there were for criminals on a planet without an active police force or prison ship.

"There isn't much and anyone caught is sent off-world." He must have seen her skeptical expression. "The planet is large, but the stable population is tiny. We are outnumbered by guests that come here for a good time, and if they commit a crime, they are returned to their home planet for trial. It's an efficient system."

She nodded, understanding what he was saying, but it didn't seem right to deprive individuals of justice on Glaendor and expect others to pick up the pieces. Still, in the interests of diplomacy, she didn't want to start a debate about anything that could interfere with their current business.

Del-Awai stepped off the walkway. "It wouldn't be unheard of for visitors, here for a short time, to do something illegal."

It occurred to Kali that a touring band was a perfect cover for criminal activity, although what they would want with a woman from Glaendor, she couldn't imagine. Possibly trafficking—but why?

"We have a suite of offices inside the port," Del-Awai explained. "It saves having to go through security."

"Very convenient." Kali thought it was a little *too* convenient and a good way of keeping enforcement away from guests.

"We don't have a central base. Our offices are all over the place. The larger hotels pay us to have a room inside their buildings. That way, we are readily available to sort out problems as they arise."

Kali was again reminded of Avon's agenda. She had the sense that Del-Awai had been coached on what to say and probably what subjects to avoid. Well, they would see about that. She had a job to do, and time was imperative.

They walked past an unmanned reception desk. Nobody asked about weapons and no sensors went off. Kali didn't mention the pulse gun at her waist, hidden by her dark blue overcoat.

They went straight to a private room that Kali decided must be used for interviewing witnesses rather than suspects, since it had plush chairs, a large viewscreen, and a central table. That was if they didn't just hand criminals over to the hotel where the crime was committed.

When had she become so cynical? *In the cells of the Priesthood,* her brain answered before she could censor it. Now was not the time to indulge in self-pity, and she had no intention of living in the past.

A drink machine in the corner kicked out a low hum. Del-Awai gestured to it but Kali shook her head, wanting to get on with things. They needed to catch up with the band soon, preferably before they left the next planet. She had a vision of chasing them across the galaxy, always one step behind.

Del-Awai smiled and motioned to a chair opposite. Kali sank into it and, acting on impulse, scanned as far as she could reach with her mind—not going deep enough to delve, but noting the two people in the next room. Neither with any ability. They weren't a real threat, but their proximity made it obvious this conversation was being monitored.

Shaking her head slightly to clear it, she thought back to a session she'd attended on interview techniques and prayed she remembered enough to get the job done. Keep it simple with a nice open question.

"Tell me what happened."

Del-Awai's brow creased and she wasn't sure whether he was annoyed or surprised that she'd gotten straight to the point. He stood. "If you'd like to wait a minute while I get clearance for you to access the file, you can read my report."

"That's okay I've already reviewed the file." Did he really think that the TSS wouldn't have access to the report or that she wouldn't have done her homework? Perhaps he wanted a reason to leave the room. "I want to find out what happened from you directly." Then remembering diplomacy was vital, she added, "If you don't mind. You were involved in the case, weren't you? I remember your name from the file."

He paused, and she saw him consider his options. If he said no, then she would ask to speak to the security guard who was involved, and if he admitted his involvement, then she would proceed to ask questions. Kali resisted the urge to point out that she only wanted an answer, not his first-born child.

Del-Awai let out a breath. "Yes, I took the statement from the neurotic woman."

She smiled, sure the unnecessary judgment was meant to rile her. "Go on."

His contempt was apparent. "The woman…"

Kali interrupted, "Lola Beri?"

He nodded once. "She called to say that her friend, Darlia Ferrangi, had been kidnapped. At first, she said that the two had been on a night out and stayed over in a hotel. Apparently, they'd had some fun with a wealthy businessman before sharing transport home two days later.

"They live within a five-minute walk of each other, but Ferrangi never made it to her house." He gave her a knowing look. "A common enough occurrence for the locals."

Kali caught his emphasis on the word locals and surmised that he wasn't originally from Glaendor. Although, thinking about it, she imagined that most people migrated to the planet to work.

Del-Awai continued, "Later, she changed her story, saying that Ferrangi had gone with the rock band and wasn't missing at all. But, and this was the strange thing, she refused to say what motivated her to make the first statement."

Kali frowned, trying to imagine what anyone would

have to gain from fabricating either story. "What do you think?"

He answered immediately and with an enthusiasm that made her wonder if he'd forgotten that they were being monitored. "It's obvious that the woman went with the band. Perhaps a jealous boyfriend or husband or whoever made trouble, so she gave the first version to explain the delay in reporting."

It was plausible, but Kali's gut told her that something was off. "I didn't think she was married."

"Ex-husband, then."

Del-Awai should know whether Ferrangi was married or not. There'd been nothing in the report, but any investigator would have checked such basic information. The husband, if there was one, should have been ruled out as a suspect before anyone else. It was basic stuff, but she wasn't dealing with a member of the Guard Enforcers. Del-Awai was a security guard, and it was likely that he'd had the same training as everyone else in his organization.

The lack of a husband in the report had led Kali to surmise that Ferrangi had never been married. There was another problem: Del-Awai didn't talk about Darlia Ferrangi as if he knew her, and he should.

Kali realized that the set up on this planet was a potential problem for the TSS, since it made the world an ideal base for organized crime. She guessed that this was not the first-time difficulties had arisen. It certainly explained the covert interest in her visit. The question was, should she let them know that she knew they were listening?

"Where did the band come from?" Kali knew this information wasn't available, but she wasn't sure whether it was because they didn't have it or if they were concealing it.

Del-Awai's tone became defensive. "You have to understand, this is a pleasure planet. It's not a place where we have a problem with organized crime."

Well, at least that confirmed her suspicions. They wouldn't know they had a problem until it was far too late. His comment about organized crime meant that discussions had taken place sometime in the past.

When Del-Awai next spoke, he was trying not to sound so defensive. "We don't focus too much on the comings and goings of guests. In fact, some guests have an aversion to being monitored."

Now they were getting to the heart of the matter. It was more important to keep paying guests happy than be effective. Kali smiled. She still hadn't decided what to do.

Del-Awai studied her reaction with an intensity that told her she was right. "So, it's not unusual not to know where the ship came from." He glanced at the wall where the screen was and stopped talking.

The gesture was so obvious that Kali would look incompetent if she continued to pretend that she didn't know what was going on. "What were you going to say?"

"Nothing really, it's just that the ship was an unusual design. I've never seen one like it before, and so it stood out."

There had been nothing in the report. "Do you have a record?"

"Of course, when the complaint came in, I pulled the footage from the docking station." He went to the large screen and activated it with a palm print before locating the file.

The ugliest ship she had ever seen filled the screen. Its elongated shape looked like some sort of sea creature with a bulbous head and a pointy snout. It didn't resemble the sleek TSS ships that she was used to seeing and it took her a moment to work out that the streamlined curves and aerodynamic wings designed for breaking through planetary atmosphere were missing.

Instead of standard grey, its brown paint did little to make it more attractive. The *Sepiantia* was emblazoned in white across the nose. Obviously not a ship that was designed in a factory. No manufacturer would destroy their reputation by giving such a monstrosity life. It had to be a hobby ship. Someone who had access to a lot of resources and too much time. That would make it difficult to locate since there was unlikely to be a serial number or manufacturing log that would identify the owner or pilot. Had she been alone, Kali would have laughed at the absurdity of the task.

The watching eyes kept her focused. "Do you have any footage of anyone embarking or disembarking?"

"Yes, some, but it's not detailed." He sounded apologetic. "As I said, our guests like their privacy, so we limit surveillance."

Kali stopped herself rolling her eyes and pointing out the dangers. She had to remain professional. They already thought that she was young and inexperienced and, if she was clever, she could use that to her advantage.

Del-Awai fast-forwarded the footage to a group of people on the gangway. Other than being able to count that there were four of them, Kali couldn't see any detail. She couldn't even tell whether they were male or female.

"Is that everything that you have?" Disappointment colored her voice.

"It is, I'm sorry that we can't be more help." Del-Awai gave her a tight smile. "I don't think this is a matter for the TSS."

Despite desperately wanting to punch him for returning to his agenda in such a clumsy way, she returned his smile. "Thank you, but it isn't for you or me to decide what is a matter for the TSS. We are both merely doing our jobs."

"Sorry, I didn't mean anything by it." He waited, as if expecting her to say something more. He cleared his throat. "I will see you to your ship."

"Not before I interview the witness." Kali took some satisfaction in his shocked expression.

His tone returned to the frostiness of their

introduction. "I didn't realize that you would want to speak to her." He looked at the screen, where a still of the ugly ship hung like a painting. "I will need to make arrangements."

"That's okay, I am quite capable of contacting a witness and interviewing her without help."

Del-Awai looked as though he wanted to disagree. "This isn't a question of capability Ms. Wietris. It is about protocol."

Kali returned his frostiness with her own. "It is *Junior Agent* Wietris, and let me get this straight. You don't use surveillance systems out of respect for your guests, yet you are willing to obstruct a TSS official in investigating a potential crime?"

"That is correct." Yet again, he glanced at the screen, as if for strength. "Now, if you were here for pleasure, that would be different and you would be treated like any other guest. But, in your capacity as a TSS representative, we have a duty to protect the interests of our guests." Again he sounded like he was reciting from a script, and he looked pleased to have gotten it right.

The surge of anger caught Kali by surprise. These people were the only organization protecting this planet, and their priorities were skewed by greed. The Guard Enforcers weren't perfect, especially out here, but they would provide better protection for the population.

"Mr. Del-Awai, I'm investigating a serious crime. What you suggest is in breach of the cooperation between our two organizations and could be taken very seriously by my superiors." She didn't get the chance to say more before the door swung open, revealing one of the faces behind the screen.

The man that strode in was big, and instead of the ridiculous uniform, he wore a fashionable suit. It was tailored to hang without a crease to his thighs, and it told Kali that she was face-to-face with a senior member of Avon Security. If she'd had any doubt, the way all color drained from Del-Awai's face would have confirmed it.

"An *alleged* crime." He made no attempt to disguise the fact that he'd been monitoring their conversation.

Kali didn't bother to pretend surprise that he'd been listening. "I'm glad we agree. Do you deny the TSS access to the witness?"

She felt a familiar heat starting in her chest, which would be her blood pressure rising. She took a deep breath and caught hold of her temper. Counting to ten wouldn't do it, she would need to count to a foking hundred.

"Jon will escort you planet-side." The suited man's face was hard. "That's how we work. If you are unhappy, Jon will lead you through our complaint procedure. But, Junior Agent Wietris, it will not help you with this case."

So, he wasn't refusing to allow her to interview the witness, which would be grounds for more than a complaint. Instead, he was going to make it difficult. A complaint would take weeks, if not months to be dealt with, which was why he had said, quite rightly, that it would not help her in this case.

Through gritted teeth, she forced out, "Thank you, Mr... what is your name?"

"Laemton." He didn't hold out his hand. "I'm glad that we could come to an amicable arrangement."

Kali made a note of his name on her handheld to be sure she wouldn't forget. "Then, I would be grateful if you would make arrangements for as soon as possible."

Laemton's eyes darted around the room before he nodded and left.

Del-Awai stood. "Just give me a few minutes. It's in our interest to get this sorted as soon as possible. I don't suppose you would allow me to bring her here?"

Kali narrowed her eyes. "You make it difficult to believe that you don't have anything to hide."

Del-Awai avoided eye contact. "I thought so. I'll arrange a security pass and transport." He left in a hurry.

When she was alone, it occurred to Kali that if she could

accept the findings of Avon it would make life so much easier. Tempting though it was, she couldn't do it. She had to find out what had happened to Darlia Ferrangi.

# CHAPTER 8

KALI SAT ACROSS from Lola Beri in a cheap room at the hotel-casino Satakumba. Lola had chosen the location; it wouldn't have been Kali's choice, given the single exit point and poor visibility. She was aware that there were a number of minds close by, but none caused her any concern.

Del-Awai was in a chair to her left, close enough that she could smell the scented soap on his skin—a floral scent that made her suspect he was married. His chair was angled toward her, as if she were his focus rather than the witness.

If he hoped to intimidate her, it wouldn't work. Andy was much scarier, and she was about to spend the next few months, or more, with him. She tried not to think about how this was her first real interview, or of the consequences of getting it wrong. It was exactly like training, except that she'd never before questioned anyone so close to tears.

Lola was tiny and child-like in appearance. Large blue eyes peered out from amongst the overstuffed chair. Kali thought she might be trying to become invisible. She remembered that Lola must have lied in at least one of the accounts, but why?

Kali smiled in what she hoped was an inviting way. "Mr. Del-Awai has explained who I am?"

Lola shrank back. Any further and they would need to have her surgically removed from the furniture.

"I'm not here to upset you," Kali tried to assure her, "but I do need to ask you some questions about what happened. Is that okay?"

Lola looked up as if considering saying no. Kali had only asked out of politeness and planned to continue regardless. She waited and, eventually, Lola must have realized that there was no choice because she nodded.

Kali rushed to get the script over with quickly. "Good. I'm required to tell you that this will be recorded for the purpose of fairness and may be used as evidence." Lola turned even paler, and Kali fought to keep an open mind. "Can you tell me about the band?"

Lola's expression turned to surprise and Kali wondered what she'd been expecting. She'd wanted to ease in gently in the hope of persuading Lola to let her guard down, but now she wondered if something more direct would have been better.

"I know this might not sound relevant, but it is." What Kali really wanted to ask was, what did a seemingly sensible woman see in a loud, brash band?

Lola's eyes lit up. "They were like nothing we'd seen before."

"What was so special?"

"They played music from the lost colony of Earth—so unlike anything else in the Taran worlds. We'd never seen anything like them. It was amazing. I wouldn't have blamed Darlia for going with them." Her face tightened as she remembered why Kali was here.

Lola broadcasted every emotion to such an extent that Kali wasn't certain whether it was real. If only she could read Lola's thoughts for a few seconds, then she could be sure.

Kali glanced at the report on her handheld. "You work here?" According to the first screen, both women worked at the Satakumba.

Lola nodded and didn't offer anything more. She probably cleaned the room where they sat and either loved or hated every minute, but which was it?

Kali barely resisted banging her head on the fake wooden table. She was going to need more time than was available to establish a rapport since Lola was either a very good or very bad actress.

"So, was it a girls' night out?"

"Yeah, Darlia didn't get time away from the kids very often." Lola slapped a hand over her mouth. When Kali didn't respond, she said in a small voice, "I don't think she liked leaving them with her mother."

Kali noted her use of the past tense. Did she know that Darlia was dead, or suspect it? And why worry about mentioning the kids unless she'd been told not to by someone. She glanced at Del-Awai, but he looked just as mystified.

There'd been no mention of Darlia having children in the report. That was a significant omission and proved beyond any doubt that there had been no thorough investigation.

Lola's eyes darted around. At one point, she opened her mouth and then shut it again. Kali waited, allowing the silence to stretch but it only resulted in Del-Awai checking the time on his handheld. At her glare, he folded his hands in his lap.

Lola couldn't be scared of him, could she? Although she hadn't appeared to take any notice of his presence, that didn't mean anything.

Kali turned to Del-Awai. "Could we have a minute alone, please?"

He didn't want to leave, but Kali adjusted her posture to make it clear that she wasn't about to back down. She couldn't take the chance that Del-Awai had threatened Lola and she hadn't had the opportunity to report it.

Del-Awai glanced around as if searching for an alternative to leaving the room. Kali waited, her determination growing with each wasted second. With a sigh, he rose and slowly left, letting the door slam shut.

Kali turned to Lola, who was wide-eyed and frozen like she was about to be dinner. "Now that we're alone, what are you frightened of?" Lola didn't respond. "Is it Mr. Del-Awai, because you never have to see him again. I can make a call..."

Lola shook her head. She cleared her throat and Kali thought for a second that she was going to say something, but she resumed staring.

"Was Darlia the sort of woman to leave her children while she went off and had adventures?"

Lola looked down and away without attempting to answer. Absentmindedly, she cracked the little finger of her left hand before working her way through each finger, one at a time.

Inside, Kali cringed at the sound but looking at Lola's vacant eyes, she would bet that Lola didn't know what she was doing. A bit like when Kali chewed her nails.

So, Lola wasn't ready to trash her friend's reputation completely, no matter what incentive there was to change her story. Kali was sure that Lola was lying, she just didn't know why, and it didn't appear that she was going to get her to talk with this line of questioning.

Kali was considering trying a more forceful interviewing technique when Del-Awai opened the door. "Have you almost finished?"

She narrowed her eyes, quite prepared to take out her frustration on the man monitoring every word and waiting to smooth over any threat to the planet's main businesses. Darlia wasn't important enough to the authorities for them to make much effort to find her.

Del-Awai ignored the hostility radiating from Kali and returned to his seat, resuming his position, hands in his lap.

Kali decided that he wasn't worth it, and turned her attention back to Lola. If they'd been alone, Kali would have asked why Lola was lying, but an honest answer could put the woman in danger. One thing had become evident, this silence wasn't Lola's choice.

Lola had relaxed slightly when talking about the band, but now she'd backed further into the cushions. The poor woman couldn't lift a drink without spilling it, her hands were shaking so much.

The reputation of the TSS wasn't *that* fearsome. Was she scared Kali would find out she'd killed her friend and was trying to cover it up? That didn't feel right. There was nothing about Lola that indicated she would be capable of such a callous act.

Del-Awai glanced at his handheld again. Kali didn't have any grounds for dragging the interview out for much longer.

She decided to be more direct. "What happened on the night of the twenty-third?"

"I told you, or I told him anyway." When Kali didn't say anything, Lola added, "I've talked about it over and over."

"I want the truth, and if I'm going to find your friend, I need to know what happened."

Something flickered in Lola's eyes. She looked at the ground and pressed her lips into a white line. There was something stopping her from talking, Kali just couldn't think what it might be.

Kali looked down at her handheld. "I have your statement here. Would you like me to read the bit where you state that Darlia was with you on the night you now claim she'd left?"

The color drained from Lola's face. At first, she didn't respond, probably trying to think of a plausible reason for the inconsistencies. "I suppose if that's what I said..."

"I have already explained why I need the truth. Lies and misdirection have consequences, and I'm struggling to understand why you wouldn't want to help the investigation to find your friend."

Kali's chest tightened, and it took her a moment to realize that the sensation came from Lola. Fear for her friend? Without thinking, Kali skimmed Lola's mind. She recoiled.

The woman emanated fear, her thoughts darting around so that nothing made any sense at all. Kali was tempted to go deeper, sure that answers were there, but it would be a violation of TSS ethics. Kali was not in dire need, no matter how much it felt like it. There might not even be a crime. She couldn't justify the intrusion and wished she could check with Andy that it was the right decision.

After that brief glimpse, Kali knew she wasn't going to get anything from Lola. "Okay, we'll leave it there, for now."

What more could she do? Lola was determined not to tell her anything, and Kali wasn't even sure she was capable of talking.

Kali nodded to Del-Awai. "We're done here."

She noted his satisfied expression and was grateful when he didn't say anything. As they left, Lola was mumbling under her breath. She hadn't displayed any of the relief that Kali had expected at their departure.

As she reached the door, Kali forced herself to say, "Thank you for your time."

Lola looked as if she'd forgotten how to speak at all, and Kali thought she was going to burst into tears. She considered trying one last time to see if Lola had changed her mind but remembered the chaos in her head.

They left, with Kali walking ahead of Del-Awai. She didn't want a conversation with him.

Andy had been right to question her suitability. She couldn't even get the facts out of one tiny woman. Something had happened that night Darlia disappeared, and Lola Beri was living with the consequences.

# CHAPTER 9

TREGAREN WAITED. IT made no sense to take unnecessary risks. He'd been hiding for so long, it was second-nature to be patient and cautious.

He couldn't see Lola Beri from this position. If she dared to move, he'd blast her pathetic hide back into the chair. After a few minutes in his company, she should know how to behave. Tregaren wouldn't show himself just yet. They might come back because they'd forgotten something or wanted to surprise Lola into telling what she knew.

All those years ago, the idiot leaders in the Priesthood had lost their way and talked of merging and becoming one. How was that ever going to be a good thing?

It didn't matter for those that had no individuality, ambition or weak abilities, but Tregaren had plans. The thought of losing his brilliant mind had made him twitch. That was why he'd chosen to go on the run, despite the risks. It had been touch and go whether he'd escape after the leaders ordered him detained.

He should be grateful to the TSS for destroying the Priesthood and freeing him from a near-constant vigilance, but their betrayal cut deep. The TSS had been set up to obey the directives of the Priesthood, not go their own way.

The Sietinen family was the most dominant of the High

Dynasties, and now that they were also at the helm of the TSS, they had too much power. Tregaren recognized the threat they posed by having command of such significant political and military might. Worse, the people had embraced them, and it made him sick. Once Tregaren had secured his immortality, he would recreate the Priesthood of old and take care of the great TSS, but until then, he had to be careful.

As expected, Lola remained frozen in place. Tregaren moved on silent feet, once he was sure that Avon and the TSS weren't coming back. His lips curved slightly as he rounded the chair and took in Lola's wide, terror-filled eyes. It was rare he got to wield power like in the old days.

She made a low moaning noise, more animal than Taran. Tregaren narrowed his eyes; he hadn't meant to break her. Taran minds were even weaker than their bodies.

Kali Wietris, Tregaren had caught the name and would remember it. She might be different. She had the ability and youth; an ideal candidate to allow him to make desperately needed progress.

More than that, Kali made his blood sing. Mika was powerful, and yet he suspected she was stronger. Mika hadn't fought Tregaren's control in years, whereas he suspected that Kali would fight with everything she had. He had to hurry if he wanted to catch her.

A shiver went down his spine. Was he really considering tangling directly with the TSS? Dangerous, but Kali was too good a candidate to pass up. Besides, she'd come here alone.

Tregaren brought his attention back to the present and Lola, who needed to understand that there were consequences to opening her mouth. He hadn't hurt her yet, because she'd been too pathetic. He conceded that the Priesthood's reputation had helped, and he'd only needed to threaten her family to turn her into a blubbering, cooperative mess. Although, at first, she'd questioned his authority. She'd been so sure the Priesthood was finished, but he would see about that.

Throughout the interview, she'd been aware that he was close, listening to everything. He couldn't allow her the space to make a mistake.

Tregaren had been ready for the Junior Agent to use telepathy. Whether she hadn't out of misguided principles or a lack of training, he wasn't sure.

Now, when he scanned Lola's mind, he found her running through every word she'd said, analyzing it for anything that might anger him. It was good that she was scared, but he had to make sure that she didn't feel safe enough to talk to someone when he had gone.

It would be easy enough to kill her, but that would raise the alarm. Even the incompetent law enforcement on this planet would investigate a death or the disappearance of a recent witness. Worse, they'd be duty-bound to inform the TSS. It was too risky.

Kali seemed too invested to accept Avon's version of events. If Tregaren hurried, he could finish with Lola and catch up with Kali before the investigation put him in danger.

Lola reminded Tregaren of a rodent, trying to remain still and small in the hope he would forget about her. Not likely. She could ruin everything, and he wouldn't leave anything to chance. She wouldn't open her mouth to anyone, not even her lover, by the time he'd finished with her.

"I didn't tell them anything!" The words burst out of Lola in a rush.

"You aren't a convincing liar." Tregaren paused, considering what to do next. "I have been wondering how to ensure that you do not talk to anybody ever again."

She shrank. "No, you said... I did everything you wanted. It wasn't my fault that..."

"It *was* your fault. If you'd been more convincing, you would have eradicated any doubt. Want to know what I think?" He didn't let her reply. "I think you want them to investigate." The desire was at the forefront of her mind. He sighed. "But, I'm willing to work with what I've got."

"I didn't tell them anything."

"Perhaps you would like to choose one child to take the blame?"

Lola was on her feet, hands balled into fists. "Leave the children alone!" she screamed.

Tregaren stepped back, unprepared for the outburst. He'd only withdrawn from her mind for a second since nothing about Lola had indicated she would resist.

The walls weren't soundproof. Anyone could hear her yelling. How hadn't he anticipated her reaction?

Her blazing eyes remained fixed on him, so he caught her surface thoughts without trying. *"He's leaving. If he goes near the children, I'll claw his eyes out."*

She was actually thinking about attacking him. He couldn't believe that she would have the nerve. He reached out with telekinetic hands and grasped Lola's throat, squeezing to cut off her air. She would never make another sound.

Her hands flew to her neck, futilely scrabbling at her throat to free the invisible vise. Fingernails left welts on her pale skin.

Just a touch more pressure and she'd be dead. It was so easy to inflict irreparable damage to the neck.

Tregaren entered her mind out of curiosity. It was full of images of children. She tried to stay on her feet and failed, sliding onto the floor as she slowly suffocated—such ineffective survival attempts. No wonder the Priesthood was like gods to these people.

Now, Tregaren remembered why killing her hadn't been part of the plan. He left the room, taking his telekinesis with him. He still remotely observed Lola's frantic gasps for oxygen as she found she could breathe again.

She would bruise. That couldn't be helped, but he didn't

think she'd talk.

It was best to go after Kali before she reached the safety of her TSS ship. *"Kali Wietris, where are you?"* He wanted to send the telepathic call out but kept it in his own head, too afraid she would answer and bring the whole station down on him.

If the area was less densely populated, she might sense him, anyway. He would check the bar in case she had stayed close to watch Lola. She might have been thirsty or wanted to talk to the fool that accompanied her, but as soon as Tregaren stepped into the bar, he knew she wasn't there. The place would have been brighter if she'd lingered.

*Wietris...* The name was familiar. Following his hunch, he sat and searched, limiting the parameters to dynastic families. As expected, he got an immediate hit.

Wietris was a Lower Dynasty from the First Region of Tararia. That explained Kali's dark hair and eyes. If she went missing, her family wouldn't have the limitless resources for a prolonged search the way one of the High Dynasties might, though going after anyone highborn was still a risk. He'd need to consider it.

About to close the device, he saw a headline: 'Kali Wietris Rescued from Secret Priesthood Breeding Program'. The photo under the headline was unmistakably a younger version of the woman he'd seen less than an hour ago.

Interesting, but unsurprising. The Priesthood had targeted women from the lesser dynasties for their strong bloodlines and more frequent occurrence of abilities than the general population, which made them ideal for incubating clones.

That settled it. If she'd been suitable for the Priesthood's program a few years ago, it was a sign that she'd be perfect for his needs, especially as his other subjects didn't have her power. The Priesthood had been in a position to be fussy about who they took for their program, whereas Tregaren had been forced to take anyone Mika had identified as having some ability.

With this new information, Tregaren decided to alter his plan to intercept her in the station. Her ship would be easy to find. Even flying covertly without the TSS logo emblazoned along the side, TSS ships were easy to pick out from civilian vessels.

Although, he hadn't dared to try and read her mind, it was obvious she would attempt to follow Mika. Tregaren would make sure that Kali Wietris didn't lose the trail that led directly to him. There was only one thing that mattered, securing what he had lost: immortality.

# CHAPTER 10

ANDY WAS WAITING in the doorway to the flight deck when Kali returned to *Journey IV*. He was doing his best to appear casual—so much so that she was suspicious. On closer inspection, his face was tight and shoulders tense.

She stopped. "Were you worried?"

"Of course not. I knew you'd be fine." He leaned against the wall. "How did it go?"

His question reminded her that she would have to explain what happened. She sighed, frustrated at her failure to get the information they needed.

"Nobody cares." She went past him to the flight deck and flopped into the pilot's chair. "The witness was scared." She paused to analyze the interview. "No, more like terrified. I used everything I could to try to get her to tell me what really happened. There were a couple of times when I could see that she wanted to, but she didn't. I was afraid to waste too much time." She stopped, realizing that she was about to defend her decision.

Andy opened his mouth and shut it again. He sank into the chair next to her and sat on his hands like she did when trying not to bite her nails.

Kali's smile was strained. "I know what you want to say—that she was frightened of me using telepathy to ransack her mind, but that wasn't it. There was something else going on. Her behavior wasn't normal. Strained. Indecisive about how much to tell me. It wouldn't take a telepath to notice that."

"You didn't look into her mind?" Andy asked sharply.

Kali shook her head, tapping at her handheld. "I won't lie, I wanted to. But in training, they drum into us the consequences of unauthorized telepathy. I just kept it to a high-level gleaning, like the code dictates."

"Sorry, it's just that I know how tempting it is."

"You think I'm impulsive, but I'm not *that* bad." She typed 'Higgs Boson Bruisers' into her handheld. Without waiting for the search results, she continued, "Of course, the planet's security force can't tell us where the ship went because they don't want to upset their rich guests by monitoring them."

Andy tilted his head. "And how are you?"

She frowned, irritated by the interruption. Noting the irrational reaction to a reasonable question, she did as Andy had suggested and tried to connect with her present physical state.

There was a great deal of tension throughout her body, but her mind was surprisingly clear. She didn't want to get side-tracked by focusing on her issues. It was much more satisfying to examine Lola's interview and try to work out what was going on.

"It's weird, I haven't felt anxious at all. Too focused on getting the job done, I guess."

Andy smiled. "Good, that's exactly what I hoped."

She grinned for the first time in what felt like ages. "You think you're so clever."

"I'm the best." He returned her smile. "Sometimes, it's about using what you've got and turning it to your advantage. There's always something you can do." He nodded to the nav console. "Where are we going next?"

"That's a good question. I'm still annoyed that the *Sepiantia* left Glaendor three days ago and nobody can tell me in which direction they headed." Kali glanced down at her handheld and saw that the search results had loaded. "Ah, *there* you are." She smiled up at Andy. "We're off to Zeron to see The Higgs Boson Bruisers. It seems that they advertise where they're playing next."

Andy smiled back. "Good thinking." Then more seriously, he added, "Although, I'm not sure why they would announce their whereabouts unless they're legitimate." He clamped his mouth shut.

Kali was getting used to identifying when he wanted to say more, but she knew he was walking a fine line between strictly observing and wanting to successfully complete the mission. "Perhaps they're stupid," she offered. "Or, they might be trying hard to appear as if they have nothing to hide."

Andy nodded, and she could see from his expression that he was fighting not to say anything that might be interpreted as assistance.

"Perhaps I should go back without Del-Awai and see Lola again, just in case he made her nervous." Even as she said it, she knew he hadn't been the problem.

"It's up to you," Andy said the words carefully, as if they might tell her what to do.

He pulled out his own handheld, probably to write a report about her. Still, talking it through had been useful and she'd got more information than she'd initially thought.

"No, I think it's more important to rule out the band in case they have the victim." Andy didn't look up so, she knew it was the right decision.

Kali found information about Zeron much more limited than Glaendor, probably because Zeron's visitor numbers were vastly lower.

"Zeron. An archaeological colony, about two hours' jump from here—very different from Glaendor. According to the promo, the Bofs are playing three nights. We should catch them."

"Archaeology? As in digging out the remains of an ancient civilization?"

Kali scanned for more details because Andy was correct, that didn't make sense. She laughed. "No, they're digging deep into the planet's core to study its formation. Apparently, it has some unusual properties, but that's not what they do now."

"So, it was a mining colony?"

"If you want to call it that, go ahead. Personally, I think a mining colony might be more useful." She didn't lift her gaze from the device. "I'm trying to find out who's rich enough to indulge in the sort of research that's going to lose them more than the net worth of Tararia. It sounds like a pet project."

"I wouldn't bother. The super-rich know how to cover their tracks. How does the planet make a living now?"

Kali gave up searching. "Apparently, once they'd dug out a load of tunnels, they used them for food production. Even more conveniently, there was a whole workforce in need of employment. So, basically, it's one huge factory."

"Underground food production?"

Kali frowned as she read, "Some sort of bacteria that likes dark, damp conditions to produce edible protein."

"It sounds delicious. I'll treat you to dinner while we're there."

Kali grimaced. "It can't be worse than what the Priesthood fed me." She shuddered, quickly shaking off the memory. "Oh, by the way, I managed to get Del-Awai to reluctantly agree to send me a copy of his updated report, but I wouldn't put it past him to fudge things."

"Well done. I'll get someone to check their systems for the real copy."

She frowned. "Are you allowed to do that? Won't it be interpreted as helping?"

"Perhaps, but there's a woman's life hanging in the balance here."

Kali felt herself blanch. "Don't remind me. I feel like she

needs someone with more skills than me to work on her case."

Andy looked over at her. "Don't sell yourself short. You discovered that the witness was unreliable. Did you get a sense that she was making the whole thing up?"

"No. I caught... it was on the surface. I couldn't stop from catching an impression of her concern for her friend. I don't think she could have faked that. Also, she was really uncomfortable—like telling me anything went against her moral code or something."

"Okay, so something happened that made the witness back-track on her original interview, and it was significant enough to make her lie."

"That's how it felt."

Andy looked thoughtful. "I have a bad feeling about this."

Kali knew what he meant. *What sort of threat would make Lola abandon finding her friend?*

# CHAPTER 11

EACH BANG ON Mika's door drove a spike of pain into his head. He dove out of the shower, cursing as water sprayed the mirror in the tiny cubicle. His arm hit the sink, eliciting another swear. With one hand clutching a towel at his waist, he left a trail of wet footprints across the carpet.

After checking the video screen, he yanked the door open. "Stars, Owen, what is it now? I only left you guys five minutes ago." His attention moved to the half-empty whiskey bottle dangling at Owen's side, and he sighed. "You cannot have drunk the entire bottle since I left you."

*Trying to manage them is worse than babysitting children.*

Behind Owen, Luca leaned against the wall as if needing support to remain on his feet, but Mika knew from experience that it wasn't so easy to tell when Luca was under the influence. He had a habit of appearing drunk when sober, and sober right up until the point he collapsed.

"I thought the whiskey might help, man, with what I've got to tell you," Owen said.

An elderly couple walked past the door, peering in at Mika's mostly naked body. The woman gasped and put her hand over her mouth. They didn't look like the club's usual clientele, and Mika could only imagine why they were slumming at this end of the planet.

Luca grinned. "Don't burst his bubble, lady."

"Come in before we get arrested." Mika moved away from the door to give them room.

Owen opened his mouth but stopped when Mika held up a hand. "Not until I'm dressed." He headed back into the bathroom cubicle. "Owen, don't start with a statement like that. I need more preparation time."

"But..."

The bathroom door slammed shut, cutting off the rest of Owen's response.

Mika muttered to himself while dressing. What with the headache and his other worries, he didn't have the patience today.

*How did I end up on a backward planet in charge of a bunch of crazy idiots, trying to avoid doing what Tregaren wants?*

He had just decided to dry his hair before facing whatever problems the painful pair needed him to sort out when someone banged on the door.

Mika snatched it open. "Owen, what..."

"You need to hurry your ass up, is what." Owen offered the whiskey bottle to Mika—tempting, but he shook his head. "We need to go get Caryanne," Owen continued.

Mika knew what that meant. "You left her alone while she was wasted?"

"Hey, she was still conscious when we came to find you, and you know how she gets if you try to get between her and alcohol."

"Scared of a little, itty-bitty woman?" Luca jested from the chair in the corner, where he had a leg hooked over one arm.

Mika averted his eyes. He didn't need the sight of Luca's manhood outlined in the impossibly tight jeans burned onto his retinas.

"Too foking right. I didn't see you wrestling the glass from her hand."

Luca smiled, staring at his cowboy-booted toes. Mika wanted to slap them both, but he knew from experience that getting angry would be a waste of time and energy.

Knowing better than to leave them alone in his room, Mika gestured to the door. "What are we waiting for?"

Owen led the way out, while Luca lurched to his feet and then very deliberately put one foot in front of the other. Mika watched, fascinated as Luca made his slow, torturous way to the corridor. If he wasn't drunk, he deserved an award for best actor.

Mika made sure the door was locked. "Go lie down, Luca. You look like you need the rest."

"Can't, there's a girl."

Mika pressed his lips together to stop from responding. Trouble often started with a sentence like that. Later, it would be followed by, "I didn't know her father was anyone important", or "I didn't know her friend was the jealous type", or "what time was I supposed to be onstage?" Still, Mika would deal with one problem at a time, because when Luca was like this, there was no explaining it in a way he'd understand.

Mika conceded that he might have been doing this whole band management thing wrong. Was there such a thing as a 'Crazy Band Management course'? Until he found one, he had no choice but to make things up as he went along.

The Bruisers were his first band and almost certainly last. He wasn't sure how he'd fallen into the job, except there had been a need and he met it. He'd had a ship and wanted to travel, and the Bruisers had to get around to gig. They hadn't told him that his job description included being the only person taking responsibility for everything that went wrong.

Except for Honk, the band members spent their off-time boozing and abusing whatever substances were available, wherever they happened to be at the time. They'd watched too many vids of the Earth bands they emulated.

Mika had tried to explain that Earth bands probably

wouldn't do those things if they had the technological sophistication of the Taran people. Stars, most of the wild lifestyle depicted in the vids was probably exaggerated. Mika had pointed out that Keith Richards couldn't have taken the vast quantity of substances he claimed and have lived for so long, but they wouldn't listen. The vids were the band's blueprint.

Caryanne was different. With her, drugs and alcohol were an illness. She could only go a few days before obliterating herself with whatever substance was available. It acted as a reset, and she would be okay afterward.

Mika had hoped that she would last until they left Zeron; one of his many fantasies. Her self-destructive cycle wasn't sustainable but trying to stage an intervention mid-tour would be an even bigger disaster. Between the five band members, the clock was always ticking down to the next crisis.

"What have you done this time?" Mika muttered under his breath as he stalked ahead down the narrow corridor.

"It wasn't us, man," Owen thought the question was meant for him. "This dude in the bar challenged Caryanne to a drinking game. I really don't think she's going to be good to go on tonight. Perhaps if we force her to puke, we might have a chance." In a quieter voice, he added, "Or, if we get her to the infirmary."

Mika gave Owen a hard stare. "You think that they're going to entertain a drunken guitarist in the infirmary? They would charge more than we've made before they'd agree to treat her. Then they'd probably charge extra just to make sure she never did it again."

"I know, I know. It's just, you know Honk won't go on without all of us."

"We'll have to sort her out the old-fashioned way." Mika increased his speed.

Luca caught up. "What's that?"

Mika stopped and decided that Luca was sober enough

despite his meandering gait. "Lots of black coffee."

Owen and Luca shared a skeptical look.

Mika shook his head and hurried on. They were probably right, but it was the same problem every single time, and he wanted to avoid having the same foking argument.

The band needed to play without Caryanne. It wouldn't be perfect without a guitarist, but it would be good enough.

Stars, he could stand-in for her, but apparently, he wasn't cool enough, nor was his musical ability good enough. He resolved to learn to play all the instruments to avoid dealing with the same problem, time and time again.

Perhaps a decent manager wouldn't tell them to play any shite, knowing the Zeron audience would love it, regardless. They would dance, clap and, most importantly, buy drinks.

The trouble was these guys took their music way too seriously. They talked about making art as if that absolved them from earning a living. Mika snorted. He wasn't sure where drinking, drugging, and fornicating fitted into making art.

He was used to tiptoeing around their sensitive personalities, but he wasn't in the mood today—not after his conversation with Tregaren last night. There were too many things that could go wrong, and he wanted them all to grow up.

His gut told him that they needed to move on sooner rather than later, even if that meant letting Tregaren have the woman he'd found. The isotope would stay in her system for some time, but they had to be gone before Tregaren reached the planet. If not, their cover would be at risk, and someone might start to ask questions.

Mika's chest tightened. What did Tregaren do with the women Mika identified for him? That same question bothered him, more and more.

The trouble was, they had committed to play another night, and the band wanted a night off. Fortunately, the venue wasn't fussy about which nights they played as long as they brought in enough business to make a profit.

Mika heard raised voices before he reached the bar. As he rounded the corner, he saw Caryanne leaning on... no, more like collapsed, across a table. Three people stood around her, and he only recognized one—the bar manager. Great, they would be lucky if they didn't get kicked out.

The manager raised his eyes until his brows disappeared into his hairline. He shook his head slightly as if unable to believe what he was seeing and pursed his lips.

Mika took a deep breath and smiled. "Surely, this isn't the first time you've had to deal with someone who's out of it?"

The man, whose name Mika had forgotten, nodded. "It's not, but I don't usually employ them, and never so early in the afternoon." He checked the time on his handheld. "Isn't she due on-stage tonight?" He tugged on her arm but didn't get a response. "Don't tell me you don't need her. I saw the band last night, and they weren't all that great even with all five."

Mika couldn't help grinding his teeth. There wasn't anything he could say. Best just to get Caryanne out of sight.

"What's that about our music?" Owen squared up to the manager, who Mika now noticed had arms like he bench-pressed a shuttle or two before work.

Mika sighed. It had been a mistake not to insist that Owen and Luca return to their room. Now, he would pay the price.

"Do you want to give her another shot?" the bartender asked, his face hidden behind a grey beard so that Mika couldn't tell if he was serious or not. "Might revive her."

"What?" Mika wondered why he was proposing more alcohol. "No more shots. She's had enough."

The bartender sauntered over. "It's okay. Don't worry, we do this all the time."

# CHAPTER 12

ANDY WAITED UNTIL they had docked at Zeron's capital station to suggest Kali get some sleep. She needed to be fresh before her next challenge. Plus, it was an opportunity to contact Saera in private. He stood in front of the viewscreen in *Journey IV's* conference room and initiated the call.

Saera answered immediately, apparently on the couch in her living quarters. "Hey, Andy. Is everything okay?"

He smiled. "We're fine, but there are a couple of issues I need to discuss with you while Kali is asleep."

She sat up. "Why? Do you have concerns?"

"Nothing like that, I just want to be cautious of her overhearing something that might inadvertently help her and void my assessment. I feel like I'm already interfering too much, even though I'm trying to bite my tongue."

"It's difficult to be an impartial observer sometimes, especially when you're not."

Andy considered taking offense at the implication that he was too invested in Kali's success, but then realized it was true.

"It doesn't help that the stakes are higher in this assignment than they are for most internships," Saera continued.

"Which is what I keep telling myself. But, all the same, I think I've been treating her more as a partner rather than staying in the background as an evaluator."

The Lead Agent nodded. "Were we dealing with any other student, I'd be concerned. However, in Kali's case, what's most important to evaluate is how well she works with others. She's a natural loner, and she's always excelled in her training when she's on her own. Why do you think I was so insistent that *you*—a highly experienced field Agent with zero experience taking a back seat—evaluate her?" She smirked. "I told you I was good at this."

Andy couldn't help but smile back. "All right, you got me."

Saera turned somber. "How is she?"

Andy swiveled in his chair. "Kali's doing fine. She doesn't seem to have any trouble focusing on the right things and making difficult decisions. No outbursts and she's behaving like a professional." He paused. "But none of this is actually what I contacted you about. I'm pretty sure we're onto something serious. Do you remember the case?"

She nodded, her brows drawing together.

"Well," Andy continued, "the witness changed her story, but Kali said she was terrified. Not only that, but it sounds as if the planet's law enforcement is ineffective."

Saera's full attention was on him now. "Really? I thought they had a decent private police force. Avon, wasn't it?"

"Yeah, but it is literally a security service—one that serves the interests of big business over those of the population. They're too concerned with protecting their wealthy clients' right to privacy to be effective in eradicating organized crime."

Saera made some notes. "Okay, I'll get the local Captain of Guard Enforcers to investigate. They can elevate the situation as needed."

"Thank you. Can I let Kali know?"

"I don't see why not." Saera leaned back. "Now, what

did you really need to talk to me about?"

Andy mirrored her position. "Kali thinks the witness was threatened, which means this assignment is a lot bigger than we thought. The band has to be involved somehow, but they can't be acting alone. I'm worried about what we're going to uncover."

Saera nodded. "When we came up with this assignment, we thought the *Sepiantia* might be taking the women with them, either with or without their consent. The main test for Kali was whether she could deal with the probable antagonism from the authorities. We didn't envision that she would be in real danger."

"I'm not sure how much to help, given that things are turning out to be more complicated. Oh, I forgot to say that the victim has dependent children, which makes it unlikely she abandoned them. So, there's a possibility that we're dealing with an organized trafficking case."

Saera gazed off to the side and remained silent. Andy didn't interrupt, recognizing her need for thinking time. It made him nervous because he realized that she was considering aborting the assignment altogether.

Finally, she said, "As you know, we don't have the resources at the moment. Continue with the investigation but keep a closer eye than normal and intervene where you feel you have to. When it comes to her evaluation, we can look at whether she has achieved the skills needed to function as an Agent regardless of your input. But Andy… "

"Yes?"

"Don't stifle her. Give her the chance to do things for herself and don't be afraid to test her. I trust you to use your judgment on when to get involved, but do try to let her take the lead." When he started to say something, she interrupted, "I know that it's a balancing act, but while I don't want her to take unnecessary risks, I want her to realize her potential. I'm sure that Kali is quite capable of investigating a trafficking case. It is only that we wouldn't have asked her to do it alone."

Andy nodded. "Okay, I will endeavor to both allow her to display her skills and look out for her safety. Is it always this hard?"

Saera smiled. "Yes and no. Each student is different. Kali is certainly complicated, but it probably doesn't help that you might be on the trail of well-resourced traffickers. Given the similarities to Kali's past trauma, this will be an ideal test of her ability to emotionally regulate. Just stay alert in case it is anything worse."

"I have all the luck." Andy chuckled. "At least I should get to see the band play."

She studied him, making him conscious that he couldn't hide much from her. "I can see that's important to you."

"Only because it will be great." He couldn't keep the enthusiasm out of his voice. "Of course, I won't forget that I have a job to do."

Saera's tone was serious. "They might be criminals, Andy. There's very little information on this Mika Hendri character. It seems he lived in the outer colonies and their record keeping is atrocious."

"I know, and if they're up to something illegal, I'll have no hesitation in dealing with them."

Her shoulders dropped. "Good, I hope they turn out to be innocent, but we still have at least one missing woman, possibly more."

"Darlia Ferrangi is our priority. At the very least, we need to find out what happened to her so that her family can have closure. Although, I'm sure that Kali hasn't given up hope of finding her alive."

—    —    —

"Who was it that said, 'history repeats itself'?" Saera asked her husband as soon as the call with Andy had ended.

Wil had been listening in on the exchange in the lounge of their quarters. Everyone in the TSS had long since gotten over the potential conflicts of interest of the High

Commander and Lead Agent being married; the pair had proven the value of their working relationship countless times over the decades. "I really hope this is only a simple case of trafficking."

"I can't help but think it sounds a lot like..." She didn't need to complete the thought.

The Priesthood's perverse genetic experimentations and secret cloning program had impacted their family more than most. Their own daughter had been temporarily captured as a would-be surrogate, before she escaped. The experience had confirmed their worst fears about the Priesthood, though they hadn't needed more motivation to remove the organization from power.

One of the most difficult professional decisions they'd ever had to make was to allow the prisoners to remain on the Priesthood's island. The Sietinen Dynasty had needed the pieces in place to mount a political revolution with the other High Dynasties. That decision to wait had allowed the Priesthood to capture Kali and at least a dozen other young women. Saera would never fully forgive herself for not finding a way to intervene sooner.

"None of the Priesthood should have survived," Wil murmured.

Saera wanted to believe that more than anything. The final telepathic assault on the Priesthood had crippled its members, but if anyone hadn't been a part of the telepathic link... Her gaze met Wil's.

"I always knew there was a possibility, but I wanted so badly to put them behind us."

"Me too." Saera sighed, sinking deeper into the couch.

Wil moved to sit next to her. "If a member of the Priesthood *is* behind these disappearances, it's not safe for Kali to be going after them alone, or even with Andy."

"Who else is there to send?"

"I should really be there myself." While Wil was the most telekinetically gifted person alive—with the possible exception of his and Saera's two children—there were too many other pressing issues to have the TSS High Commander dashing around the galaxy trying to track down rogue Priests. He knew as much, and Saera didn't need to make the point.

"Once there's a specific target, we can find a team to redirect," Saera went on. "I can't think of anyone to spare for the search right now."

"I never thought our resources would ever again be stretched as thin as they were at the end of the war."

"Of all the times for the Empire to try to tear itself in two."

Wil shook his head. "Launching one political revolution opened the door. If only people realized what we saved them from."

Saera took his hand. "We'll make it through this one, too."

"I hope Kali doesn't try to play the hero. Andy has his own impulsive streak, and he still doesn't listen to me."

"It's tough to see how much people have changed from when you first met them, especially when you've spent a lot of time apart."

Wil grimaced. "Forever an awkward teenager in his eyes. Fantastic."

She laughed. "I don't think it's *that* bad. But, I mean, you were roommates. You get to know a person in a different way."

"It's true. Some relationships transcend the reporting structure." He eyed her meaningfully.

She nodded. "We're surrounded by good people. We need to trust them and their training."

"I do. We'll act when the time is right."

# CHAPTER 13

THE TSS TRANSPORT ship shuddered as the docking clamp locked on. Kali glanced up from the screen where she'd absorbed just about all there was on Zeron's people and culture. "Docked already?"

"Sometimes arriving in a TSS ship makes things easier and sometimes harder. Thankfully, this planet doesn't appear to have anything to hide," Andy called from across the flight deck. "Find anything interesting in your research?"

"Apparently, there are great pieces of art hidden in the tunnels, designed and executed by local talent, and all unsigned. It's very secretive since it's illegal."

Andy shut down the engine and began the preparations to secure the *Journey IV* —tasks Kali had been expected to perform on the previous leg of their journey.

Kali raised an eyebrow. "How come you're helping me all of a sudden?" She jumped to her feet, struck with a pang of panic. "I haven't failed already, have I?"

"No, of course not. I had a conversation with Agent Alexri about how to proceed, in light of the escalating concerns, and we agreed that, although my primary role will continue to be to observe you, I could offer more help." At her frown, he added, "You are still being assessed."

Kali stared at him for a long moment, only slightly satisfied. "You can't wait to sample the local food?"

"Um." His earlier cheerfulness had gone, and he sounded distracted as he checked the readouts. "Let's get changed. We can't go barging in as TSS Agents."

Kali had thought the same and had already put in contact lenses, which she hated with a passion, to hide her bioluminescent eyes. It wouldn't take long to pull on jeans and a t-shirt. Her boots were fine.

"Aren't you staying on the ship?" she asked the Agent.

"No, I thought I'd come with you."

Kali frowned. "This shouldn't be too dangerous."

Andy looked up. "Kali, you have no idea what you are walking into. Nobody knows anything about these individuals, except they stop on distant planets supposedly to play music. It's worrying that there is so little information about them."

Something wasn't right, other students didn't get help. But, arguing wouldn't get her anywhere. "Are we taking weapons?" she asked, returning to the task at hand. She headed for her cabin to change.

Andy's voice drifted through the ship. "Don't think we'll need them with the two of us and it might be difficult if we're undercover, but it's better to be safe. We should be able to conceal pulse handguns."

Kali quickly donned her civilian outfit, grabbed the handguns and returned to the flight deck. Andy was still making his own preparations, so Kali took the opportunity to review a map of the immediate area. According to the promo post, the Bruisers were playing at a hotel nearby. She supposed it made sense that they wouldn't travel far from the central docking station. They would presumably have limited time before they needed to leave the planet.

"I'll work out the easiest route to the hotel." The frown stayed etched on her face. "Everything is contained in a network of tunnels. It should be a pretty straight shot."

"All right." Andy scanned the flight deck, checking to

see that he hadn't forgotten anything and made his way to the exit. *"Let's go."*

Kali jumped at the unexpected telepathy. When would she stop doing that? She should have practiced more when there'd been the chance. The problem was, she didn't really like having anyone in her head.

She grabbed her backpack and followed. It still didn't feel right to have the Agent helping her rather than being a silent observer. Clearly, Andy wasn't telling her everything. Did he speak to Agent Alexri because he didn't trust her to do what needed to be done, or didn't he trust her to keep herself safe? Whichever the case, it wasn't good.

She drew a deep breath. *There's no point worrying about it now. Just prove that you can do the job.*

They exited the ship through the side hatch and out into an enormous domed hanger. Ships were clamped to the outside of the dome, invisible once inside. Nothing distinguished the docking portals from each other, except for a number. Kali made a mental note of their number: 11420. Without it, she doubted they would be able to locate their ship again without help.

Kali stood on the top level of a metal walkway that branched in all directions to the various numbered hatches. It would appear anyone could walk to any ship as long as they knew the ship's allocated number.

The ground must have been over five hundred meters down. Looking through the metal slats made her dizzy.

"This way," Andy called from her right.

Kali tore her eyes from the tiny people scurrying below to see Andy waiting by a lift to take them down. *Good, an elevator!* More like a metal box. She briefly considered walking, but Andy's impatient expression warned against it.

The descent took seconds, and they stepped out onto compact soil. Close up, everything was brown. The walls, floor, and ceiling looked as if they had been chiseled and blasted out of the rock, which they probably had.

Kali had read that there was no atmosphere on the planet's surface and nothing grew, resulting in everything being contained underground in the network of tunnels.

A small woman in a purple jumpsuit intercepted them with a forced smile. "Welcome to Zeron. My name is Edlira, and I'm one of the local police on shift. How can I assist the TSS?"

It wasn't clear if Edlira was her full name, and Kali waited for Andy to respond until it became clear that he expected her to handle the interaction. *Right, so now he's observing.* She'd need to work out the cues for him shifting between evaluator and investigation partner.

"We're here to investigate a group of visitors to your planet." Kali belatedly realized that it would have been a good idea to let the authorities know that they were on their way, although there hadn't been much time. "The people we're looking for might be able to help with our inquiries into a missing person's case."

Edlira visibly relaxed. "We don't have many strangers on Zeron. Do you want me to try and locate them?"

"No, thank you, we know where to find them."

Edlira took a step back, the color draining from her already pale face. "In that case—"

"Could you help us to blend in a little more?" Kali was busy scanning their surroundings, where everyone wore the same jumpsuits but in different colors.

"Of course, please follow me."

She looked at Andy, who appeared to be trying to hold back a smile. *"What's wrong with her?"* she asked him.

*"At a guess, she thinks we've used powerful telepathy to find our persons of interest."*

Kali shook her head. *"That's mad, it would take extremely powerful telepathy with all these people."*

*"Exactly."*

Edlira led them to a row of metal boxes where, in response to Kali's dubious expression, she explained, "The jumpsuits are manufactured to your specifications."

Kali had used plenty of body scanners for custom clothing, but the metal stalls looked more like a storage locker than a fitting room. She didn't need telepathy to see that Andy was silently laughing at her reaction to the setup, so she reluctantly stepped inside the booth Edlira indicated.

The interior had a sharp, tangy smell that was difficult to identify. When Kali lifted her arms, they made contact with the cold walls before they were at waist height. Kali suppressed a shiver.

There was a window just below head height, which made it slightly less claustrophobic. Based on its position, all the inhabitants must be as short as Edlira. Kali supposed it made sense if they'd moved around in tunnels for generations, they would adapt to the environment. However, she didn't believe that the planet had been inhabited for that length of time. Perhaps the work had just attracted short people.

Edlira tapped on a display screen outside the booth. "Since you want to blend in, I have programmed for administrator color. That way, nobody will pay much attention to you."

*So, the color of their jumpsuits denotes their job.* That hadn't been in the information packet Kali had read. She took a deep breath and filled out her chest as a laser scanned her body. It would be better to have the garment too large rather than too tight.

It took a few minutes for a blue light to appear, indicating that the process was complete. By that time, Kali was considering leaving anyway. Folded grey cloth appeared from a chute at knee height. The material was light and felt like cotton. At least it wouldn't be unpleasant to wear.

It was awkward to disrobe and dress in the limited space, and Kali wondered how Andy was getting on with his larger frame. Finally, she was ready to leave the booth.

Andy appeared a few seconds later, wearing a

matching grey jumpsuit. The fabric pulled tight across his chest and she laughed, doubly thankful she'd thought of filling her lungs in time.

Andy shook his head, a frown on his face. They might look ridiculous, but there was no doubt that they blended in better, although they were still too tall. Kali wasn't going into any booth to sort that out.

Edlira stood to one side until she had their attention. "You will find hand sanitizers in every public place. Please be sure to use them."

*I guess their medical nanotech isn't very sophisticated around here.* Kali looked at Andy in time to catch him nod.

Edlira wasn't finished, "You will need to leave your weapons here." Kali opened her mouth to object but Edlira continued, "If not, you will set off alarms wherever you go."

Kali conceded that it would be inconvenient to alert everyone to their presence. *"I suppose we have other more covert weapons,"* she said to Andy.

Once they had placed their weapons in a secure storage locker Edlira gave an awkward half-bow. "Is that everything?"

Andy bowed back. "I guess so."

As Edlira walked away, Kali asked, "Wouldn't it have been sensible to keep her around?"

"I'm not sure that I trust her. She was a little *too* helpful."

Despite the vague answer, Kali knew what he meant; she was uncomfortable with the way that the woman was clearly afraid of them. Kali realized that she hadn't really been out in the world as a TSS trainee, so hadn't encountered the types of reactions that her instructors had warned her about. Until very recently, use of telekinesis by anyone not associated with the TSS was illegal—one of the many things that had changed since the Priesthood's fall.

Centuries of propaganda had relegated those gifted with abilities to be forced to the outskirts of society. Those perceptions were slow to change, especially on insular worlds such as Zeron. Still, Kali thought they could have gotten more out of Edlira if they'd tried.

Andy set off toward a tunnel and Kali ran to catch up. "I thought this was *my* mission?"

As they reached the entrance, she saw an information screen with a list of destinations.

"Yes. Sorry, force of habit." He stopped to look at the screen. "But, hurry up."

She couldn't hide her irritation any longer. "What's going on?" He should just tell her if she'd failed or didn't trust her judgment.

Andy didn't seem to notice her annoyance. "They're on stage in about forty-five minutes. I don't want to miss the beginning, and we don't know how long it'll take us to get there."

Kali pointed. "Twenty-five minutes, if we get one of those." Five sleek, bullet-shaped crafts hovered together near to the tunnel mouth. "Transport shuttle-cars."

"Great." Andy grinned, which made her want to punch him.

This was a fun time for him, whereas for her it was her future. *Coward*, she wanted to say, except he couldn't be. Not with what he must have done in the war. Yet, how could he be so cheerful when she'd failed? Perhaps, he couldn't be bothered to tell her or didn't respect her enough to be honest. Well, she wasn't going to be able to keep quiet for much longer.

They boarded one of the small shuttle-cars. Inside, there was room for four people, which was weird.

"Wouldn't it make more sense to have larger shuttles?" she asked as she strapped in.

Andy was busy examining the interior when a warm female voice spoke, "What is your destination?" He glanced at Kali.

"The Adheres Hotel," she stated.

"Arrival in twenty-three minutes and thirty-four seconds. Please take a seat."

Andy sat and fastened his straps. Only then did they set off down one of the tunnels at speed.

A walkway ran down one side of the tunnel but there wasn't anyone on it. Kali saw that the shuttles had to be small to fit in the narrow space. When they met another coming the other way, their shuttle reversed until they reached a wide area. White lettering on the wall spelled out 'passing place'. Under the artificial white light that was similar to daylight, the walls looked like sandstone with flecks of sparkling silver.

"What's that?" Andy pointed.

Kali leaned forward for a better look. "That must be the illegal art." She couldn't keep the excitement out of her voice. "It appears overnight."

Now that they'd noticed one piece, more jumped out at them. They maneuvered past another shuttle-car and sped down the tunnel too fast to see anything. Kali caught glimpses of shapes but no detail.

After what felt like no time at all, the shuttle-car slowed. "You have arrived at your destination. Your journey-time was twenty-four minutes and forty seconds."

They pulled up in a cavern in front of wide stone steps leading to a set of double doors. About twenty people filed through one side into a dark interior.

Kali stared around at the cavern. "Wow."

The ceiling was covered in intricately carved fish, mammals, and creatures Kali had never even heard of, all rendered in minute detail. Carvings extended down the walls and partially across the floor, giving the appearance that they were approaching a holy temple rather than a hotel.

Wide arced steps led to a heavy metal door, etched in all manner of plant-life. Kali spotted a couple of birds nestling in the leaves.

"Do you think we have to pay for the shuttle-car?" Andy asked, scanning the interior of their vehicle for instructions.

Kali shook her head, still distracted. "I don't think so. Maybe it's charged automatically."

She didn't think that was likely, as nobody had taken any payment details, but they'd find out soon enough. As soon as they got out, the shuttle-car moved a short distance away. Presumably, it was waiting for new passengers.

"It's a bit bright," Andy said, staring at the closed half of the vibrant red metal door.

Kali struggled to take her eyes from the masterpiece on the roof, but she glanced at the door. "Apparently, establishments can be identified by their different colored doors. Anywhere that offers lodgings has a red door."

"What happens if a business offers more than one thing?"

Andy sounded cheerful now they were here. Should she say something? Ask him why he'd really come along? She thought she'd done all right so far. He hadn't given any indication that she'd done anything wrong and had reassured her about her conduct on Glaendor.

"No idea. There was no mention of that in the information I read."

She pulled up the file to check, and Andy nudged her arm. "Make some effort to blend in. Didn't they teach you anything in training?"

She felt the familiar urge to punch somebody and instantly remembered what he said about checking her body and mind. As soon as she did, she realized that he was annoying her deliberately.

She took a deep breath. "You did that on purpose to provoke me into hitting you."

He grinned. "I did, indeed, and you acted brilliantly. Punching me needs to be way up on your list of unapproved activities."

When they got closer to the door, Kali spotted large mammals amongst the carved plant life. They looked like bears dancing in a circle with their huge paws raised in celebration.

"It's beautiful," Andy breathed next to her.

The man in front of them, wearing a light-green jumpsuit, turned. "You are strangers here?"

So much for blending in. There was no point denying it. "We're here to see the band," Kali replied.

He nodded as if it made perfect sense to travel across the galaxy to watch a bunch of people play instruments.

Andy's eyes shone as he peered into the dark interior. Kali wasn't sure that he was acting. She suspected that he was genuinely excited about watching the performance.

"This planet is dead, except for vats of bacteria," the green-jumpsuited man mumbled. "People want to make things better in any way they can, even if that is through creativity." He scuffed his boot along the floor. "It's a shame the government doesn't see it that way. They want people to work, work, work and make money for them." He spit into the dust.

Kali would have liked to find out more but they were moving, and it became too noisy to talk. At first, she thought the band was already playing, it was so loud.

A man half her size read her palm print on a handheld biometric scanner, and she wondered whether the absence of her details in any database would prove to be a problem. It didn't seem so because he let them both inside without asking any questions.

Once they were in the main hall, it was evident that the sound was coming from overhead speakers and the stage at the far end stood empty of people. Kali couldn't believe that so many people had lined up to watch the music she'd heard. The place was crowded, and she couldn't move without stepping on a foot or bumping an arm. The low-level lighting didn't help.

Andy didn't seem to notice. His eyes were alight with excitement, and she wondered if he'd come with her simply to see the band play. She fought to suppress her anger at the thought that seeing their performance was more important to him than making sure she graduated. Besides, where had he found a love of Earth music? If he wanted to see it so much, he could have hopped down to the planet itself. She would ask him once they were back on the ship.

Over the loud music, he mouthed the words at the same time as asking telepathically, *"Do you want a drink?"*

Was this another test? *"I'll just have juice."*

*"No alcohol?"* He seemed surprised.

What did he expect? *"Not while I'm working."* Kali smirked at the superior edge to her telepathic voice.

*"Ah, but you have to blend in."*

Kali wasn't going to worry about failing anymore. She had a job to do if she was going to find Darlia.

Andy was in front of her again. This time, instead of heading to the bar, he was going toward the stage.

*Stars, what is he doing?* She grabbed his arm. *"I thought that we were supposed to be undercover, scoping the place out?"*

He paused, leaning close enough that his breath tickled her ear and said something. She didn't think she would have heard him if he hadn't spoken into her mind at the same time. *"I'm worried they'll notice us and run."*

She shivered and looked around, noticing how much shorter everyone was than them. They were going to stand out in the crowd no matter what they did. She conceded that wearing grey jumpsuits was not going to offer adequate camouflage.

*"Doesn't that go against our objectives?"* She tried harder to explain, *"I mean—"*

*"Do the people here appear sophisticated, Kali?"*

She had to concede that the way the people around them were drinking and chatting in their different colored jumpsuits, they were unlikely to be hoarding vital secrets. It didn't change the fact that Andy had changed the parameters of their mission without discussing it with her first.

Kali wished again that he would be honest and tell her if she was making a mess of things, especially as she couldn't think what she'd done wrong. If she'd already failed, what was she doing here? Unless he needed her, or worse, just wanted to see the band play.

*No, that would be cruel!* Andy wasn't cruel, as far as she could tell. No Agent should have that quality.

"What about those drinks?" She asked loudly.

He grinned. "We'd only spill them."

Kali shook her head, not knowing what he meant and afraid to find out.

The energy of the club was almost physical in the way it bounced off the walls, and despite her churning innards, Kali couldn't help being affected. She felt light-headed from the laughter and hum of voices. The occasional shout rang out, calling for the Bruisers to come on stage.

Some danced, although how they found the space to move, she didn't know. It was a far cry from the orderly queues that had formed outside.

The stage contained all manner of equipment, from musical instruments to speakers and amplifiers. Kali had never seen anything like it. She hadn't been to a concert since she was a kid, and even then, it had been a very different affair. There had been seats and an empty stage, which had changed in a kaleidoscope of lighting. Compared to one person standing on a stage without a piece of visible equipment, she couldn't imagine what all of this stuff was going to do.

The stage itself wasn't huge, although it was raised so that people would be able to see from wherever they stood. Like everything else, the high domed ceiling had been chiseled out of the rock.

A banner fluttered at the back of the stage with the band's name painted in an amateurish scrawl that must have been deliberate. Spotlights picked out individual instruments and metal poles.

Of course, there were no windows or natural light. The thought of not having access to the stars brought back the feeling of claustrophobia that Kali had experienced in the booth. Everything was artificial and underground.

It wasn't only that, but the man in the queue had suggested that people were only on the planet to work. Little effort had been put into making the environment attractive to the point that people had resorted to adding their own art, and she thought that should be a crime.

The information packet had claimed that this was the only hotel on this side of the planet. It was no wonder that there were so few visitors.

It was remarkable that a scarceness of natural beauty prompted the creativity streak that had resulted in the ceiling outside. Perhaps that was why so many people had packed into the hotel's concert hall tonight. Yet, nobody behaved like the workers the man outside had described, even with their matching jumpsuits and small stature. They were too free.

A man with dusky skin and shining blue eyes tapped her arm, tipping an imaginary glass to his mouth. She understood that he wanted to buy her a drink even though he didn't know her name. It was strange. She politely declined, scanning the surface of his mind for ill intentions.

After that, Kali stayed close to Andy's back. It was the right decision because the crowd was growing denser the closer they got to the stage. They were near the front, towering over the audience, when the lights dimmed. The crowd roared.

Kali swung around, searching for the threat, wishing she still had her weapon.

Andy grabbed her arm. *"It's okay, the band is coming on."*

With wide eyes and big grins, the sea of faces behind stared past her to the stage. Someone winked at her, and she swung to face the front, not wanting to stand out more than she already did.

The music coming out of the speakers changed. It elicited another roar from the crowd. A sweaty man almost touching her shoulder, started to jump up and down in time to the music. Alarmed, Kali tried to move away but there was nowhere to go.

Andy pulled her close to him. *"Just enjoy it."*

She might have been reassured if he hadn't shared the same rapt expression as everyone else. It felt like they were in the middle of a cult and she was the only one not drugged. Still, for the sake of blending in, she tried to do as he suggested. That was until a girl who didn't look old enough to drink wandered onstage. She picked up an instrument and ran her fingers over the strings, producing a metallic sound. A guitarist, Kali knew from her research.

Another woman appeared, swaggering onto the stage as if she was high. She folded long limbs behind a barrage of drums. Bright blue hair caught in the overhead spotlight as she bobbed up and down, producing a beat that hit Kali in the center of her chest. The music was physical and so far beyond her experience, she thought she might die.

Kali screwed her eyes closed. *"I'm not sure about this."*

Andy shifted from foot to foot.

*"Are you possessed?"* she asked.

He laughed. *"They haven't even started yet."*

# CHAPTER 14

THE POUNDING BASS vibrated through Kali's chest. She'd been to parties and on one occasion experienced hearing-damaging music, but never anything like this. She had an urge to move, not dance exactly—it was more of an insistent pull on her hips.

Andy was still behind her. Not touching, thank the stars, but it proved impossible not to be very aware of the way he was dancing. The movement was building, and it was as if he was controlled by the music like a puppet.

This was far outside of Kali's experience. In the past, she'd listened to soothing sounds meant to calm her nerves before sleep.

Tanya liked listening on her headphones to music that might be a step closer to what was coming from the stage. Despite the alien environment, a reckless, rebellious part of her was thrilled. It wanted to connect to the exuberant energy that stemmed from sharing a passion.

The crowd roared again as smoke drifted across the stage, obscuring the drummer and wrapping around the legs of the willowy, blonde guitarist. She cocked a hand to her ear, encouraging the audience to shout louder.

Kali's attention was so fixed on her that at first, she didn't notice the figures appearing out of the smoke. The two women played together until, with a thunderclap, everything was bathed in color and light.

A shiver went down Kali's spine. People danced, deliberately banging into each other and not caring, while some sang along with every word.

She glanced at Andy to see a big grin, and yet, she could tell he was holding back. He would be as bad as the rest if not for his official capacity. The analytical side of her brain saw the reinforcing cycle of music driving the crowd, and the crowd driving the music.

With no time between songs, the unnatural energy built, as the band jumped straight into the next song and the next, stopping only briefly to say, "Hello Adhere!"

Kali was being carried along by the plaintive, almost sensual sound of a golden metal instrument—a saxophone—when awareness pierced her fevered state. She went from awe to wariness within a heartbeat. Someone was watching her, and not just anyone—someone with a lot of ability.

The probe that tested the strength of her shield was either untrained or incompetent, but forceful. The all-consuming music faded into the background as adrenaline focused her mind.

Sensing he wasn't anywhere behind, she scanned the crowd in front. It was hard to pick out details in the dark, and the flashes of blinding light only made it more difficult. She could see that everybody was facing the stage. Andy was the only one staring at her with a question in his eyes.

Kali nodded once, knowing that he'd pick up on the subtle signal. It was a warning that she didn't want to use telepathy since it could alert their stalker.

Andy's gaze returned forward, sharply enough that she knew he was searching. Despite her height, nobody paid any attention to her.

It wasn't until the spotlight on the stage moved right that she saw him: a silhouette behind the band, light reflecting from his pale face. No wonder Kali hadn't spotted him immediately. He was barely visible and was too far away to see any detail, but she sensed him staring in her direction.

She grabbed Andy's hand and squeezed. The spotlight swung away and the man was lost in shadow. She strained her eyes, trying to see anything, but when the light returned, he was gone.

Andy tapped her shoulder and they weaved through the ever-moving crowd. People parted as they headed for the edge of the room, finally reaching a door at the rear of the stage. Surprisingly, nobody made any attempt to stop them as they slipped out.

Thankfully, it was brighter in the corridor despite dark-green stone walls. They hurried away with the music becoming increasingly muffled the deeper they went into the hotel's basement.

Kali's ears buzzed from the earlier abuse and it felt as if her head had to readjust to the real world. Regardless, she kept her senses alert for any sign of a psychic attack. It occurred to her that this could be a trap to lure them away from a populated area.

The corridor ended abruptly in an empty basement with industrial-sized elevators dominating the center. A smooth rock floor caused their footsteps to echo alarmingly in the chamber. So much for stealth.

*"Anyone could be hiding amongst those."* Andy gestured to rows of aluminum boxes that were stacked ceiling high. *"This must be how they get the equipment in and out."* He finished scanning the area and headed for a flight of stairs.

*"Did you see him?"* Kali asked, breathing hard as they raced upstairs.

*"Just a shadow, but I felt him try to get through your shield. It's too much of a coincidence that he knows how to use his ability. There are so few places that teach telepathy."*

Good to know that Andy was thinking the same thing. The man couldn't have gone far and he would find it difficult to hide from them.

They had started up the second flight when Kali sensed his presence at the same time as he appeared above, jogging down. When he saw them, he froze, which was the only option as far as Kali could tell. They were too close for him to successfully flee.

A flash of something crossed his face. If Kali didn't know better, she would have said that he recognized her. She was sure that she had never seen him before, and he couldn't know her. How long had he been watching her in the crowd?

*Fok it.* Kali wasn't going to let Andy take the lead. She didn't know what he wanted, but until he told her differently, this was still her assignment.

She closed the distance to the suspect. "TSS, we need to speak to you."

As Kali had hoped, the mention of the TSS had an effect. In fact, she had never seen the color drain so entirely from someone's face. He tensed, and she readied for him to run or attack, but then his body sagged and he nodded.

"Perhaps we could go to your room," Kali suggested. They didn't need to announce who they were to the entire planet.

She expected him to argue. After all, they hadn't any weapons and no arrangement with local law enforcement, but he obviously didn't know or care. Whatever was going on, he was behaving as if he was guilty.

Andy stayed a step behind, and more importantly, remained quiet. Good, perhaps she could show him that she was capable of getting the job done.

Nobody said anything as they walked four flights to a hotel corridor lined with rooms. Kali stayed alert for signs of a trap, since it was still possible that this had been engineered. She would have been happier if the man had argued or tried to put up a fight.

He stopped at a door and pressed his palm to the screen. It clicked open and they followed him inside to a poky room in which they all barely fit at the same time.

Kali took a deep breath, determined not to mess up this chance. "Who are you?"

# CHAPTER 15

MIKA COULDN'T THINK as the two TSS Agents invaded his room. The space had felt small before, especially when Owen and Luca were in there, but now it was downright cramped.

He should have said that they couldn't come in when they'd asked. Should have asked to see identification, but he hadn't. It wasn't just the shock of being confronted by the TSS, something he'd been afraid of since he started this voyage. No, it had been seeing her so unexpectedly.

Of course, he'd seen her at the concert. As usual, he'd been attracted to the bright aura of someone with abilities. He'd thought that she looked like Kali Wietris, but it had never occurred to him that it actually *was* her. That was why it had seemed so pointless to ask for identification. He knew very well who she was and that she had joined the TSS. It was just such a surprise to meet her in person.

When Tregaren had told Mika what he expected him to do three years ago, he'd remembered the news feed about the women who had escaped the Priesthood. Worried about what he was getting involved in, Mika had wanted reassurance that this was different and so he'd read everything he could find.

That was how he first found out about Kali Wietris and

what she'd been through. She was mysterious as she didn't give interviews. Nobody was sure what had happened to her, but sources close to her family suggested that she'd been recruited by the TSS.

As he searched for somewhere for the Agents to sit, he thought again how he shouldn't have brought them up here. It was too personal with his dirty laundry at the foot of the bunk and his lounge pants hanging from the door. He resisted the urge to race around, stuffing clothes in drawers and tidying away his belongings. At least they would see that he had nothing to hide. No women stashed in the wardrobe. He caught himself; he shouldn't think like that, since they might not be there about any women.

How much *did* they know? What was he going to tell them? Had they already read his mind? He didn't think so. Tregaren had taught him basic shielding, and he hadn't detected anyone probing his head. Perhaps this was nothing to do with him and merely a coincidence that they'd shown up tonight. He had to be careful that he didn't give himself away. *Act confident, you've got nothing to hide. You are not guilty of anything.*

There was only one chair and the bed. *Nothing to hide, remember.* Mika gestured at the bed because it was big enough for them both and he took the chair, only realizing as he sat that the chair was lower than the bed.

Neither Agent had said anything since they entered the room, and the silence was starting to become uncomfortable. Sweat beaded along the back of Mika's neck.

Stars, the band would be finishing soon. The last thing he needed was Owen or Luca bursting in and making things worse.

"How can I help the TSS?" When his voice came out sounding steady, it gave Mika a small measure of confidence.

Despite being a similar age, Kali answered as if she were in charge, and Mika suspected that she was the one to watch. "You can start by telling us who you are."

He wanted to argue that they should introduce themselves first but was too relieved that they didn't appear to know him. "Mika Hendri. I manage the band."

It occurred to him as soon as he spoke that he should have given them a false name. No, they would check with the hotel and that would look incredibly suspicious if it didn't match. Better to stick to the truth as much as possible. Thank the stars that this was the last night of the gig. It didn't matter that the band wanted a night off, they would move on tomorrow.

"I'm Junior Agent Wietris, and this is Agent Renteria, we're investigating," Mika held his breath as Kali paused, "a crime."

She was watching for a reaction, and he didn't know how much he'd already given away. TSS Agents were known to use all sorts of techniques to get what they wanted.

*Stay calm, wait it out and for fok's sake, act ordinary, or at least innocent.* How did he even do that?

Kali was still speaking, "...understand that you came via Glaendor." She stopped.

*They knew where the* Sepiantia *had come from. This has to do with... No, don't think about it.*

"Was that a question?" he blurted out.

Kali frowned. "I hadn't got to the question, Mr. Hendri."

"It's just that I want to help, but the band, they'll be finished soon and need a hand packing up. We don't have any roadies, you see. We do everything ourselves, and there's a lot of equipment." *He was babbling.*

"Roadies?"

He blinked. "You don't know what roadies are?" At her frown, he added, "Of course not, why would you?" Mika glanced at the man who hadn't said a word and received a polite smile in return. "They are... someone who moves equipment for entertainers."

There was a note of impatience in Kali's voice when she

replied, "That's great, but the sooner we get on with the interview, the sooner you can leave, okay?"

Mika found himself nodding. What was he doing? He hadn't done anything against the law. It was ridiculous how they could make him feel so bad, so guilty just by asking some questions.

Mika found his voice. "I'll give you five minutes before I ask you to leave, not because I'm unwilling to be helpful but because of necessity."

The skin around Kali's eyes tightened and she compressed her lips. She didn't like that, but Mika felt better. Nobody said that he had to put up with harassment.

"This is a serious matter, Mr. Hendri —"

"Mika, call me Mika."

She raised her eyebrows. "A woman went missing from Glaendor, immediately after your band left."

He knew it. They were investigating the woman, and they would find out about the others if they didn't already know. He had to assume that they knew. It was the only safe course of action.

"Well, I'd like to help you, but you say she disappeared after we left, so obviously, we didn't have anything to do with it."

Kali's eyes narrowed. "How do you know that she was seen after you left? Someone in the band could have killed her and dumped her body."

*Oh no, she's right. How could I know that?* Because that had been the plan. It was always the plan. The women would be seen at a minimum of the next day to divert suspicion away from the band. People always blame outsiders first, particularly if they're untrustworthy party-animals. But, Mika couldn't say any of that.

"I assumed, with you saying 'after' we left." His voice was steadier than it had any right to be. "Anyway, I really have to go now."

He stood, and the two Agents got up. With a surge of triumph, he took two strides to the door and pressed his hand to the biometric lock. Kali's gaze—not Kali, Junior Agent Wietris—lingered on the screen, and he saw the sheen of moisture he'd left behind.

Their eyes connected, and she gave him a wide smile. "We can wait. Don't try to leave until we've finished our conversation."

With that, the two Agents left ahead of Mika. He glanced at Agent Renteria as he passed, but his face gave nothing away.

As soon as the door clicked shut, Mika leaned against it, breathing heavily. *She knows.* There had been no doubt in her eyes that he was guilty. What could he do? All he'd achieved so far was putting off the inevitable charge of conspiracy to kidnap and for all he knew, worse.

There was no time to comb through the entire conversation, looking for clues because the band really would be playing their encore. Five more minutes and they would be coming off stage, demanding attention.

Mika hurried to the comm screen. He had to make time to talk to Tregaren. This brush with the TSS could have too many wide-reaching implications.

For once, Tregaren's face appeared on-screen immediately, as if he knew there was something wrong. It wasn't a leap since Mika wasn't calling him at the time of one of their scheduled calls.

"What is it?" Tregaren snapped. "I don't have much time." He echoed the words Mika was about to say.

"The TSS is here, and they're suspicious. An Agent and Junior Agent came to see me, wanting to know about the missing woman from Glaendor."

Tregaren interrupted, "Which Agents?"

Mika stared at him for a few seconds, struggling to understand why it mattered. Unless he already knew. Unless he had already seen Junior Agent Wietris on Glaendor. Mika went cold because that made sense.

"It's the T-S-foking-S. That's all that matters." It was easy to turn fear into anger. "What are we going to do?"

Tregaren smiled, sending a shiver down Mika's spine. "What was the female's name?"

"What has that got to do with it?" He was stalling, and that never worked with Tregaren.

The ex-Priest's predatory smile widened, waiting. When Mika refused to respond, he said, "Why don't you invite Junior Agent Wietris onto your ship?"

Mika's mouth dropped open and he shook his head. "This... she's not like the others. She's been training for years to use her abilities. I don't even know if my mental shield will hold if she starts to probe."

"It will hold. I trained you." Tregaren's expression was serene. "I will see what my contacts can find out about her."

Mika had given too much away and now he would pay the price.

"And don't worry," Tregaren soothed. "I'll handle her."

Mika felt sick. Tregaren was playing with him, just like he always did. But this time, it could have significant consequences.

"What do you want with her?" Mika forced the words through his constricted throat, while he tried to think how to be smarter, sneakier than Tregaren. He was searching for a way to win but didn't really want to know what happened to the women he was complicit in abducting. "What would I even tell her?"

"That is for you to work out. And, Mika," Tregaren's eyes glowed through the screen, "remember that I have no use for your friends."

Mika's whole body jumped as a rhythmic banging started on the door. He snapped off the transmission and swung to face the door.

Muffled, excited voices came from the corridor outside. Mika's heart was racing, and his hands felt clammy as he again placed his palm against the biometric lock.

As soon as the door clicked open, Owen and Vaira tumbled through. They were busy jabbering at each other. At first, Mika couldn't tell what they were talking about.

Then, he caught one word—police—and thought that his night couldn't get any worse.

Within two minutes, they proved him wrong.

Owen burst out, "Caryanne has been arrested."

# CHAPTER 16

DARLIA WAS INSIDE some sort of locker, but it could just as easily be a metal coffin stood on end. She knew it was locked, so why the fok did her mind have to make things worse?

Her brain was definitely against her. If not, why hadn't she been able to think of a single decent plan? She didn't think that demanding to be let out counted. Had that ever worked in the history of the universe? She doubted it.

Besides, she didn't know for sure who had kidnapped her or what he wanted. His manner of dress reminded her of the footage of the Priests she'd seen when the TSS had cleared out the Priesthood's island on Tararia after the organization's dissolution. They'd said that nobody needed to be afraid of the Priesthood's twisted justice—that Gifted didn't need to hide their abilities. Was that true?

She'd never paid attention to the politics on the central worlds, like many people born and raised in the Taran outer colonies, but now she wished she'd followed what had happened to the Priesthood after their fall. Could members of the organization still be operating in the shadows? If they *were* still out there, then no one was safe, no matter how remote a world.

He'd said something about her having ability. That

certainly *sounded* like the former Priesthood's rhetoric—
assuming he wasn't talking about her ability to raise
children or to keep a job and run a home. But *her*? She'd
never read someone's mind or levitated an object. There
were only the whispers she could sometimes collect from
the wind, though that was hardly like the Gifts she'd heard
about. This man was clearly insane, Priest or not.

It was best not to draw his attention. The foker was
there whenever she closed her eyes, and while the locker
was hideous and smelly, and she could barely scratch her
nose, at least he couldn't sneak up on her. She would hear
him well before he got close enough to touch her. She
shivered at the thought of his vile hands.

Light spilled through the cracks. Her eyes had adjusted
to the point where she could see her hand in front of her
face. The metal looked flimsy and she wondered if she
could warp the door enough to escape.

Darlia had always thought that she would fight back in
a kidnapping situation. How little she'd known about how
scared it was possible to be. She sent a silent apology to all
those victims she'd read about—the ones where she had
secretly thought, "I would never let that happen to me. I
would fight."

It hadn't been at all like she'd imagined. She'd never
had a chance to fight, and even if she had, her weak body
would have betrayed her and she'd have been no better off.

He'd been in her head. It was the only explanation. No,
he couldn't do that, he'd just made her think he could. He
wasn't a Priest because the Priesthood was gone. Wasn't it?

Darlia's breathing had gone shallow again and she
made an effort to fill her lungs, worried she'd
hyperventilate and pass out. It had happened earlier when
he'd put her in the box, and it was only as darkness crept in
at the edges of her vision that she had gotten herself under
control.

She focused on the hum of the air filtration system. It
was the only thing she could hear, but it didn't give her any

clues about where she was.

There was an occasional shudder, which suggested they were moving, traveling far from her family and everything she'd known. It didn't help to think like that, but her mind didn't seem to care.

*What does he want with me?* She didn't have money or wealthy relatives, which left her mind and body. He'd already made her do things she didn't want to. Stars, she'd walked right into this box. She had sensed him directing her mind, compelling her—making his desires her own. Whatever he had planned for her, she might not be able to resist.

Regardless of the odds against her, she couldn't give up. Couldn't accept that she would never see her daughters again. She would do whatever was needed to live— whatever it took to take her home.

Darlia braced her shoulders against the back wall and pressed her knees into what she thought was the door, pushing the metal outwards with all her strength. Something gave. Panting, she dropped back down.

She hit the door with the palm of her hand. The suddenness of the action surprised her. Vibrations traveled up her arm, numbing her shoulder for a few seconds. She wanted to cry out with the pain but instead channeled it into hitting the metal in the same spot. The space was too tight to build up much force and it felt useless, but then she noticed the dent, small but real.

Darlia smashed her palm into the same spot harder this time, causing her forearm to throb. It was difficult to get much momentum in the tight space so she threw her shoulder against the door again and again without waiting for the pain to register.

The thud reverberated around the tiny space, making her ears ring and her head throb. She didn't stop. Her whole arm was numb now. The dent was growing, bending the edges of the door. It wouldn't take much more force to make it buckle open, and that spurred her on.

She was desperate. There was no capacity in her head to consider how she would escape the ship if she got out of the locker. All that went through her mind was if she just put in a bit more effort, it might be enough for her to escape.

One more strike and it burst open, falling outwards to crash on the floor. A tall shape loomed millimeters away from where the door lay, but all Darlia saw was his red eyes. He must have worn contact lenses before, because she would have remembered if they had glowed. There could be no doubt what he was now. Only Priests had red, glowing eyes.

The figure moved over the wreckage, blocking out the light. "Oh, Darlia, I'm not finished with you."

—    —    —

The bar was empty except for an elderly man sweeping the floor with an actual brush. Kali wanted to ask why they didn't use a cleaning bot, but she couldn't be bothered to move from the table she perched against.

She yawned. "It's late."

"Early." Andy studied his handheld from where he leaned against the bar.

"It would only be early if we had actually been to bed."

Andy ignored her comment. "Finally, some intel on Mika Hendri."

Kali chewed her thumbnail, tasting the silicone covering and wondering when Andy had put in the request. When did Andy get the chance to talk to Headquarters about the situation? More importantly, what else had he discussed? Had he talked about her, and had anything been decided?

"Andy, we need to talk." She hadn't planned to say anything, but once the words were out, she was glad. She didn't think she was being unreasonable. She needed to be clear where she stood with this assignment.

He looked up startled. "There's information here about—"

"Yes, I'm sure you have vital information, but this is more important," she plowed on before she lost her courage. "Have I failed my internship?"

Andy frowned. "Why would you think that?"

Kali fought to hide her annoyance, but it colored her voice. "You're supposed to be observing, not accompanying me to interview suspects, and certainly not helping with an investigation."

His face cleared. "Oh yes, but I thought I explained that Saera... Agent Alexri said that—"

"I know that you were supposed to play a more active role, but I'm confused. What am I supposed to do?"

Andy walked over to pull her hand away from her mouth, ignoring her death-glare. "Kali, I am truly sorry, I should've clarified the situation." He glanced at his shoes. "I might have gotten so excited about seeing the Bruisers that I didn't take the time to explain properly."

Kali couldn't let herself relax, not yet. "Okay, I can see that." She understood his eagerness better now that she'd actually experienced the concert.

"I spoke to Agent Alexri, and she agreed that I would go with you." He put up a hand when she opened her mouth. "No qualified Agent would work a potentially dangerous assignment like this alone." He was about to say more but stopped.

"What? Tell me everything." When he hesitated, she added, "You owe me for allowing me to believe I'd failed."

Andy gave her a hard look. "You wouldn't be using my mistake for your own ends, would you?"

She met his gaze. "I just want to know."

"Um, I have to say that you are doing well under the circumstances. For instance, you haven't tried to punch me yet, which I take as a good sign."

Kali shook her head to hide suppressed laughter since she had fantasized about punching him many times. "So, I still have a chance?"

"I can't say too much about how you're doing, but I haven't observed anything that would be grounds for disqualification. Now, let's get on with it."

"And, you're going to let me lead the investigation?"

"Of course." He shrugged. "Don't forget, you are my first trainee. I might have gotten a little carried away."

Kali let relief spread through her. She didn't know what she would do if she failed the internship. This was all she'd wanted to do for the last seven years. Besides, they still hadn't found Darlia, and Mika Hendri clearly knew something he wasn't telling them.

She pushed up from the table, feeling lighter than she had since leaving the ship. It would be better if Andy didn't find out how much she really did want to punch him. She set off.

He hurried after her. "Where are you going?"

"Well, there's no doubt that Mika was lying to us, and I don't think we should let him get away with it. Let's go and help, roadie."

Andy laughed. "No, that's what they'll call us if we help the band—roadies." He grabbed her arm. "Don't you want to hear what I've found out?"

*"Sorry, with all the drama, I forgot that you had information."* She switched to speaking telepathically to stop anyone from overhearing their conversation.

Andy checked the corridor but it was clear. *"Mika Hendri was born on a ship-building colony called Veraria— to a war-hero, no less. There's no information about his father, but it sounds like Mika was technically gifted. There was a rumor that he built his own ship, which would explain the strange-looking craft. What I wouldn't give to search the Sepiantia."*

*"He doesn't look techy."* Kali reddened as soon as she'd spoken the thought. "Come on," she said before Andy asked her to explain why she thought Mika didn't have the physique of someone who tinkered with equipment all day.

There was a commotion ahead, and they turned into the hall to find the blue-haired drummer—Vaira Destuti—sobbing against a speaker. Mika and the singer—Owen Bruiser—were in the middle of a shouting match.

Kali couldn't understand a word Vaira was mumbling and made it a priority to find out what was going on. She grabbed the arm of the oldest band member as he moved to comfort Vaira.

"What's going on?"

The guy looked startled but answered, "Caryanne has been arrested."

"Caryanne Westlaen?"

"Yeah, our guitarist." He turned back to Vaira. "Ah, come on now. She'll be fine. Nobody has been locked up more than our Caryanne, and she always gets out okay."

Kali raised an eyebrow; that information hadn't been in any report. Unfortunately, now wasn't the time to go into it. "What has she done?"

"They wouldn't tell us anything."

"What *did* they say?" She would do better trying to get information from the rock wall.

The man ran a hand through his black hair, inadvertently revealing a poorly done patch of transplants at the back of his head. "Just that they were taking her to the station to be charged." He held up a hand to forestall her. "I don't understand why they wouldn't say more but they wouldn't."

Kali controlled her desire to shake him. "What's your name?" she asked, even though she already knew the answer.

His frown deepened. "Honk Da Moog."

Kali suppressed a laugh at hearing it said aloud. "Do your best to explain."

The bass player stumbled past, pushing an amplifier or speaker—Kali wasn't sure which it was—and the two men exchanged a glance.

Honk saw Kali's frown. "He was checking that I'm

okay."

She watched as Luca almost rammed the equipment into a door. "He looks too drunk to help anyone."

Honk chuckled. "If Luca looks drunk, it means he's sober."

Kali didn't try to make sense of the statement. "Anyway, as I was saying, do your best to explain, and we'll see what we can do to help." Whatever she'd been expecting from the band, this wasn't it.

Andy walked toward her with an expression of disbelief that made her want to raise her eyebrows.

"Go on, why might Caryanne have been arrested?" Kali pressed.

Andy shrugged. "Nobody knows for certain but she went home with a local—a fan."

Kali stared blankly. "Went home?"

Andy snorted. "She went with him to his accommodation for sex."

"Oh..." Kali pressed her lips together because she had almost asked why and could only guess what sort of response she would have received.

Honk sighed. "Apparently he wanted more. She never does more, so it seems he made a complaint and it's been taken seriously, which is just crazy."

"We're supposed to be leaving tomorrow," Vaira spoke her first intelligible words.

Kali had read that law enforcement on the planet was strict about anything that could escalate into trouble within the small community. "Okay, we'll see what we can do." She looked up to see Mika striding toward them.

"He looks like trouble," Andy muttered at her side.

Honk wandered off, carrying a small case. He seemed happy to abandon Vaira now that she had stopped crying. Kali suspected that he didn't want to get caught in the middle of an argument.

*"I sense an opportunity to find out more,"* Kali said telepathically to Andy before flashing a greeting smile to

the approaching band manager.

Mika came to a halt in front of Kali. "Did you have them arrest Caryanne?"

The accusation surprised her. "No, Mr. Hendri. This planet has its own laws and customs." Despite what she'd told Honk about helping, she added, "We are not here to interfere."

Andy shifted slightly, and she could almost hear his approval. Thankfully, he stayed silent.

"Mika. Call me Mika, not Mr. Hendri." He dropped his voice. "I'm sorry about what I said earlier. Can you help?"

"Of course, we can try. Shall we go and find where law enforcement has taken your... is she your employee?"

He frowned. "No, Caryanne is more than that." Then he seemed to realize that he'd implied something that he didn't mean. "She is a friend as well as a colleague."

Kali suspected that she might get on well with Mika if he wasn't hiding things from them. This was her opportunity to get him to let his guard down, and she intended to make sure that she didn't waste it.

# CHAPTER 17

WHEN MIKA LEFT the hotel with Junior Agent Wietris, Agent Renteria had stayed behind—probably to keep an eye on the band and make sure they didn't abscond, or perhaps to see what he could discover with Mika out of the picture.

If only the TSS knew everyone the way Mika did. None of them had the skills to survive on their own, let alone run. At least when it came to the band, Mika had nothing to worry about. They didn't know anything that would interest the TSS. Honk might have an illegal stash somewhere but he wasn't likely to let that slip unless someone held him by his feet out an airlock.

The ride to the station was strained. Mika didn't think Junior Agent Wietris cared one way or another about the uncomfortable atmosphere, since all she seemed interested in was getting a glimpse of the artwork. She wasn't likely to see much at these speeds, but he liked her fascination with it. Anything that made her less scary and more of a regular person was good.

They paused in a passing place where someone had painted a glorious picture of the star system. The Junior Agent's eyes were wide as she took in every detail.

Mika laughed. "Do you know your mouth is hanging open?" He nodded toward the wall. "We had the same on my planet."

She gave him a questioning look.

"I have a theory that if it is suppressed, imagination leaks out of people however it can," he clarified.

"Is that your explanation for the appearance of your ship?"

He laughed at the unexpected honesty. "On my home planet, art wasn't important. Functionality was all that mattered, which is sad. That approach stifles innovation."

"What made you different?"

His voice was quiet when he answered. "My mother." He needed to stop her from asking more, so he said the first thing that came into his head. "How come you haven't delved into my mind?" He realized how rude the question was as soon as the words were out of his mouth. "Sorry..."

She raised her eyebrows. "We have to follow rules. Can you imagine how people would see the TSS if we read minds every time it was convenient?"

Her explanation made sense. She stared at him too long, and Mika guessed she knew about his shield. Of course, she knew. He waited for her to say something, to ask how he had learned about mental guards without any official training, but she didn't. It was just as well, since he didn't have an answer that he could share.

"Everyone probably believes you do it, anyway." He looked at his hands. "At least, I did."

He felt her eyes on him. "That's one of the few honest things you've said."

Mika's cheeks grew warm. It was true, but there was nothing to be done so, he changed the subject. "Thank you for helping me with Caryanne. She's a bit... special."

"What do you mean?" Junior Agent Wietris sounded genuinely curious. "And, we haven't gotten her out of trouble yet. I have the feeling that while the authorities are cooperative, they aren't overly friendly to the TSS."

The shuttle slowed and took a branch tunnel before passing through a narrow opening into a courtyard, where it stopped in front of a large fish-shaped fountain. Water spouted high from the fish's open mouth.

Mika was surprised by the artistry, since everything else he'd encountered during his short stay had been fundamental and practical, aside from the spontaneous artwork. He had the impression that such extravagant displays were frowned upon. He wondered at the fountain's significance outside the law enforcement building.

"I hope this isn't a trap," he muttered under his breath.

Junior Agent Wietris climbed out of the shuttle to walk once around the structure. "Decadent for a planet that has to import all its water."

She was already at the top of the stone steps, pushing the heavy midnight-blue door wide. She didn't look as though she shared his trepidation. Since there was no other choice, he took in a deep breath and followed.

Inside, the building was more impressive than the fountain. The ceiling rose into a high dome with a single, curved reception desk in the center of the space beneath.

Tapestries softened rock walls, projecting a much-needed air of warmth. They depicted full-color scenes from the planet's history. Artistic license must have been in play, because Mika was sure that the workers never toiled with pickaxes in the tunnels; they would have operated machines that cut through stone.

Junior Agent Wietris had reached the reception desk. Her voice echoed around the vaulted space, making any attempt at a private conversation impossible. "Please check whether she is here."

The woman behind the desk took her time using the comm link. "I have someone from the TSS here." In a voice full of disapproval, she said, "She wants to speak to the arresting officer of the off-worlder brought in earlier." Mika didn't catch the response.

The woman ended the call and stared at the Junior Agent, not at all intimidated by her. "You will have to wait."

Mika crossed the polished marble floor, each footstep reverberated off the walls. The space was probably calculated to intimidate. It was doing a good job.

Junior Agent Wietris gave him a tired nod when he reached her side. "I've just—"

The desk clerk interrupted, "Who is this?"

"Mika Hendri. He is here to assist with the case."

Mika recognized her tone from the first time he'd met the Junior Agent and clearly remembered how it felt to be on the receiving end. He didn't want to swap places with the receptionist.

"We are not open to the public. People have to have an appointment or a reason to be here."

The Junior Agent opened her mouth, no doubt to give a blistering reply, when she noticed a man striding toward them. She ignored the receptionist, focusing on the newcomer.

The man wore a black jumpsuit and Mika couldn't help wondering what it signified. *Is black covert operations?* Stars, he could be a cleaner for all Mika knew. As the man got closer, Mika changed his mind. No cleaner had ever projected such arrogance.

Junior Agent Wietris didn't look impressed by the new arrival. Mika thought that was a bad thing, especially when she glared at him as if he'd already insulted her.

The man hadn't reached them before asking, "Can I help you?"

Junior Agent Wietris didn't answer until he stood in front of her. "You can explain what is going on."

At least, the man in black didn't pretend not to know what she was talking about. "Shall we go somewhere more private?" He was already moving into the building.

In Mika's experience, it was never good when someone failed to introduce themselves, but the Junior Agent didn't waste energy getting annoyed. She flashed Mika a look that he was unable to interpret—probably some sort of warning.

*What does she expect me to do?*

They followed the nameless man deeper into law enforcement clutches. Mika suddenly understood the real reason Renteria hadn't come with them. As long as he was out there, somebody knew what had happened to them and could press the authorities for their release. He realized how vulnerable he would have been on his own. There was the band, but nobody was likely to listen to them.

Mika almost bumped into Junior Agent Wietris when she stopped in a doorway. He peered around her shoulder at the room ahead. What he saw reinforced his dark thoughts. It couldn't be someone's office—not with the lack of anything resembling comfort and with a surveillance camera mounted in the corner of the ceiling. Four chairs surrounded a round table, all of which were fixed to the floor.

The Junior Agent tensed, facing the man who now stood by the table. "Who are you?"

"I'm in charge of this investigation. That is all you need to know. Now, if you'd like to take a seat, we can get on with this."

"What exactly *is* this?" Junior Agent Wietris gestured to the interior of the interrogation room.

"It's obvious." His expression was cold. "We need to establish if a crime has been committed, and, if so, obtain redress for the victim."

Mika wanted to object. Rather than listen to them, the authorities were going to use their visit to gather evidence against Caryanne.

Junior Agent Wietris' jaw clenched. He wasn't expecting her to willingly march into the room and sit in one of the four chairs, but that was what she did.

"The other side, if you please." The officer pointed to the chairs at the far side of the table.

Mika wanted to put his hands over his head to protect himself from the explosion he was sure was coming, but nothing happened. The Junior Agent didn't move.

Mika scanned the man's mind and immediately felt a

cold detachment and determination to get the job done. His irritation was well controlled. Measured thoughts skimmed the surface of his mind, *"Off-worlders have to be made to understand that they cannot do what they want."*

Mika realized that the man was staring at him and hurriedly went to sit next to Junior Agent Wietris, wondering why in these circumstances, she didn't use telepathic influence. He tried to catch her eye, but she refused to look at him.

There was no way to ask, but he had the sense that he had annoyed her. Perhaps she detected his use of telepathy. He wanted to apologize and explain what he had seen in the officer's mind, but couldn't say anything. Unless...

He reached out telepathically. *"Can you hear me?"*

Her attention didn't waver in his direction, and yet, he heard, *"Stop."*

Wow, she *had* heard him. Tregaren was the only other person Mika had ever spoken to mind-to-mind. He'd spent all his life hiding the ability. She had told him to stop, but he wanted more than one word. Couldn't she see that they could work together to get Caryanne out?

With an annoyed huff, the officer finally sat in a chair on the opposite side of the table, glaring at Mika. "I have to warn you that the use of telepathy in any government-run or owned building is highly illegal and carries a significant prison sentence."

— — —

Kali hated interrogation rooms, even when she was the one doing the questioning. It brought back unpleasant memories of her time with the Priesthood—not that they had bothered to talk to her. Either they hadn't seen her as a person, or, more likely, they viewed all people who weren't a member of their organization as being no more than primitive animals.

In retrospect, that explained why she hated certain

things. Most of all, being locked up and feeling like she couldn't leave of her own free will.

Mika sat quietly. She had no idea why he'd attempted telepathy at the worst time and hoped the warning had been coincidental. *Doesn't he know that we're most likely being monitored?* No doubt the chair she sat in was collecting data about her blood pressure, heart rate, and oxygen levels. She had known that was a risk as soon as she stepped into the interrogation room.

If they were lucky, their brain activity wasn't being recorded by remote sensors, but Kali wasn't willing to take the chance. She hoped Mika now understood that it wasn't a good idea to use his ability in the presence of law enforcement on an unfamiliar world.

On being shown to the room, Kali had considered leaving, but despite the lack of overt security measures, she suspected they would have been stopped. She decided to do what the officer wanted, because if they resisted, there was too high a chance they'd be locked up and stuck until help arrived.

Kali would have to trust Andy to get them out if necessary, but in the meantime, she needed to take the chance to find out what was going on and discover more about Mika in the process.

The officer left them alone, but neither spoke since any innocent conversation could make matters worse. On his return, the officer slid into the seat opposite them, face expressionless.

Kali risked skimming his mind, much as Mika had done earlier but with more confidence of remaining undetected. She'd cringed when she'd sensed Mika's telepathy and had to hope that the officer hadn't known what was happening. This wasn't the same. Kali was only gleaning impressions on the surface where it was less likely to be discovered and deemed an offense.

He wasn't happy. She caught his name—Percy Joabe—and filed it away for when needed.

A loud crack made Mika and Kali jump, and for a second, she'd thought she'd been caught in the act.

The officer had slapped the surface of the table hard. "You will answer all questions truthfully."

Kali narrowed her eyes. Anger flared, catching her off-guard. She almost reached across the table with her telekinesis before Andy's warning played in her head. *Why do I want to slap Joabe's face so badly?*

A combination of tension and a loss of control created additional stress. The unexpected sound had almost shocked her to act—as always anger was her default response. At least she hadn't reacted. That would have been a mistake.

That's what Joabe probably wanted. She didn't have to read his mind to know. He was looking for any excuse to detain them, thereby solving his problem. Even though she understood what was happening, her anger remained, ready to erupt at the slightest provocation.

Wrestling the impulse to let Joabe know what he was really dealing with hurt, but she didn't think Andy would be impressed if she was involved in a diplomatic incident.

"Your employee is charged with committing a serious offense." Joabe stared at Mika as if he was just as guilty as Caryanne.

"I don't understand." Mika struggled to meet the man's gaze, and Kali wished he would pull himself together and not give in to the bully. "I mean, from what I understand, she had consensual sex with someone who wanted a relationship. That's not a crime."

"You have described the circumstances surrounding the incident, but that wasn't what she was charged with." When Mika's expression remained confused, Joabe continued, "This is a small, intense community contained underground, and there are laws. If we didn't take a strict stance, many people could be infected by one person's irresponsibility. You were all issued a copy of our civil codes upon arrival."

Kali closed her eyes, trying to center herself. She thought she knew what crime Caryanne had committed and it was ludicrous, but that didn't change reality. They were going to have to deal with the situation, regardless of its absurdity.

Mika still looked confused so, for his benefit, Kali said, "Can you spell out what she's done, please?"

Joabe's frown threatened to cause his eyebrows to meet in the middle. "Caryanne Westlaen is charged with sneezing in a public place and refusing to decontaminate the area within a reasonable timeframe."

Mika's mouth dropped open. When he tried to speak, Kali kicked him hard under the table. She didn't care if anybody saw the blow since it was more important that he didn't utter whatever was on the tip of his tongue at that moment.

Joabe had already noted Mika's expression. "The expelled air from one sneeze reaches speeds of one-hundred-fifty kilometers per hour, or more."

Mika started to laugh. Kali couldn't really blame him. She wasn't sure whether it was the seriousness with which Joabe described a sneeze or the absurd nature of the law, but it was hilarious.

Joabe continued as if anything he said now could alter Mika's reaction. "The accused made no attempt to sneeze into a tissue or her elbow."

Mika wobbled on the edge of his chair, holding his hands to his sides, laughing. Kali struggled to keep her face straight while her stomach muscles clenched as she held in the snicker. It was only the seriousness of their position that stopped her from joining Mika in rolling around in hilarity.

"It transmits nasal droplets and saliva through the air and is one of the primary ways that infectious diseases are transmitted."

If he didn't stop soon, there would be nothing she could do except join in.

"She should have immediately used a sanitization station after sneezing."

Unable to contain her amusement totally, Kali smirked. "Sanitizer was mentioned, but I don't think that constitutes warning us of the law." A law like that would need spelling out to visitors.

"A copy of our codes is relayed to each ship with the docking instructions."

*Well, shite. Andy... you and your foking obsession with getting to the concert in a hurry.*

Kali struggled to remain composed. "What happens now? Is there a trial or something? What if she is found guilty?" She asked the questions mainly to stop Joabe from reciting more sneezing facts.

"A decision will be reached in the next fifty days—"

Kali shot to her feet. "Fifty-days? For sneezing?"

"Yes, we don't appreciate outsiders interfering with our laws, which are in place to keep everyone safe."

"How is sickness even an issue? Don't you use medical nanotech to prevent disease like every other world? Caryanne was probably just sneezing from the dust! Her own nanites would—"

"Our beliefs and customs are our own business."

Mika gripped his stomach, crippled by a new round of laughter. "The dust!"

Things deteriorated quickly after that, until Mika and Kali found themselves locked in a cell together.

Kali crossed her arms. "Okay, that could have gone better."

Mika watched her warily from where he sat on the lone bench along the back wall of the stark white cell. "I thought that you were going to refuse to give up your handheld."

"I did have to consider it."

She hoped that Andy would appreciate the way she conducted herself. Despite the situation and the feeling that there was a fist around her throat, she chuckled.

"What are you laughing at?" Mika sounded miserable.

She supposed he'd exhausted his capacity for amusement for the time being. "It's just that I have a reputation for having a temper, but we basically got locked up because you found Zeron's laws so funny." She didn't mention that she thought Joabe was looking for an excuse. "It's just Andy will never guess the reason we're enjoying Zeron's hospitality."

"Agent Wie—"

"Call me Kali, since it looks like we'll be spending what's left of the night together." She sounded exhausted to herself and couldn't be bothered to hide it. "I wonder how long it will take them to find out everything about us?"

Mika hesitated. "Why do you think they kept us together? I mean, I'm glad they did. I just thought it would further their ends if we were separated. Isn't that how you normally deal with criminals?"

Kali smiled as it occurred to her that she could further her investigation into Mika while keeping her mind off being caged. "They'll be monitoring us for anything they can use against Caryanne and possibly us. We'd be unlikely to say anything worthwhile to ourselves."

She walked the three paces that were the extent of the floor space. "Andy will get us out, don't worry. So, with that in mind, you could tell me a bit about yourself. What do you like doing? What led to you managing a band that could have been from Earth?"

Mika leaned back against the white wall. "There isn't that much to tell. I built a ship to escape the planet I grew up on." He laughed, and it sounded a touch hysterical. "That sounds impressive when I say it out aloud."

"You built a ship?" Kali heard the disbelief in her voice, even though that's what she'd read in her research. "All by yourself?"

"My mother helped..." He trailed off.

"She helped, and then what happened to her? Was she just helping you to escape or...?" She stopped when she saw Mika's face drop. *Shite, something awful had happened to her.* "She's not dead, is she?"

Mika shrugged. "I don't know." He looked down at the hands in his lap.

"Let's talk about something else." She would see what she could find out when she got back to the ship. For now, she recalled the video image they had of the *Sepiantia*. It was a unique design and the ugliest ship she'd ever seen, but she wasn't going to offend him immediately after causing him pain. "How do you even begin to build a ship without a whole factory?"

He took a long breath in and smiled weakly. "That's the thing. I did have access to a factory. Our colony built ships. That's all they did and because I had talent, they wanted me to develop my skills. So, they gave me access to what I needed." He hesitated. "I never expected to keep the *Sepiantia*." Mika looked away.

Kali frowned. "That does seem strange." There was something he wasn't saying. *Keep him talking.* "I wouldn't know where to start. Flying is hard enough." She remembered the disastrous flight that almost ended her internship before it had begun. She'd wasted too much time running away from things. She flopped down next to him and whispered, "Caryanne can't be far away."

Mika didn't say anything, and she wasn't sure whether he was afraid the microphones would pick up whatever he said or if he just didn't care anymore.

"How did you become a band manager?"

"Just in the wrong place at the wrong time." He smiled weakly. "They needed transport, and I needed a job. Anyway, I was sucked in as soon as I heard those high-energy guitar riffs and booming rhythm."

Kali wasn't sure what to make of that, so she changed the subject again. "I think we should leave." She said it more to see what his reaction would be than because she meant it. She did have faith that Andy would come through; except, he might see it as part of her evaluation. "Shite."

He met her eyes then. "What?"

"It just occurred to me that Andy might want me to deal with this situation."

"Well, we can't break out, anyway. We'd never get off the planet."

Kali went quiet. How could she determine the best thing to do without having all of the information about others' intentions? Whatever she decided, it could be wrong.

If only she could use telepathy to find out more... but, she was pretty sure that this was not the life-threatening situation to constitute using her gifts. Telekinesis could no doubt free them, but breaking out wouldn't fix their problems. While the *Journey IV* would ultimately be allowed to leave—because who wanted an argument with Wil Sietinen—Mika's ship would be detained.

There had to be another way. Anything but negotiation; she would rather fight her way out. She took a calming breath. *Punching people in the face isn't how Agents behave.* Diplomacy was exactly what she needed right now, as much as it pained her to admit.

Kali had to assume they were on their own, since there was no guarantee Andy would come for them anytime soon. She was going to have to talk her way out without losing her temper. *Are we doomed?*

# CHAPTER 18

MIKA COULDN'T AFFORD to stay on Zeron much longer, not with Tregaren about to arrive. He didn't say anything because it was evident that the authorities weren't going to be bothered about his schedule.

"Kali..."

The Junior Agent stirred where she was curled up on the bench, and Mika couldn't help thinking that it was a shame to wake her because she was pretty when she was asleep. He felt oddly protective of her, being locked up together like this. He hated that once they were released, he still had to persuade her to come aboard the *Sepiantia*. He really didn't want to go through with Tregaren's plan.

It had sounded impressive when he'd told Kali that he'd built the *Sepiantia* with his mother. He'd been lucky. The technology and expertise had been available, and Tregaren had ensured that people wanted to help.

Why had he never thought about that before? Tregaren never did anything that wasn't in his own interest. Why had he wanted Mika to complete the project?

Mika didn't want to think about that now—not when the answer was obvious. Tregaren's plan had always been for Mika to search out Gifted women. That was why he wanted Kali on Mika's ship.

Mika had been a willing shipbuilder, since it was the only worthwhile activity on Veraria. The entire colony was obsessed with designing and building ships, limiting the options for anything else to do. Mika might have grown up with similar inclinations if it hadn't been for his mother; and, though he hated to admit it, even Tregaren had played a role in providing a different perspective.

Still, flying was something else entirely. Despite the mandatory flying lessons that all students were expected to take, nobody anticipated that Mika would be the one captaining the *Sepiantia* once it was complete. They hadn't taken account of his mother teaching him everything she knew about piloting.

Mika smiled, remembering the way Kali had failed to point out how ugly the *Sepiantia* was, which must have been to spare his feelings. He liked her for that alone. When she came aboard, she would see its beauty.

"What time is it?" Kali's voice was full of sleep.

"Early morning. Don't worry, I don't think our captors are awake yet."

"I need to pee." She said in such a matter-of-fact tone that he guessed it bothered her.

"Don't worry, I can face the far wall." Then he answered the obvious unspoken question, "I went while you were still asleep."

There was a bathroom area inside the cell, but without running water—just a spray that smelled of chemicals. *There probably wasn't enough water for people after they'd filled the fountain.*

Kali had just finished when the door opened, revealing their hard-faced interrogator. Mika jumped to his feet, ready to... do what? He was clueless about how to handle the situation.

"Good morning, Officer Joabe. Or should I call you Percy?" Kali greeted.

*How? Oh, she didn't!* Mika grinned. He couldn't help it, especially when the man took an involuntary step backward. *Percy Joabe.* That's the last name he would have put to the guy's face.

Kali didn't pause. "Technically," she cocked her head, "despite you warning us that telepathy is illegal, I'm not allowed to read your mind, anyway. But if you broadcast your thoughts so loudly that it's impossible not to pick things up, what can I do?" She shrugged. "Sorry, but you know how it is."

Joabe had gone as white as the wall, and Mika found himself leaning forward to watch. Genius, she had reminded him what she could do if pushed and was using the TSS' reputation against him.

"Now, I'll admit that I thought about breaking out last night. You might have overheard my conversation with Mika. However, it would obviously be better if we could come to an amicable arrangement."

Joabe straightened and managed half a smile. Mika realized that something had changed, because this wouldn't have been his reaction yesterday.

"Please," Joabe gestured out of the cell, "this way.

*Definitely* not the same reaction. Kali raised her eyebrows as she glanced at Mika. She looked pleased.

Mika couldn't move out of the door fast enough. "I've spent too long in here." Then he hastily added, "Though the company was great."

The sound of a commotion drifted down the corridor, and Mika slapped his forehead when he recognized Owen's booming voice. As a singer, his distinctive vocals carried even when he didn't mean it to.

"This gets better and better," Kali said under her breath. "Let's hope we don't all end up in jail."

"Your... colleagues are in reception. We tried to encourage them to leave, but they believe that you need rescuing."

"I'm sorry—" Mika started to say.

Kali cut him off. "All the more reason to get this sorted as soon as possible."

Joabe paused at the interrogation room, down the corridor from their holding cell, and Mika's heart hammered as he anticipated the hours to follow. Then, with a sigh, Joabe walked past, stopping at a comfortable office instead.

This room couldn't be more different from the other spaces. Images that were probably from the planet's surface covered the walls. The areas that weren't covered were shaded orange. Bright padding covered the chairs, and there was a drink machine in the corner.

Mika followed Joabe into the office and then realized that Kali remained in the corridor.

"Aren't you forgetting someone?" When Joabe looked blank, Kali said, "Caryanne." He started to respond, but she continued, "There's nothing to discuss until we know that she is okay. She has special..."

"Needs," Mika finished for her.

Mika saw Joabe's jaw tighten ever so slightly and guessed that he wanted to order them back to the cell. An unnatural silence lasted for a couple of heartbeats.

Joabe scowled as he spoke into his comm. "Bring Prisoner 415 to my office."

*They actually refer to those charged with a crime by a number!*

Mika looked at Kali, tempted to speak telepathically and then thought better of it. He didn't want to become number 416.

Mika sat in the seat Joabe indicated, too exhausted by stress to argue. Kali ignored the gesture and stayed near the door. Joabe also remained standing, shifting from foot to foot. His face wasn't so blank today, and Mika detected displeasure in the set of his mouth and deepening of tiny frown lines. His attention remained fixed on Kali.

Mika had heard what Kali said about not being able to use her telepathy, but those rules didn't apply to him. He didn't work for the TSS, so he didn't have to conform. Of course, he risked breaking Zeron's laws, but if he was going to be any use in getting them out of here, he had to take a chance.

He skimmed Joabe's mind. It was different from what he'd felt yesterday when there had been more arrogance and less fear. What could have changed? Joabe had always known that Kali was a member of the TSS.

Mika went in deeper. Joabe didn't have any family, and the job was everything to him. He was going on holiday next week for the first time in five years. *Not relevant.* There it was: Joabe had been sure that Kali's position in the TSS was in the Militia division and thought that she didn't have any abilities.

Mika saw how Joabe had made a mistake. The TSS didn't have a significant presence in the outer planets. Why would they bother sending an Agent to a world that had such a basic infrastructure? Then, Kali had proved who she was when she'd said his name. Whatever Joabe had planned for them that morning had to change. There was no way the TSS would leave one of their precious Agents locked up on a backward planet.

Mika paused, that was a point—how come he warranted *two* Agents? He thought about what he knew and realized that he should be as worried as Joabe.

Caryanne appeared in the doorway wearing a fuchsia jumpsuit. Apart from the way the garish color changed the hue of her skin, she looked surprisingly well.

"Mika, it's lovely to see you," she frowned, "even here."

He got up and put his hands on her shoulders, looking into her eyes. "Are you okay?"

Tears welled but none fell. "I am alive."

"Did they hurt you?" Kali asked from nearby, her voice sharp with a threat.

"There is no past or future, only now."

"What?" Kali said.

Mika intervened, "I'll explain later."

Joabe rummaged in a drawer and produced their handhelds. "You are free to leave."

"Without charge?" Kali asked.

*"Don't push it,"* Mika sent telepathically before he realized what he was doing.

He had no idea if Kali could hear him. She didn't give any indication, but she did stop talking.

"You are free to go without charge, but Ms. Westlaen, you will not be given another chance. Make sure that you cover your mouth in the future."

Caryanne looked confused. "There is no future, only the present."

"Let's go." Kali grabbed their handhelds and headed out before Joabe could change his mind.

"Thank you," Mika managed before racing after the other two.

They didn't stop until they were in front of the fountain. Caryanne looked confused. She was still wearing the jumpsuit. Mika was a little jealous of Caryanne at that moment. She didn't have the stress of getting them off-planet—of working out the length of time to take-off, and how he was going to get Kali on board.

Mika noticed that a mesh bag containing folded clothes hung from Caryanne's shoulder. "Perhaps you should get changed. We'll draw unwanted attention walking around with a prisoner."

"In the shuttle-car," Kali said. "I don't want him to change his mind and come looking for us." She was already moving toward one of the automated vehicles waiting nearby.

Caryanne followed. She was always compliant when she didn't know what was happening. He suspected that sometimes that was how she ended up in bed with someone she didn't know.

As soon as they were inside the shuttle-car and heading back to the docking station, Mika asked, "If you didn't use telepathy, how did you get his name?"

"Like I said, it was unintentional."

Mika wasn't sure whether to believe her or not, but she

met his gaze. "Revealing that information was a calculated risk. I took the chance that they wouldn't have the guts to make us disappear."

"Stars, they wouldn't have done that, would they?"

Kali didn't answer. Mika supposed that he should know better by now. This world wasn't the peaceful working colony it pretended to be.

# CHAPTER 19

KALI KNEW THEY were running out of time. Darlia's time was even shorter, wherever she was.

Mika had invited her to see the *Sepiantia*—clearly proud of the work he'd put into constructing it himself—but she wasn't sure whether to accept. She *did* want to investigate the ship to see if there were any potential ties to Darlia's disappearance, but something was making her nervous about going.

"Andy, stop ignoring me and give me a straightforward answer," she demanded of the Agent. After leaving her in a holding cell overnight, the least he could do was offer his opinion about whether the *Sepiantia* was worth seeing on the inside.

He looked up from the console. "I can't do that; this is your internship. If I start giving you all the answers, you'll fail."

Kali slumped in the chair. "Sorry, it's just... I thought."

"No, it's my fault. The lines got blurred and made things confusing." He sighed. "There are bits that we might need to work out together."

"Thank you for being honest about that. It helps."

"As to what you should do, listen to your training and instinct. That's the only answer I can give that doesn't compromise us both. How could you make it less risky?"

Kali nodded. Okay then, she was on her own but she could make decisions. She had been doing that all her life.

*Yeah, usually the wrong ones.*

After spending the night together as prisoners, she knew Mika better, but she couldn't say whether he was guilty of a crime or not. There were things she didn't know and those odd moments where she'd sensed he was holding something back. Then again, how was she going to find Darlia unless she took a chance?

"I'm going."

"That's not such a good idea."

"You just said—"

"I know, but you're proposing going alone into hostile territory."

Kali wanted to make light of his concerns, but she couldn't because of her nagging doubt. "How about if I get some of the band to come over here as an exchange of sorts?"

Andy halted whatever he was going to say and slowly nodded. "That would be a compromise, but he still might not care enough about them for that to be effective."

"Well, we have to investigate. We have no other leads." Kali knew that her impatience came through in her voice and tried to get it under control. "The only other option is if you came with me, but that's likely to increase the risk since if we both disappear, there'd be nobody nearby to help us."

She couldn't believe that she was talking about Mika like he was a sneaky criminal—the same man who'd risked himself to get Caryanne released from custody. Yet, Andy was right; she needed to trust her uneasy feeling that something was amiss.

All the same, gut feelings didn't make Mika guilty. She was certain he was hiding *something*, but it might be unrelated to their investigation. At the end of the day, her priority was to find Darlia. While she couldn't see Mika deliberately hurting anybody, she really didn't know him. She couldn't let him go until she was satisfied with his innocence.

"I need to inspect that ship to make sure that none of them have anything to do with Darlia going missing." She picked up her handheld. "I'll send one of them over here as insurance, if I can."

Andy nodded. "I like your idea to reduce the risk, but be careful."

"It might not work and Mika might not care, but it's the best I can do."

"Still don't like you going over there alone, but I knew that's what you'd decide."

"It's a shame that you haven't got anyone to bet against." She initiated a comm link to the *Sepiantia*.

"That would be unprofessional." She heard him add, "But, I do talk to people."

She was chuckling when Mika answered the call. "You're not coming," he stated before she could say anything. He looked slightly relieved.

"I was going to say that I will. Do any of your band members want to see the inside of a TSS ship?" She figured she'd make it sound optional rather than a condition, for starters.

Mika paled.

*Well, that's not a very enthusiastic reaction.* Kali smiled. "Why don't you ask around now, while I'm still here and then we can make arrangements?"

They stared at each other. Kali didn't know what she was going to do if he refused. Darlia was still missing and she needed to check she wasn't on that ship.

Mika activated the ship-wide communication system. His image faded, though the comm link was still open. Kali sat back in her chair, aware of Andy not voicing the same thing that she was thinking.

A minute later, Mika's grave face appeared. "Caryanne and Honk are on their way over."

"Okay, great! Andy will give them the grand tour." She ended the transmission and turned to Andy. "I guess this is happening."

"The *Sepiantia* isn't docked too far from here. As soon as you get there, give me a telepathic shout."

"Okay. Try to make Caryanne and Honk comfortable—it's better if they feel like guests rather than collateral."

"I know how to throw a good party," Andy acknowledged. "Be careful."

Kali left to brave the lift in the docking bay, following directions to bay 2113. It was much easier now she had familiarized herself with the layout of the station. After passing an excited Caryanne and Honk on the walkway, she knew it was the right direction.

The entrance was identical to theirs, aside from the number next to the outer hatch.

*"Andy?"* she tested the mental connection.

*"They're here,"* he responded immediately.

Kali stared at the closed hatch for a second, hoping that she was making the right decision. *No turning back now.*

The hatch swung open to reveal Mika waiting for her, a huge grin on his face. "Welcome aboard the *Sepiantia*." With a sweeping gesture, he invited her inside.

Kali wasn't sure if his eagerness was a product of pride for the ship or was a cover for nerves.

She took her first cautious step into the ship, her senses on high alert. To her surprise, the air was fresh with the faint smell of a forest after rainfall. "Wow," She reached for Andy, *"I've never seen anything like this."*

Relief came through Andy's telepathic link. *"I can still hear you."*

Disorientated by the strange environment, Kali reached out a hand to steady herself on a patterned wall of moving purple and orange. The wall was solid enough, but she had sunk into the floor. She looked down to find herself standing on a spongy substance that gripped her feet.

"It takes a little getting used to, but don't worry, it won't be long before you are more comfortable here than on a planet." Mika beamed. "You're getting a peek into my mind. I had free reign to use my imagination when designing her. I started when I was eight, which is why it gets a little crazy."

Kali forgot her surroundings for a second. "They let you start designing a ship at eight years old?"

"Yep, they recognized my genius." When she looked at him, he said, "I'm not even joking. What better way to motivate a boy than letting him build his own ship?"

Kali shook her head. It seemed like madness to her.

"When designing a ship, it's about getting the best function for the lowest cost. Each one is built to be efficient, unless commissioned by someone rich enough to afford fancy. My people tend to have a limited imagination. I was lucky. I started designing before I was influenced by sensible."

"They allowed you a lot of freedom at great risk." She was thinking aloud.

"I'd already proved to have the skills they were looking for." Mika sounded defensive.

"Sorry, I'm just fascinated, that's all."

"I was part of a project run to improve innovation."

"And, they let you keep the ship?"

Mika headed down the corridor. "Let me show you around."

The change of topic wasn't subtle, but she let it go—for now. She followed Mika.

The floor sucked at her feet slightly. She was surprised that with each step, it was easier to walk until she felt more steady than usual.

"I can increase the traction," Mika said, gesturing at the floor. "It's invaluable if we lose pressure and makes getting around in zero-G easy."

"What about the walls?" The word psychedelic came to mind.

He hesitated. "Yeah, well, they're just fancy because I

wanted the *Sepiantia* to be unique."

Kali thought about it and realized that it was also a good way of hiding control panels. Anyone boarding would have a hard time with basic operations until they knew the *Sepiantia* intimately.

Mika's excitement at having her on board had dimmed and she wondered if it was something she'd said. If so, things were only going to get worse.

"This way." Mika headed along the corridor toward the center of the ship.

"I can't wait." She didn't add that a tour wasn't the real reason she was there; he would find that out soon enough.

"Where is everyone?" She couldn't hear any sounds other than the air filtration system.

"Oh, it's too early for them; they'll be asleep for another few hours yet. You only got Honk because he hadn't been to bed yet, and Caryanne doesn't exactly keep normal hours."

Kali glanced at her handheld to confirm the time. "It's not early."

A soft alarm started. There was no urgency to the sound and Mika didn't appear concerned.

"Don't forget that they basically work nights." Mika canceled the alarm from his handheld.

"How is Caryanne?"

"Okay. She's just Caryanne—you know."

Kali didn't know and wasn't in the mood to let him off the hook. "Tell me. Explain what you meant when you said she's 'special'."

Mika stopped. His expression became uncertain as he considered a response.

Voice hardening, Kali said, "Why don't you try the truth?" She wondered if she was going to have to remind him who she was.

"I wasn't going to lie. It's just that I don't know how to explain." At her determined expression, he held up his hands. "Okay, okay. Caryanne had a traumatic past, which means she can't cope with worrying about the future."

Kali worked through what she knew. "So, when she says that 'there's only now', she means it. There is no past or future."

"She puts her energy into the present moment, believing that all pain comes from the past or future."

*That's tempting.*

Kali nodded. "So, once she was locked up, the present became scary, as well."

"I think so, she hasn't talked about it." He let out a little laugh. "Well, I suppose she wouldn't because of her mental state. It means that she can't function very well without assistance."

Kali was quiet, thinking of how she could relate to Caryanne. She'd done the same, in a way. She'd tried not to think about what had happened in the past. Only, she wasn't so successful, which was just as well because Caryanne didn't appear to cope very well out in the world.

*"Kali, just checking in."* Andy's voice was in her head.

*"I'm fine."*

"Anyway, the galley is this way." Mika continued with his tour of the ship.

She glanced at him, wondering if he could sense her conversation with Andy. It was likely that he could, but after the tension of the last few minutes, Kali was glad to move around. The galley more closely resembled a planetside kitchen than anything Kali had seen on a spaceship. There was even a range with gas flames, which seemed like a terrible idea for a spacecraft, but Mika insisted it was safe. Kali touched a state-of-the-art coffee machine and decided that she would forgive the ship its eccentricities for that alone.

The rest of the finishes were modern and practical, as well as being quirky and unique. She couldn't help thinking that it reflected Mika's personality. It was more about the aesthetic feeling of the space, like her parent's house, rather than being a simple vessel for getting from one place to another. Such attention to environment made sense, considering the *Sepiantia* was Mika's home as well as his way to leave Veraria.

None of the cabins were the same, and no attempt had been made at uniformity. The lounge had a garish purple wall, which clashed violently with green floor tiles. Kali wondered how Owen coped with the sight when he had a hangover.

She expected the flight deck to be standard, since it was the heart of operations, but Mika hadn't worried about that. There were no seats, only four brown blobs of goo surrounding a wraparound console. She couldn't make any sense of the control interface—dark and moving, with no discernible buttons.

"What in the...?" She trailed off.

Mika approached one of the brown blobs. "Here, I'll show you how they work."

He sank into a goo, which sculpted to his shape. "Try it."

Cautiously, Kali sat on the nearest blob. The cool material molded around her, conforming and supporting her body. When she moved, it flowed to accommodate the change in position.

"There's no need for restraints of any kind. It will keep you in place in the event of a crash.

A familiar panicky feeling rose in her. "What if I want to get up?"

"Just touch the release mechanism here." He pointed to a switch, which was easily reached on the righthand side, near the base.

When activated, the seat returned to blob shape, pushing her up and out at the same time. She stood and sat once again a couple of times to try it out. "Where did you find this tech? I've never seen anything like it in the central worlds."

"A researcher on Veraria stumbled across it while trying to improve escape pods. The big ship manufacturers didn't seem interested in licensing the tech, for whatever reason—probably because it looks weird."

"It does. Huh."

"Tabatha's a genius. She invented the flooring material, too," Mika explained.

"You worked with her on the ship?"

"She was more of an acquaintance. I kept to myself a lot as a kid."

Kali turned her attention from the chair to the viewscreen wrapping around the front of the flight deck. It was presently a dull gray, which was a strange contrast to the bright colors everywhere else.

"Oh, here." Mika touched the mysterious black control console, and the enormous screen sprang to life.

Kali's mouth involuntarily dropped open. The entire curved wall appeared as if it was open to the stars. "How do you get anything done with that view in front of you?"

Mika relaxed for the first time since she'd arrived. "Awesome, isn't it?" He had avoided her eyes while he'd showed her around, and it had taken her a little while to realize that he was nervous.

"When are you and the band leaving Zeron?" she asked, considering her options.

She could make him delay his departure or follow him to the next planet, but to have any hope of finding out what was going on, she needed to get him to open up.

"We need to be on Fureron for a gig tomorrow night." He checked the time. "I've scheduled departure in two hours and sixteen minutes." He swallowed. "There's something I need to ask you."

She waited.

He cleared his throat. "Would you travel with us, just as far as Fureron? It's only a few systems over, so it wouldn't take long, but it would give us a chance to talk."

It would solve one problem, but she was suspicious. It was too easy. What did he want to talk to *her* about? It didn't sit right.

*"They're planning to leave in just over two hours,"* she

relayed to Andy, realizing it had been too long since she checked in. *"Destination is Fureron."*

*"I'll look into it,"* he replied.

Andy had said to listen to her gut, and her instincts told her Mika wasn't interested in an innocent chat. As much as she found herself liking him, despite his obvious eccentricities, she didn't trust him.

"There are things I need to tell you, but we don't have time before we need to leave," Mika explained, as if he'd read her mind. "We have to get there tonight so that the Bruisers can meet with the stage lighting crew to get everything set before the gig tomorrow night. I'm not trying to be difficult."

"What takes more than two hours to explain?"

"It's complicated... and I have other things to take care of before we leave."

Kali knew what Andy would say, but she was torn. She needed to find Darlia and even though there was no sign of her on the *Sepiantia*, Mika was connected to her disappearance in some way. Perhaps not the rest of the band, but Mika was different.

*He wants to talk, so I should hear him out.* The chance to do that away from the insane authorities on Zeron was even better. Kali nodded her agreement. "Very well, we'll meet you there on the planet." She was pleased with herself for making a firm decision. It was a good compromise that didn't risk her failing the mission.

"Fine." Mika didn't look happy as he busied himself making entries into the bizarre command console.

*"I'm heading back,"* Kali relayed to Andy. *"Mika wants to talk, but it'll have to be on Fureron."*

*"All right. I haven't had a chance to look up the gig venue yet. Caryanne and Honk have a surprising number of technical questions for a couple of musicians."*

She started for the door. "I'll send Caryanne and Honk back over. We'll see you on Fureron."

Mika's head snapped up. "Why don't you stay a little

longer?"

A warning went off in Kali's head. "I don't think so." She hurried for the exit. "I'll see you soon."

"Kali, wait." His voice was urgent. "Kali—"

She wasn't listening. *"Andy, there's a problem."*

He responded immediately, *"Get out of there now."*

She dashed toward the hatch, but she found the outer hatch was sealed. "Fok." Panic set in. *"I think I'm trapped."*

She marched back onto the flight deck to find Mika wringing his hands.

"Open the door," she demanded.

"I'm sorry, it's—"

Rage blotted out the panic. Kali punched him, releasing all the anger she'd been holding back since receiving her internship assignment. She caught him on the side of the jaw. His head snapped back as the force swung his body away from the console. At the same time, her professional sensibilities took over and she gripped him in a telekinetic vise.

"Open the foking door."

# CHAPTER 20

MIKA MADE AN unintelligible sound. Kali had hit him—
*actually* hit him.

In his stunned shock, it took him a moment to realize
he was being gripped by an invisible force. An electrical
hum filled his ears. Kali's naturally bright aura was blazing
now.

His brain formed words, but his mouth wouldn't work
properly. His jaw ached. "I was trying to explain that I
can't." The words came out slurred as if he was drunk. "The
station blocked the hatch when they brought our departure
time forward."

"They what?" Kali glared at him.

"I'd requested an earlier window a while back, before
we arranged the tour. They never confirmed, so I didn't
think it'd been approved. I thought they'd give a warning. I
mean, I'm missing two members of my band!"

Most of what he said was true, except he didn't tell her
that he knew bumping up the window would trap her on
the ship, and he'd known the exact time that would happen.
He had wanted to let her go, and he couldn't explain why
he'd done what Tregaren ordered—trapping her here and
leaving his friends in the hands of the TSS. He hadn't
wanted to do any of it, and yet he had.

Kali quivered with barely contained rage. "I want systemwide access."

Mika stared at her. "It won't do you any good—" The telekinetic vise tightened around him.

"Give me access. Now."

Mika's face throbbed from her punch and the pressure around his chest was making it difficult to breathe. He didn't want to experience a full-on telekinetic blow, so he did as she demanded. It occurred to him that he couldn't overpower Kali physically or psychically, not with her training, and she wasn't likely to trust him. Somehow, he had to gain her cooperation.

"There, you have unrestricted access to the *Sepiantia*, but the system interface is designed for me only."

Kali released her tight grip on him, but he still sensed a loose hold. She began checking the communication log, scrolling through messages as if she owned the ship.

Mika massaged his jaw. *She hit me.* His brain still couldn't deal with that fact.

The comm link beeped with an incoming message.

"Answer it," Kali instructed.

"Sepiantia," he answered.

An automated voice came over the speaker. "Cleared for take-off."

Mika and Kali stared at each other. He could see her weighing her options. Given how the authorities had reacted to a sneeze, she couldn't abort take-off without an element of risk.

"Sepiantia, please acknowledge."

"Understood," Kali replied. Her breathing was slower and she appeared calmer until she turned in Mika's direction and he saw her expression.

*"Torture and dismemberment."* The words appeared in his head.

He didn't dare respond to the threat with anything as intimate as telepathy. Considering how he felt after a punch, Mika would rather avoid finding out what it felt like to have his arms pulled off.

An upbeat chime sounded over the speaker. "Please hand over control so that the station can guide you out."

Kali grimaced, but she nodded for Mika to proceed. "Do it. We will wait for *Journey IV* as soon as control reverts back to the ship."

Mika addressed the onboard computer, "Sepiantia, allow station access."

"Granted."

He didn't hear the dull thud of the docking clamps release, but the view on the front screen displayed transit away from the planet. The shift into space was so smooth, they hadn't felt a thing. Mika had to act before control of the ship automatically returned to him.

— — —

Kali kept a close watch on Mika while checking the readings, but she was still unprepared for the blast of telekinesis. She instinctively reinforced her mental shield before realizing that the attack wasn't aimed at her.

The *Sepiantia* shuddered as the ship was ripped away from the remote guidance assistance. *Stars, is Mika trying to get us all killed?*

An angry voice came over the speaker—too angry to be automated. "Unauthorized use of weapons is an offense and we will take whatever measures necessary to protect the planet."

*What an overreaction. It isn't like anybody was at risk.* "What weapon?" Kali bluffed. She knew exactly what had happened when she'd felt Mika's badly controlled blast of telekinesis, but she wasn't going to admit to anything. "We don't know what's going on." She glared at Mika, challenging him to contradict her.

He looked away, which was good because she was quite prepared to throttle him at the first sign of defiance.

"That force came from the *Sepiantia*." The voice paused

and Kali had the impression that a discussion was going on out of earshot, before continuing. "We received information about how dangerous you were from the local police. An attack on our systems will not be tolerated."

*So that was Mika's plan. Make sure that we are seen as a threat to stop me from taking the* Sepiantia *back to Zeron or waiting for the* Journey IV. Kali might have been impressed with his duplicity if she wasn't so mad and worried.

"It's sixteen hours to Fureron. Are we waiting for the Zeron authorities to shoot at us, or are we jumping?" Mika asked, daring to fiddle with the nav console.

Kali ignored him and spoke into the comm link, "Who am I speaking to?"

Another male voice said, "You have forty-five seconds to leave Zeron airspace before we take offensive action."

Kali didn't bother to argue since it wouldn't achieve anything; the authorities wanted them gone. Percy Joabe had obviously shared his experience and someone must have been watching to know that she was on the *Sepiantia*. She understood for the first time why the policy on the use of telepathy was so strict.

Forty-five seconds wasn't enough time to do anything. She had no idea how long the *Sepiantia's* shields would hold up against bombardment by planetary missiles and didn't want to find out.

Kali reached for Andy with her mind since their link was firmly established. *"We have a problem."* She gave him a brief outline of the situation while making a quick entry on her handheld.

The same voice came through the speakers. "Twenty seconds."

Kali swallowed. *"Andy, we need to jump. We'll meet you at Fureron in sixteen hours."*

"Count down ten, nine, eight..." The voice had reverted to the metallic sound of a machine.

"Jump," Kali shouted at Mika who was busy inputting coordinates.

*What is he doing?*

"Six, five, four..."

"Mika, jump, now!"

The ship hummed under Mika's touch and he stroked the console. The view outside the front display changed to shimmering blue-green light as the ship slipped into subspace.

— — —

Andy put a hand to his head as his telepathic link with Kali was ripped away. The *Sepiantia* disappeared from sensors and he stared at where she had been a second before.

Caryanne sobbed. "Mika left without us." There were tears in the corner of her eyes.

Honk put an arm around her. "It's okay." He looked at Andy for reassurance.

Andy's smile was automatic, but he wasn't sure he managed to hide his worry. "They had to leave quickly, and we're going to meet on Fureron."

*I should have stopped Kali from going over there. It was too risky.*

He opened communication with the station. "This is the TSS *Journey IV* requesting immediate departure."

There was a delay before a male voice responded. "The first available window is in one hour and forty minutes."

"That is unacceptable." Andy's response was immediate. *What were these fools playing at?*

Again, there was a delay before anybody responded. "We are not able to make exceptions."

"This is an emergency. I need to follow the *Sepiantia*." Feeling his patience slip away, he added, "The TSS requests an immediate, emergency departure." *They will listen to me.*

It was hard to concentrate with Caryanne crying in the background. Honk was murmuring nonsense about them going out together on Fureron in a few hours. *We have to get off this planet first.*

"Honk, why don't you take Caryanne to choose a cabin."

Thankfully, Honk nodded and led her away, just as the speaker crackled. "We will allow departure in thirty minutes."

"You will allow departure in thirty seconds. I am pursuing an investigation and if you do not comply, a formal complaint with be logged with TSS Headquarters. Then you can expect a lot of attention—"

"One minute and thirty seconds to the nearest window."

Finally, a reasonable response. "Accepted."

Andy prepared to follow the *Sepiantia*, hoping that the gnawing sensation in his gut was a result of the Zeron protein diet and nothing else.

# CHAPTER 21

WITHOUT TIME TO work out proper coordinates, Mika had only taken them outside of Zeron's space traffic control zone, but now he needed to somehow get them to the meeting point. He could feel Kali's eyes on him while he programmed the next jump. *Stay calm. You have a plan and she needs you. Nobody can fly this ship except you,* he tried to assure himself.

When the proposed route of beacon locks appeared on the nav console, Kali looked dubious. "It can't possibly take sixteen hours to get to Fureron, even with the most rudimentary civilian jump drive."

Mika wasn't stupid; he'd fed Kali just enough information to cover his actions. He would only reroute to the real coordinates, once Kali relaxed and wasn't so vigilant. She had to drop her guard at some point, although he had his doubts, looking at her now. He had to keep everyone happy while making sure that nobody found out what he was really doing. His throat tightened as he thought about the impossible task ahead. *Don't dwell on it.*

"Well, that's where we're heading. You might be overestimating the capabilities of civilian jump drives—the TSS has spoiled you."

Kali's nostrils flared. She was clearly furious, but he'd

already told her about the misunderstanding with the departure request. It was a flimsy excuse, but it was the best he'd been able to come up with on short notice. Her abduction needed to look like an accident.

Not for the first time, he wondered if he should have disobeyed Tregaren. If he had, it would have only been the second time in his life that he had gone against the ex-Priest's wishes.

The last time, he'd lost his mother. She was probably dead, but until he knew for sure, he had to try to find her.

"There's nothing more to do for now. Would you like a cabin for the voyage? We have an extra," Mika offered.

"Maybe in a bit after I've gotten to know the ship's controls."

That wasn't what Mika wanted to hear. He set about trying to distract himself, doing anything that meant he didn't have to think about Kali and what lay ahead. She had helped get Caryanne out of jail and he'd gotten to know her a bit in the process. Without her, he suspected that they would still be on Zeron, waiting for a trial date.

Mika watched as Kali became increasingly frustrated, trying to work out why the ship wouldn't respond. Nobody else could fly the *Sepiantia*; he'd had to do something to make sure that Tregaren couldn't take control. The *Sepiantia* required a neural link to back up major commands and, for now, it was configured to Mika alone.

Eventually, the ship dropped out of subspace at its first scheduled cool-down stop—or so Kali would think. She finally accepted defeat and went to use the facilities in the guest cabin, freeing up Mika for his next order of business.

He didn't want to contact Tregaren. He put off the call as long as he could, but on one of the cool-down stops for the jump drive, he eventually excused himself and went to his quarters. If he didn't do what Tregaren wanted, there would be consequences—if not for his mother, then for the band. Yet, he knew better than anyone what Tregaren was capable of so, how could he hand Kali over? He felt as though he had swallowed a weight as he put the call through. It was as if his hands worked independently of his brain.

Tregaren's harsh features appeared, shrouded in darkness. His expression of irritation smoothed into a half-smile.

As always, Mika stayed alert, trying to identify anything in the background that would tell him more about Tregaren's whereabouts or what he got up to when alone. It was a wasted effort because he immediately recognized the interior of the ship.

"She's here," Mika said the words before he could change his mind.

Tregaren nodded once and the screen went black. It was sensible to keep the transmission short, considering Kali's ability, but still, he couldn't help being exasperated by the abrupt end. *Let it go. That's the least of your troubles.*

Using the remote access terminal in his quarters, Mika activated the subspace communication jammer so Kali would no longer be able to use her handheld. Since the comm link wouldn't work in subspace, anyway, she wouldn't notice until it was too late.

Taking a deep breath to steady his nerves, he initiated the independent jump-drive that nobody knew was installed—an incredibly rare device for any civilian ship to possess, secretly salvaged from TSS wreckage during the war. It had been Tregaren's gift to Mika for work well done. Mika had always hoped to use it to escape his adversary one day, allowing untraceable transit without the use of the SiNavTech navigation beacon network, but that time hadn't come yet.

If Kali checked their course on the flight deck nav console, it would appear like they had begun the next jump in their scheduled journey after the requisite cool-down period. Kali would no doubt be diligently watching their progress toward Fureron, but she'd be in for a surprise when they reached their true destination.

— — —

Andy's stomach had a knot the size of a large shuttle. Somehow, he'd managed to lose the *Sepiantia* with Kali on board. Saera should never have trusted him with a trainee.

The *Sepiantia* must have transitioned into subspace, which meant that they must have an unregulated independent jump drive.

*This is bad. Very, very bad.* Andy scrolled back through the readings, searching for any clues. The sensors picked up a spike in heat and radiation a fraction of a second before the ship disappeared.

He braced himself on the console, not liking what it implied. He had the impression that Kali thought that Mika was an unlikely suspect, and yet she hadn't been comfortable going to the *Sepiantia*. That was why he was now carrying two extra passengers, both of whom were crazy in different ways.

With that thought, he checked where they were, thinking that it would be easier to lock them up. The camera in the lounge showed Caryanne scribbling in a journal and Honk was logged as asleep in one of the spaceship's cabins. It seemed that he had arrived with his own alcoholic supplies, which he proceeded to drink.

Andy had hoped to get some information out of them while they were separated from the rest of their party. Both had proved useless so far, not helped by the lack of time to interrogate them. Still, if he didn't ask and they knew where Mika might have gone, he would feel a fool.

He activated the comm link. "Caryanne, could you come to the flight deck, please?" When she hadn't moved after a few seconds, he added, "I need to ask you something."

She rose gracefully and without hurry. When she made it to the flight deck, her journal was still in her hand.

One look at her unfocused eyes and Andy wasn't sure why he was bothering asking her anything. At least there was a chance of Honk sobering up at some point as long as he didn't discover the emergency alcohol stashed in the commander's office. Caryanne was playing by a whole different set of rules. There was none of the earlier distress that she had displayed when the *Sepiantia* took off unexpectedly.

"Your boss just disappeared."

"My boss? Mika? He's our manager, not our boss."

"Yeah, well, you're missing the point." He did his best to keep the irritation out of his voice, but she didn't seem to notice it anyway. "Do you know where he could have gone?"

She cocked her head to one side. "I might never have known."

Like he'd thought, it was pointless trying to have a conversation with her. He scanned the surface of her mind and found the strangest jumble of sensations and images that he'd ever encountered. Confusion—that was her mind, and it was very effective at keeping him out.

It occurred to him that she might be using it as some sort of defense, but he wasn't willing to risk it. He was afraid of pushing past the surface and being sucked into a nightmare from which he couldn't escape. Best to wait for Honk to sober up.

In another time, he would have felt sorry for her, but for now, his priority was to find Kali. He tried not to think about how she had disappeared in the same way as the other women. Not only that, but she'd already survived that nightmare once. It couldn't be allowed to happen again. He had to find her, and fast.

*What to do first?* He could wait to see if the *Sepiantia* showed up at Fureron, but it was best to alert Saera to the situation as soon as possible. He would need help from Headquarters.

He scanned the flight deck. Caryanne had gone, and when he checked, he saw that she was back in the lounge. Honk remained in his quarters. Andy initiated the call.

Saera answered quickly, and from her expression had guessed there was trouble. "Tell me the worst."

"I've lost Kali."

He explained what had happened, and when he'd finished, Saera asked, "What are you planning to do?" There was no anger or condemnation in her voice.

"Our options are limited. The only thing I can think to do is to wait here at Fureron to see if they show up. However, Kali's final message to me said it would take sixteen hours, so it could take a while to find out if this is a false alarm."

Saera was thoughtful. "Yes, if they aren't tied to a beacon, they could be anywhere."

"Our only hope is to find someone who has spotted them and can give us an idea in which direction they went." Andy slumped. "The ship is distinctive at least."

"If they made an effort to lose you, I doubt they're headed your way."

"I know, but what else can I do? Pace a track in the flight deck." Neither of them smiled; the situation was too serious. "We'll get her back; we have to."

"I can set up a trace on the *Sepiantia's* course along the SiNavTech beacon network. As you know, it's far from standard practice, but I know my way around the system well enough."

Andy didn't ask what backdoor permissions Saera had persuaded her father-in-law to give her. Instead, he waited and tried not to get too hopeful while she set up the trace.

Saera focused on the readings off-screen as she spoke, "The first leg of the jump went without incident, but then... they disappeared. An independent jump drive is the only explanation, as you suspected."

It was what Andy had feared. "We have to find her."

Saera nodded, returning her attention to him. "I know. I just keep thinking about all she's been through and hope that she can handle the situation."

"She's stronger than you think, Saera. Trust me, I've

gotten to know her a bit in the time we've spent together. I hate to say it, but we might have to rely on Kali to get herself out of this mess."

"I suppose she's proved herself capable enough, if a little rash and too willing to take chances to get results."

"Really, no worse than most of us at her age." He ran a hand through his hair. "My first trainee, and I go and lose her. I'm really, really sorry."

"It's not your fault. It's one of the dangers facing trainees at this stage of their training." She straightened. "Right, I'll send what back up I can and check for reports of any unusual activity in that area. I'll also put out a reward for sightings."

She looked as tired as Andy felt, but he wisely kept that observation to himself. "Okay, at least we have a plan."

He was just about to end the call when she said, "Andy, take care of yourself and remember it wasn't your fault."

"I'll be fine when we get her back."

*I shouldn't have allowed Kali to go over to the ship alone.* Hindsight was cruel when she got her claws in deep.

—  —  —

Kali wandered through the *Sepiantia*, barely noticing the way the floor sucked at her feet anymore. The corridor illuminated where she walked, fading behind and brightening as she drew closer. She remained in a bubble of light and was tempted to try running just to see if she could outrun the automatic response.

Mika hadn't told her that a neural link was needed to fly the ship, but it was the only thing that made any sense. It seemed there was a lot he hadn't mentioned.

After doing everything she could to check that they were on route to Fureron, Kali decided that she needed to make sure there were no surprises on the rest of the ship. First, it wouldn't hurt to take a few minutes to freshen up and let Mika believe that she trusted him. That way, she hoped he'd drop his guard, and she'd find out what was really going on.

Kali had taken Mika up on his offer for her to use the guest cabin, giving her the opportunity to remove the contact lenses hiding her bioluminescent eyes. The cabin was decorated in shades of green, reminiscent of a jungle, which must be the desired effect. There had even been the soft sound of distant bird calls. It might have been therapeutic if she'd spent any time in nature, but as it was, she expected a giant spider to drop down any second. As soon as she'd used the facilities, she set off to explore the rest of the ship.

The whole vessel was so different from where she'd been living for most of her life that it would take some getting used to. The bold styling made her think of her childhood and her family home. *Stars, this isn't the right time to get homesick.* The sudden desire to be back with her family made her realize just how frightened she was about being trapped on the *Sepiantia.*

There was no way the sooner-than-planned departure from Zeron had been an accident, which meant that Mika had nefarious intentions. She wasn't sure why it made her sad to have confirmation of his ill-intent. It wasn't as if he was a friend, and she had more important things to worry about.

She wished that she could be confident that Andy was close behind, but something about the stated navigation plan was wrong. It was true that civilian jump drives required cool-down periods and weren't as efficient as the specialized drives used by the TSS, but 'sixteen hours to go a few systems over' didn't check out. Either he was hiding a detour, or they weren't going to Fureron at all.

The possibility of an unregistered independent jump drive was another reason to examine every millimeter of the *Sepiantia.* She'd learned during her training that they'd become a hot commodity on the black market in the years following the war, and it wouldn't surprise her to find that

Mika had somehow acquired one to go with his bizarre collection of unique tech on the ship. If the *Sepiantia* did somehow have an independent jump drive, she was thoroughly foked. Unless she could get out a signal with her location, the ship's path would be completely untraceable.

While knowing the kind of tech she was up against was important, her other priority was to see if Darlia was hidden somewhere on the ship. Aside from concern about the missing woman, she needed to know if she was on her own or if there was a hostage to free. Her plan of action would have to take account of all the elements.

The way the control panels were concealed behind a kaleidoscope of color made Kali wonder what else Mika was hiding behind the walls. Her brain was getting used to the strange environment, and she moved along the corridors quickly without feeling nauseated. She kept her mind open as she walked, trying to feel for anyone who might be hidden behind a concealed door.

It was only when she reached the galley that she encountered anyone else. It took Kali a moment to identify the gangly young woman. She looked utterly different off-stage, and without the blue hair, it would have taken her longer to place her.

"Hello. It's Vaira, right?"

The woman turned from the stovetop but didn't smile. "Yep, that's me."

Kali was startled by her hard, hazel eyes. They'd been blue when she'd seen her after the show on Zeron. Kali's brain recorded those sorts of details automatically.

"Do you mind if I join you?" If Kali was going to conduct a thorough investigation, then she needed to interview everyone on board.

"Whatever."

It wasn't the enthusiastic response Kali had hoped for, but it was good enough. Thinking that she wouldn't get very far by launching straight into what she wanted to know, she started simple. "It must be different playing on

Zeron compared with Glaendor."

Vaira mixed batter, holding the bowl in the crook of her arm and using a wooden spoon rather than the integrated chrome machine. She poured some of the batter into a frying pan.

"Suppose."

There was a sizzle of hot fat and the air filled with the sweet smell of pancake. Kali's mouth watered.

It was clear that small talk wasn't going to work, which left Kali with two options—to test her authority or try honesty. She was sure that if she tried the first route, Vaira would laugh, which left the second.

"Look Vaira, I don't know how much Mika has told you, but I'm investigating the disappearance of a woman from Glaendor."

Vaira turned from the frying pan to Kali with wide eyes. Her surprise seemed genuine. "You think we had something to do with a woman's disappearance?"

If she told the whole truth, she risked alienating Vaira more, but now that she'd started down this route, there wasn't much choice. "Possibly. She came to your show—"

"Gig. It's called a gig." Vaira turned back to the frying pan. "Are you investigating Mika or all of us?"

"I'm investigating everyone." Kali wondered if Vaira knew that Mika had abilities and considered if there would be any benefit from disclosing the information. She decided to keep it to herself for now.

"I've never seen Mika talking to a woman for more than a few seconds. Besides, he wouldn't do that after what happened to his own mother."

The hair stood up on the back of Kali's neck. She remembered him mentioning his mother on a couple of occasions, and both times he'd been reluctant to talk. She knew something bad had occurred but had never pressed him.

Kali tried to keep her voice as casual as possible. "What happened to his mother?"

She needn't have worried. Vaira had relaxed her guard and was busy scraping pancakes onto a plate. "She disappeared, and he's been searching for her ever since."

Kali still didn't know what was going on but another missing woman was too much of a coincidence to be unrelated.

# CHAPTER 22

KALI STOOD IN a bubble of light in the corridor and closed her eyes. They were still in subspace, and she felt the effect dampen her abilities. Despite that, she could sense that Mika was on the flight deck and Vaira remained in the kitchen. Luca and Owen were at the other side of the ship, either in their cabins or the lounge. There was nobody else nearby.

*All right, no Darlia. Time to see what kind of tech he's hiding.*

She narrowed her eyes and followed the corridor, using her telekinesis to feel the edges. It wasn't long before she felt a slight change in the wall. On closer examination, she found the edge of a hatch. There was no way she would have spotted it purely by sight.

*It's past time to have a look below.* A short ladder behind the camouflage catch took Kali into the space under the spongy deck. Pipes and machinery blocked her view.

With the sort of distances that the *Sepiantia* traveled, there should have been more than one engineer monitoring the mechanical systems, but Kali already knew that there would be nobody. That meant that Mika must act as an engineer, as well as the captain, pilot, navigator, and the band's manager. *He probably also writes quantum physics theorems and cures genetic ailments in his free time.*

Kali rolled her eyes at her own sarcastic quip as she dropped into the maintenance tunnel. The crawlspace led the length of the ship, and she headed for the rear. After a few dozen meters, she reached a Y-intersection, which no doubt led to the two prongs of the jump drive. The external hardware was the same for standard and independent jump drives, with the key difference being the nav console and its satellite components in Engineering. Since Mika was happily camped out in the flight deck, Kali's best option was to try to locate evidence of black-market components in the mechanical control room.

She found an access hatch nearby and peeked through it. The overhead lights in the Engineering room were dimmed, but the space was illuminated by the readouts for the ship's systems. She dropped inside.

It only took a moment to spot the piece of equipment she'd feared she'd find: the ancillary processing core for an independent jump drive. Kali suddenly wished she'd paid more attention in engineering class.

Her worries confirmed, she began scanning the room for anything else out of the ordinary. Her heart dropped when she spotted the status display for the weapons systems—not the standard lasers to blast away an asteroid to avoid a collision, but enough armaments to rival a small military ship.

*What the fok are they up to on this ship?*

They hadn't spotted the weapons on a scan, which meant that the *Sepiantia* was also equipped with advanced shielding.

Really, it was a wonder Mika had allowed her on board, never mind come up with a ruse to make her stay. *What kind of trap did I walk into?*

While Kali didn't really care about the illegal weapons, she was bothered by the fact that Mika had left her unattended, knowing she might snoop and discover the *Sepiantia*'s secrets. He couldn't expect her to turn a blind eye, which meant he never intended her to leave the *Sepiantia*.

She was about to climb back up into the access tunnel when the main door to Engineering opened. Mika stood on the other side, arms at his sides. "Thought you might be here, but I figured you'd use the door." His cheerful tone sounded forced.

"Hey, Mika." She gave a bashful shrug as she glanced at the open access hatch in the ceiling. "Just checking out your handiwork. It's an impressive setup."

He entered slowly, hugging the side wall to face her. "I see you were inspecting our weapons system."

"You have quite the assortment."

"It's not illegal to have weapons for defense. You know, it's dangerous on the outskirts of the galaxy. It's pirate law out here."

*Is he implying that I've lived a sheltered life on Tararia?* She narrowed her eyes. "It's illegal not to declare them on your docking logs. Are they even registered?"

"I don't believe a TSS Junior Agent has the authority to request our registration documents without a warrant."

*Is he trying to pick a fight?* If so, she had no intention of making it easy for him. Okay, so she had already punched him earlier, but he'd deserved it.

Kali stared at him levelly. "I want you to stop playing games and tell me what's going on. I'll do what I can to help you get out of whatever trouble you must be in."

Their eyes locked. Mika was the first to look away, but not before she'd seen a flash of guilt. She was definitely in trouble. Nobody knew where she was.

"Whatever you've done, we can sort it." That wasn't true, of course, but Kali needed to use any tactic at her disposal.

She saw by the set of Mika's jaw that he wasn't tempted by her offer. He walked past her, deeper into Engineering. Kali tensed as he passed by the weapons console, but he continued on to the control interface for the jump drive. He checked the readings.

Remembering her success with Vaira, she decided to try being honest. It was a huge risk on so many levels, but she could hardly get into deeper trouble.

"With women disappearing, I need to know... Are you working with someone connected to the former Priesthood? I know more about their experimentations than most." His expression didn't change but she sensed his interest. "I was their captive for eighteen months."

"You survived?" He sounded wistful rather than surprised. He looked to the side even though there was nothing there before saying, "Kali, I'm sorry. I know about what happened to you."

She wasn't sure what to say. Everyone at Headquarters had known, and it wasn't as if she'd ever tried to run away from it, but she hadn't been prepared for a criminal investigation suspect to know her life story.

Mika said, "I found out anything I could about the women the Priesthood captured to produce clones."

She waited, curious as to what he was going to say. His mother had gone missing. Did he suspect that she had suffered the same fate?

Mika stopped and couldn't meet her eyes. He clearly felt guilty about something.

She didn't want to disclose any more, but she had to keep him talking. "That's why I joined the TSS, so I could help others." She swallowed; her mouth had gone dry. "I don't like to think about it, but I survived when most didn't."

"You must have had to be so brave." He met her eyes, and she saw that he wanted to know more. But why? Was he searching for his missing mother or did he wonder what had happened to the women that went missing?

What she didn't say, because she couldn't form the words, was that she'd had a son. He wasn't hers anymore, if he'd ever been. If that was true, why did she feel so bad? She hadn't even been able to find the courage to see him before she'd given him away. There was nothing brave about what she'd done.

Mika might know about it already. It hadn't been much of a secret even at the time.

Mika raised his eyes upward, as if asking an unknown deity for help before returning his attention to her. "I told him you are on the ship."

The spike of fear was instant. He'd confirmed that the threat was real and she was in danger. But she needed to know exactly what she was up against.

"You told whom?"

Mika opened and closed his mouth, and she wanted to shake the answer out of him. It was clearly a struggle for him to speak. He whispered, and it was only because every cell of her was waiting and listening that she heard.

"Tregaren."

She didn't know the name. Although, he probably wouldn't use the same name as before, not if he was in hiding.

"He's... one of them?" She meant the Priesthood but saying the name would make it impossibly real.

Mika nodded. "And he's coming."

# CHAPTER 23

IN THE BACK of his mind, Mika knew that Tregaren had to be Kali's worst nightmare. He wondered why he'd told her the truth. It was cruel. The condemnation, the anger, he'd expected didn't materialize.

"Thank you for telling me."

She'd actually *thanked* him. Instead of feeling grateful that she hadn't punched him, he felt worse.

"Take us back to the coordinates before we entered subspace on the last jump," Kali requested.

Mika shook his head. "I can't." He wasn't sure why he couldn't, he just couldn't.

"Then take us to Fureron."

"I'm sorry. There's nothing I can do about it—he's on his way. He always knows where the ship is and there's no hiding from him." He didn't know why he couldn't stop speaking. Was he trying to provoke her, looking for violence because he felt he deserved it?

"What's in it for you?" Her voice was calm, but it made him want to step back. "I didn't think you were like the Priests. Was the Mika I've seen so far just an act?"

Mika would have preferred a physical attack. "Tregaren left the Priesthood before their fall."

"You believe that? Nobody left the Priesthood and lived."

Mika pretended that he hadn't heard. "Anyway, he only wants to talk to you and the others. Women with ability have the potential to undo the harm caused by the Priesthood."

Her expression turned incredulous. "Really, you can't be that stupid, can you? He isn't going to help you. I wouldn't be surprised if he hadn't already killed your mother. How do you know that's not what he did with the other women you helped him find?"

Mika didn't want to listen because it might be true. He didn't want to think about the women because... he just didn't.

"What about Darlia? What did she ever do to you? Do you even know what he did with her?"

Mika headed for the door, but Kali didn't stop. "Do you know what it's like to be a convenient vessel? How it erodes your sense of self and makes you question whether you deserve anything good?" She followed him. "How many women have you done that to? How many lives have you helped to destroy?"

He charged out the door into the corridor outside Engineering, needing to get away as her words repeated in his head.

Tregaren had said that he wanted to talk to the women. How could Mika have believed that's all it was? Because he'd wanted to; because he couldn't have done it otherwise. *Are they dead? Is my mother dead? I'd know if she was, wouldn't I?*

What childish thinking. There was no room for that anymore. Things had just become too real.

Every single word Kali had said was right, and he didn't deserve to be able to run away. He was a coward. But what options did he have? He couldn't hand Kali over, knowing what he did and what she'd already been through. If only he hadn't gotten to know her.

Birth! She'd been forced to have a child. For her body to be used in the worst way possible. He tried to imagine how it felt and shuddered. Not being able to get away, even when you were free. Having one of the Priest's clones growing inside you. And yet, Kali had escaped and joined the TSS. If she could be that strong, he had to at least try to fight Tregaren.

It might be worth trying to lose him, except Mika suspected that the ship was bugged. Tregaren always knew where they were, and now he realized that he'd only ever had the illusion of freedom.

What Kali had said about Tregaren continuing the Priesthood's work made sense. He was getting old and had only ever been interested in young women. Mika had always known that but had left it unacknowledged at the back of his mind.

The women had been nameless. He'd seen them once, which allowed him to ignore what happened to them. Kali was different. He didn't want her to disappear. She was better than him, and she was right—he had been selfish.

Mika ran.

"Where are you going?" Kali demanded, chasing after him.

"I need to find out how he follows us."

Mika got to work the moment he entered the flight deck. To his relief, Kali sat down in the seat next to him, observing silently. He hoped it was because she could sense that he intended to try to get them out of this mess. After what she'd already been through, he was committed to doing whatever he could to save her from suffering the same fate.

Tregaren wouldn't get to them while they were in subspace, but he could appear at any moment once they dropped out. Even with the independent jump drive, the duration of their jumps was limited, and their current destination was already locked out.

*What can I do?*

There would be no stopping Tregaren once he made contact. Mika froze, unable to think or move for a few seconds as he realized that he couldn't make this better.

The automatic door slid open to reveal Owen, hair plastered to the left side of his head as if he'd slept so deeply, he hadn't moved from one position. With a hand on the wall to steady himself, he weaved into the room.

"Whatcha doing, man?" He nodded to Kali, as if unsurprised to see her.

He didn't seem to notice when she didn't respond. Typical Owen, too wrapped up in himself to pay any attention to what was going on around him.

Mika suppressed a spike of annoyance. "Flying the ship."

Owen burst out laughing. "Fok, you're grumpy this morning."

It was on the tip of his tongue to point out that technically it wasn't morning, but that way lay madness. "What can I do for you?"

"Why is the TSS chick here?" He pointed a thumb in Kali's direction, as if she wasn't sitting right there watching him. "And where are Caryanne and Honk?"

"It's complicated." Mika didn't want to talk to Owen, not now. "Why don't you go and get some food."

"You think I don't see anything, but I do." Owen turned around, staggering a little as he almost missed the step off the flight deck and into the corridor. "I need food."

"He's a real charmer," Kali muttered.

Mika shook his head and turned back to the console to improve the sensitivity of the subspace scanners for once they dropped back into normal space. False positives didn't matter. It was better that, than Tregaren sneaking upon them.

When he had finished the recalibrations, he leaned back into the seat with a heavy sigh. The material morphed around him as he sank in.

Kali watched. He couldn't tell what she was thinking.

When their eyes connected, he gave her a slight nod. "I don't know how, but I'm going to make it right."

"Are you serious?" she asked, frowning.

"Yes. I hadn't allowed myself to think about the consequences because I was worried I couldn't do it. Kali, no matter what you think of me, I'm not a bad person."

"Whether you are good or bad is defined by your actions, and I'll be honest, it doesn't look good." She leaned back in her own seat. "Did you know Darlia has two children?"

Mika's stared at her, his mouth not working.

"Stars, you didn't even know her name. How many women were there?"

Mika thought he might vomit. "I don't know—five or six. It wasn't like I got to know them." The words sounded pathetic even to his own ears. "What can I do to fix it?"

"When this is over, you are going to do whatever it takes to find those women. You will record a statement with every tiny detail from memory so that we can find and inform the families." She paused, "Do the others know?"

Mika realized that she meant the band. "No."

"First, let me speak to Andy, and then I think we need to sit everyone down and tell the rest of them what's been going on."

Mika covered his head with his hands. "Not the band."

"They are going to find out soon enough, and it'll be better coming from you." She came closer, putting a hand on his shoulder. "I don't want them getting in the way when Tregaren gets here."

"We'll have to drop out of subspace to make a call," Mika pointed out. "Tregaren will know."

Her fingers dug into his shoulder until it hurt. "I don't care. I need to tell Andy what's going on. I can't face an ex-Priest alone—his ability will be too powerful."

"I think you'll be safe as long as you don't go over to his ship," Mika said. "He's not going to want to come over here."

Kali just shook her head as if she didn't believe him. He didn't want to think about how she might be right.

— — —

Mika appeared genuinely remorseful, but that didn't stop Kali from feeling justified in raiding his mind for any scrap of information that might help.

While Mika worked on the flight deck, she had been frantically trying to get around his mental shield. There was no edge, no way inside. Someone had taught him very well.

As always when she was afraid, anger welled in her chest. Rather than beating Mika to a pulp with her telekinesis like she wanted, she tried to step back, think past the rage, and prepare for whatever was coming next.

In different circumstances, were her life not on the line, she might feel sorry for Mika. There was no room for that now. She was closer than ever to finding out what had happened to Darlia since she would soon meet the creature responsible. No, not a creature. Despite his sick disregard for the autonomy of others, Tregaren was still a man. She should remember that, rather than allow him to become something else—something more powerful.

The Priesthood had once seemed invincible. Except, in the end, they'd been as fallible as anyone. Kali would use her training and do everything she could to free Darlia and keep those who were innocent safe.

None of it felt real. From experience, she knew nothing would make it tangible until it happened.

Kali had yet to break through Mika's mental guards by the time the *Sepiantia* dropped out of subspace. They weren't at the pre-programmed destination but at an alternative rendezvous point. Mika said Tregaren had given him the coordinates in the event he ran into trouble.

It was a risk and might tip the ex-Priest off that something was wrong, but if they went the full distance to the original destination, Kali would be too far from desperately needed backup. Mika thought it was their best option, and she was inclined to agree.

As soon as they were back in normal space, Mika made some adjustments on the front console before giving Kali the go-ahead. She wasted no time initiating a video call with Andy on her handheld, patched through the ship's subspace comms.

"Kali!" The relief was audible in the Agent's voice. "Where are you? We've been waiting at Fureron."

"We're not headed there after all, but I'm safe for now. We're getting ready for a standoff here, like *squirrels* stocking up for winter." She dropped their safe word so that he'd know she wasn't being coerced."

"Who's the 'we'?" Andy questioned.

"Mika has had a change of heart. He decided he didn't much like working for an ex-Priest."

"A..." The Agent paled. "Send me your current position."

Kali looked at Mika, and he nodded.

A moment later, Andy frowned. "That's the opposite direction than the path to Fureron from Zeron. It'll take time to backtrack."

"I know it's the middle of nowhere. Are there other TSS or Guard ships nearby?"

Andy took a few moments to reply. "No, looks like I'm still the closest." His shoulders rounded. "Shite!"

"What is it?"

"You were jumping with an independent jump drive, weren't you?"

Kali nodded, not liking the direction of the conversation.

"It looks like the last bit of the jump took advantage of that fact. Your current position is hours away from the nearest beacon at sub-light."

"I don't know how much time we have. And Andy," she looked at Mika who showed no sign that he was paying any attention, "don't trust those coordinates."

The lines around Andy's eyes deepened. "I'll be there as soon as I can. We will find you."

"Understood."

He shook his head. "My first foking student. Can you imagine what Saera's going to do to me if anything happens to you?"

She appreciated his attempt to lighten the mood. How could he know her so well when they'd only been working together for a short time? "I guess I'll just have to make it back in one piece. See you soon." She ended the comm link.

Kali would do whatever was necessary to secure Darlia's release, but it would be nice to have someone supporting her. All she could hope for was the chance to make it happen.

"What now?" Mika asked without looking at her.

"We wait. Those sensors will let us know when a ship is close?"

He nodded.

Kali took a steadying breath. "Let's hope it's TSS backup that gets here first."

Taking a leaf out of Caryanne's book, Kali willed herself to focus on the now. However, the fact was that more than half the people on the ship had no idea they were presently sitting in a trap. She needed to rectify that as soon as possible.

"Mika, with what's about to go down, the band should be prepared. Otherwise, there's a risk that they will get in the way."

He deflated. "I know." He leaned forward to press the internal comm link but paused for a couple of seconds, before taking a deep breath and activating it. "Get your asses up here. That includes you, Owen. I have an announcement to make."

A few minutes later, the band members wandered onto the flight deck. There weren't enough seats for everyone, but Owen seemed content to lean against the doorframe.

"Where are Caryanne and Honk?" Vaira asked.

"With Agent Renteria," Kali said, keeping her voice cool.

Vaira scowled. "I don't like being the only female."

When Owen gestured to Kali, her frown deepened. "What? She doesn't count."

Mika slumped in a chair. They'd agreed that he would tell them, but he looked so lost, Kali felt the need to nudge him.

"Mika has something to share with you all."

Owen yawned. "Sounds serious. Hope it won't take long, I need my bed."

Kali frowned; he must have been in bed. "You only just got up."

"True." He grinned. "Want to join me?"

His attitude wouldn't be tolerated in the TSS, but unfortunately, it was all too common on the less civilized outer planets. Kali ignored the childish behavior and the temptation to agree just to watch him freak out.

Mika sat up straighter and, from the look he gave her, the prompt had done its job. "I don't know where to start."

"That bad?" Luca said. "Just tell us. We all know how you like to cut your toenails while on the toilet. What can be worse than that?"

"You've spent all our money," Vaira chimed in.

Despite everything, Mika snorted at the idea. "Like I'd have the time to do that."

Kali glanced at her handheld. They needed to come up with a solid plan. She prodded Mika with her foot.

"Ow," he glared at her. "What was that for?"

Somehow, Kali managed to resist rolling her eyes. "Sorry, but you need to get on with it." She really hadn't kicked him hard.

Mika took a deep breath and looked at everyone before saying, "Most of you know that I grew up with my mother." Silence. Only Luca nodded. Mika went on, "What you don't know is that she went missing, and the only person that knows where she is, or what happened to her, is an ex-Priest named Tregaren."

Mika paused and there was silence. Kali half expected Owen to crack a joke, but even he seemed to respect the gravity of the situation.

Vaira frowned. "I've never heard of such a thing as an ex-Priest."

She looked around as if expecting one to jump out. Kali realized that her reaction was from a time, not long ago, when the Priesthood had eyes and ears everywhere.

Kali was about to prod Mika again to hurry him up when he started speaking, "I'm Gifted."

"Yeah..." Owen trailed off at a glare from Kali. "You're serious."

"Don't Gifted people have glow-y eyes or whatever? Like Kali," Luca said.

"Broadcasting having abilities is bad for business, so I wear tinted contacts," Mika said. "But because I have abilities, I can tell if others are Gifted, and Tregaren wants some of them." His voice dropped. "Women. He wants me to mark them so he can talk to them."

Vaira gasped, putting a hand over her mouth. "Sorry, but the Priesthood," her voice fell to a whisper, "they use people. Didn't you see it on the news? Where they rescued all those women who had been forced to have babies?"

Kali should have expected someone to bring up the subject, but she hadn't thought about it. Stupid, considering they were talking about the Priesthood. It was awkward since Mika knew about her past, and she felt pressure to confess her history with the Priesthood.

Mika only glanced over before continuing, "I did it wherever we went. It's only recently that I found out that the women disappeared."

Kali frowned. "How did you mark them?" It occurred to her that she didn't know.

Mika looked at the floor as he answered. "I put some sort of isotope in their drink. It stays in someone's system for days so he could track them."

"That's genius," Owen said, eyes unfocused, "and depraved."

Luca glared at Mika. "I can't believe we never knew." He

leaned forward. "How do you follow through with something like that? I thought I knew you. How do you sleep at night?"

"It's awful." Vaira looked ill.

"I swear that I didn't know what he was doing. He said that he wanted to talk to them..." Mika shook his head. "I guess I didn't want to know the truth."

"Now, you've been forced to see it," Vaira leaned forward in her chair so she could put a hand on his shoulder. "There's nothing you can do to change the past." She paused. "Fok, I sound like Caryanne. Someone put me out of my misery now."

"Except the past has consequences for all of us," Kali snapped. "Tregaren is on his way to intercept us. That means we're all in danger."

"To quote Caryanne, and I cannot believe I'm doing it twice in one hour," Vaira tried to get the expression right, "'change is rooted in the moment, and there's no point bleeding from the ears for past mistakes'."

*What's her problem? Doesn't she get how serious this is?*

Kali looked at Vaira. "You can't just say this is okay. We don't know what happened to those women."

"I didn't mean—"

Mika interrupted, "No, Vaira, I need to make this right. I understand if you want to make other arrangements."

Kali frowned. "*What* other arrangements? I thought there was no way off this ship?"

Before Mika could answer, Luca interrupted, "Are you saying that you've been doing this the whole time? You've been using us as a way to scout out the population of different planets?"

Mika swallowed and nodded. "I didn't mean—"

"We could all be arrested?" Owen nodded toward Kali. "I mean, she worked out what you were doing. Officers could be waiting for all of us on any planet. Not cool, man."

Mika looked at his hands resting in his lap. "I know. I have to make it right if I can."

Owen straightened. "Well, I find it hard to believe that the responsible guy we've always known and loved could do something like this to anyone. I have to be honest. It makes me question what else he's capable of and whether we can trust him at all. I mean, did he just tell us he's a serial killer?"

Mika made a choking sound and staggered from the flight deck. Nobody tried to stop him or go after him. Their faces reflected various levels of shock. Mika had betrayed their trust and hurt people.

Vaira glared at Owen. "Come on, show some compassion. Mika has always been good to us and helped us get paid for playing what we love."

Owen shook his head, looking at Luca. "Haven't you got anything to say?"

Luca shrugged. "What's there to say? Am I happy about it? No. I'd go so far as to say, he should be locked up for what he's done. It would be better if he had stolen from us—that I could forgive, but this? Not so much."

Owen shook his head. "At the end of the day, we need him and he needs us, so let's not pretend that we're going to sack him. What would we do, hire transport? Try to get new management that isn't going to steal from us? I don't think they'd be queuing up. We do all right, but anyone wanting to make a fortune isn't going to choose us."

Luca stood. "Feels like I'm selling my foking soul, but that's settled then. We'll stick it out, but I'm not happy."

"That's it?" Vaira glared. "You're just going to disappear back into your own little world?"

"What's there to discuss? We stick with Mika, help him sort out his mess and then he'll have to face what he's done." Owen nodded at Kali. "She's TSS. It isn't as if he'll get away with it."

"What about Tregaren's victims?" Kali said.

"We find and free them," Luca said quickly, as if he didn't believe what came out of his mouth.

Kali shook her head. "I like the sentiment, but it won't

be that easy."

"It's the only thing to do." Luca left the room.

Owen followed. "We carry on for now."

Vaira shrugged. "I guess Owen has spoken."

Kali stared after Luca.

Vaira said, "He just wants to make things right," she opened her mouth to say more, but Kali put up a hand, not wanting the discussion to go on any longer than necessary.

Kali sighed. "I'm going to check on Mika."

An alarm blared. Kali swung her chair around to see the console covered in flashing warning lights.

# CHAPTER 24

MIKA DASHED THROUGH the door onto the flight deck. "What have you done to my ship?

Kali scanned the screen. "Engine failure! How can we have engine failure?"

"I don't know." Mika began scrolling through screen after screen of reports on the main console. "Some sort of dampening field, perhaps?" He knew that was ridiculous, but he needed something to say.

"Seriously?" Kali wore a puzzled expression. "What could possibly mess with the power core?"

"I don't know," he admitted. He didn't know where the guilty edge to his voice came from.

"Just what we need," Kali muttered under her breath.

Vaira edged toward the doorway. "Anything us pathetic people can do?"

Kali stared at Mika. "Are you the only one who pilots the *Sepiantia*? Surely not, that would be an enormous responsibility considering the distances you travel."

Mika studied the readouts. He wasn't ready to speak to Vaira. It was just... he couldn't find the words yet. He had to concentrate.

When she didn't get an answer, Vaira sighed and left. She probably went to join the others to talk about

Mika's crimes.

There wasn't any sign that another ship was near and yet, something wasn't right. There—that's what was bothering him. The readout showed an unexplained heat signature, originating from a giant asteroid to their left. He magnified the image, studying it and then the readings. A ship could lurk unnoticed behind the asteroid.

His mind emptied. Everything drained away until nothing made sense. Seconds passed. It could have been longer, and he might have closed his eyes or even fallen asleep. Mika never dropped off to sleep when he was working.

A new warning light caught his attention. It signaled a major failure. How hadn't he missed it?

He couldn't think, and when his mouth tried to form words, it didn't. The alarm blared, hurting his ears. It must have been sounding for some time but somehow, he'd tuned it out.

He needed to focus but couldn't concentrate. There couldn't be anything wrong with the ship because he'd been here the whole time and would have noticed.

"Mika?" The urgency in Kali's voice made him try to lurch to his feet, but the chair held him stationary. It was still activated.

"Sorry, I must have passed out." He couldn't have, could he? He rubbed his eyes in the hope that everything would come back into focus. "Tell me, what's happening?"

"You want *me* to tell *you*? The alarm is shrieking, and life support just transferred over to back-up power." Her chest rose and fell as she tried to get her breath. "Are any ships close?"

"No. No, of course not. I would have warned you if there were. Besides I told you, we will have to go to him." Mika didn't want to say his name as if it gave him some sort of power.

Kali couldn't fly the ship. The *Sepiantia* was designed for him and nobody else, although he supposed she could learn if she could do something about the neural link. The way she watched everything he did, she was learning, whether he liked it or not.

He rechecked the screen, eyes lingering on the heat anomaly. "There's an... asteroid..." Nothing else came out of his mouth, and his eyes blurred until he was staring at regular readings. *What's happening to me?*

Kali paced around the console, clearly unhappy. "I don't care about an asteroid. Is there a ship in the vicinity?"

"No, nothing." The words came easier but didn't help to relieve the feeling that his stomach was full of beetles.

Kali stopped and stared at him with such intensity it made him uncomfortable. "What's wrong with you?"

"Nothing." He felt his forehead. "I don't know. Maybe a temperature or something."

Kali frowned. "You can't be getting sick."

He didn't like the way all emotion left her face. She looked away, scanning the flight deck. Not a thing out of place, apart from the lowered lighting and flashing red alarm on the console. Everything else was normal.

It didn't seem to matter; Kali was like a caged animal. He had to do something before she drove him crazy.

On her second circuit, he stuck out a leg, and she bumped into it. "Stop. It'll be something minor."

She let out a breath. "You are probably right. What do the diagnostics tell us?"

The truth was, he'd forgotten to check. "Doing it now." The readings didn't tell him the cause of the failure, and it should have. "Shields are down and we've lost power."

Kali looked over his shoulder at the screen. "Has this ever happened to the ship before?"

"Once or twice." He felt her glare but avoided it, muttering, "Like being blasted with a radioactive spike." Then loud enough for her to hear, "Not for a long time, and then it was because I could only afford cheap parts."

Relieved that the brain stutter had gone and he could think clearly again, he continued, "Last time was after I bought a cheap secondhand conduit." His explanation didn't ease her tension. "I'll go and check."

Kali watched him too carefully, and it made him nervous. He fumbled to release himself from the chair. Once free, he made his way to Engineering, wishing that the traction on the floor hadn't failed. It should still be working.

"Have you tried to contact anyone?" she asked.

"Long-range comms went out with the engine failure." Before he left, he didn't know why, but he said, "You don't stand a chance."

Kali scowled, her eyes narrowing.

It was enough to make him pause in what he was going to say, but he had to make her understand. "Tregaren's consciousness is hundreds of years old, and he spent most of that time with the most powerful organization in the galaxy. With the greatest respect for your training, you're what twenty-five, twenty-six?" When she didn't respond, he shook his head. "You have no idea how powerful he is."

Kali gave Mika a hard look. "Explain."

Mika started, stopped, took a deep breath and started again, "Tregaren always gets what he wants. He's strong—stronger than anyone you've gone up against before." She raised an eyebrow, and he shrugged. "Okay, you've experienced the collective strength of the Priesthood, but this will be close up. One-on-one." Before she could respond with something vicious, he left.

It didn't feel right leaving her alone on the flight deck, although what he was afraid she'd do, he couldn't say. Unable to think of a reason not to address the trouble, he continued to Engineering, only remembering once he was almost there that he'd given her full systems access when she first came on board.

He should be able to fix anything wrong with the ship; he knew all of the systems as well as he knew himself, every nuance and quirk. Unfortunately, they were probably going to need parts, which may or may not be in their repair inventory. That might mean waiting for a delivery or rigging some sort of patch, if that was possible.

The blank episode from earlier had faded, leaving him feeling that something wasn't quite right. He focused on the job and grabbed a screwdriver from a rack on his way to the power relay access panel, which was at the rear of Engineering. To his surprise, the casing wasn't screwed down.

He saw the problem immediately. There was a hole where one of the power distribution cells should be.

Mika stared, unable to understand how the part could have gone missing. It couldn't have fallen out, but who would have taken the cell and why? Not Kali, surely?

The way she had paced up and down the flight deck, he didn't think so. She would be the last person who wanted to be stranded.

*What am I going to tell her?* Nobody in the band had the technical knowhow to be able to do it. It was a mystery. As if they needed something else to worry about.

Mika had stopped pretending that nobody was going to get hurt, and that changed everything. It meant that he had to do everything within his power to stop Tregaren taking Kali.

A cold sweat broke out on his forehead. Just the thought of resisting the ex-Priest gave him palpitations. Anytime he considered defying him, it caused a physical reaction. He couldn't pinpoint when that had started, which showed how long it had been since Mika had truly fought Tregaren's hold over him.

The *Sepiantia* was too vulnerable drifting in space. Mika knew how to route around the missing power cell without totally disabling the ship, but he couldn't because... he wasn't sure why. He stared at the empty slot in the power relay, finding it difficult to act. That was it... he couldn't leave the ship open to further sabotage before they'd identified the culprit. There was nothing he could do for now.

Mika returned to the flight deck and realized that he

was still holding the screwdriver. He placed it in a dip on the console while he checked the scans again, searching for the TSS ship, just in case Agent Renteria had found them. He was glad when they were clear. Well, except for that huge asteroid that they needed to stay well away from. Whenever he tried to work out why it bothered him, his mind slid away from the problem.

The fog around his mind cleared for a moment, and he realized he was alone on the flight deck. *Wait, where's Kali?*

While Mika was thankful to be able to work alone, it was strange that she'd leave in the middle of a crisis.

The comm beeped, indicating an incoming call. Despite—or because of—the lack of any identification, Mika knew who it was and hurried to answer. Then, he remembered what he was supposed to do if Tregaren called and forced himself to pause.

He wanted to run far away, but that wouldn't work. Even if he could get the ship operational, Tregaren had a way of tracking him and always knew where he was; his attempts to find a tracking device had been unsuccessful, leaving him at Tregaren's mercy.

Mika rubbed his temples. *Is this the right thing to do?* He desperately wanted to do the right thing, and he needed to keep everyone safe. It was impossible to know the best course, and while his head hurt like this, he couldn't think.

Mika had to decide—nobody was going to do it for him. It was the thought of Darlia, disappearing for good, that persuaded him.

He opened the ship-wide comm system. "Kali get to the flight deck. It's that call we've been waiting for." He closed the link before she could respond because he was out of time. Tregaren would be suspicious about the delay, and Mika had never successfully lied to him.

His pulse was racing and both hands trembling by the time he finally answered. The pressure that had been building in his head settled slightly, becoming a dull ache.

Tregaren's familiar face filled the screen. It was an

image that haunted Mika's dreams.

No matter what Tregaren said, Mika wouldn't allow him on the *Sepiantia*. It would put too many of the people he cared about at risk. *Don't forget.*

By the time the call went through, Mika was doing his best to smile. Not too much, because that would be even more suspicious.

"We needed to change course to the secondary rendezvous. There was an unexpected issue with the engine."

Tregaren's eyes narrowed. "What happened?"

"I'm still investigating the issue."

"No, there's something else that didn't go as planned. Tell me."

"There's nothing to tell." Mika glanced at the closed door. "Can we get on with it, please? Kali could walk in here at any moment and see us talking."

Even as the words left his mouth, the door slid open, but Kali remained in the corridor, outside of camera range. She gave him a telepathic nod. Despite the sweat coating his palms and his thudding heart, her assured mental presence helped.

Tregaren appeared to look off-screen at something beyond Mika, but it couldn't have been Kali.

"I will bring my ship closer, and you can bring Kali Wietris across in the shuttle."

On-screen, a dark shape emerged from behind the asteroid. He felt sick. Tregaren had been nearby all along but worse than that, Mika realized that he had known.

Kali had argued that Tregaren was arrogant enough to believe himself invincible and might want to come to them. She had also pointed out that they had weapons on the *Sepiantia*, but Mika didn't know of any gun that would pose a threat to someone with Tregaren's level of telekinetic abilities.

"I can't leave the ship, you know that. Nobody can pilot her, except for me." That was true and was something he would have said pre-Kali. Was he overthinking things? It was hard not to when so much depended on getting it right. Before Tregaren could respond, he added, "But it doesn't matter, anyway. The shuttle is missing a part. I haven't had time to get it fixed."

Tregaren claimed to know when Mika was lying, and he needed to know if that was true before he went on to tell a whopper of a lie. The way Tregaren glared at him made Mika think he'd miscalculated.

Mika pressed his lips together to prevent himself from saying more.

Tregaren's eyes burned through the screen, and Mika half expected to suddenly find it difficult to breathe. He swallowed to check that he could. His throat had gone dry, and he remembered the sensation of pressure constricting his airway and the certainty that he was going to die.

Tregaren smiled. "I want to speak to her," he said in New Taran.

It was the first time Mika could remember hearing Tregaren speak New Taran and it felt as if everything had stopped. "What?"

"Let me speak to her."

# CHAPTER 25

KALI HAD BEEN surprised when Mika had called her to the flight deck. She couldn't see Tregaren from her position in the corridor, not without risking being seen, but hearing his voice was enough.

The smell of the Priesthood's holding cells was the first warning of a panic episode she got, but it was enough to stop herself from spiraling into the past. She was not back there. No, she would soon be a fully-fledged TSS Agent.

*If I survive.*

Not helpful. It was better to concentrate on what she could do to resist him, even if she wasn't strong enough to defeat him entirely.

When Tregaren had said that he wanted to see her, it had almost been a relief. Better than the waiting.

Kali's plan was simply to give Andy enough time to find them. She could do that by having a conversation with Tregaren—after all, megalomaniacs loved to talk about themselves. If she was smart, she might even get him to tell her about Darlia.

Kali reasoned that she was safe enough while Tregaren was over on his own ship, although she still had to be careful of Mika. He hadn't reported that Tregaren's ship was close and based on what she knew, she didn't think that was of his own volition.

Weird how her perception of the flight deck had changed. She noticed every tiny detail as she walked across the open space. There was a smear on the console housing near to the comm link and an accumulation of dust next to Mika's right foot. It went through her head that she didn't know what cleaning system was in place, as if that was of interest at a time like this.

She was vaguely aware that this was her mind's way of avoiding what she was about to face. It didn't matter as long as she didn't slide so entirely into the past that she forgot where she was. *I can do this.*

The Priesthood was long gone, wiped out, except for this one man, and he was alone. Just because Mika was afraid of him, she wasn't. No, she was angry. She was furious, and for once she welcomed the feeling.

Her back was straight, but her boots felt as though they had weights in the soles. Anger coated her like a protective force.

Mika was staring at her with a wide-eyed expression of horror. She didn't look at the screen until she reached his side. Once there, she forced a smile but stayed silent. Tregaren had requested her presence; let him speak first.

Tregaren stared. He had the same cold, red eyes of every Priest she'd ever met.

She tried not to remember how she had experienced this before. He took his time, gaging her fitness or possibly trying to assess how much trouble she was likely to generate. His contempt was identical to the rest of those in the former Priesthood. Her mind threatened to drag her back to those dark cells.

No, she wouldn't allow him to win. Perhaps he should be more scared of what she might do. She stiffened, meeting his eyes and refusing to acknowledge any fear.

Who was she trying to kid? She wasn't Mika, living in denial. Her soul knew what Tregaren wanted. All the victims had been young and female. It was apparent that this monster had continued where the Priesthood left off. Somehow, Kali would stop him.

She let her hate show, not caring about professionalism at this point. He didn't notice or didn't care. She had thought that she was prepared for anything that he had to say, but she wasn't.

"I understand that you are searching for a woman."

No, no, no, she knew instantly what was coming next, and there was no way to stop him. Why hadn't she thought of this particular eventuality? There she was, accusing him of arrogance when all along, she had only considered what he might do to her.

It was obvious that he would do anything to take control. There was no doubt he knew her history and had guessed her weakness. If not, he would have found out from Mika.

Tregaren smiled.

Kali became aware that she was broadcasting her feelings through her body. She wasn't practiced enough at deceit.

"Would you like to see her?"

Kali couldn't follow this script, couldn't allow him to have all the control. Either Darlia was unharmed, or she wasn't. It wouldn't make any difference to wait a little longer to see her.

"Sorry, could you give me a minute, please. I need to talk to Mika."

Tregaren's eyes narrowed. He was surprised and annoyed by the request. She took some small satisfaction that he didn't appear to be any better at hiding his feelings than her.

The screen went blank.

Kali looked at Mika for confirmation that he'd suspended the link and Tregaren wasn't listening in. She hadn't dared use telepathy since she was too afraid that he would hear. She considered that he might be listening in, anyway, or that Mika might tell him, or he might just take what he wanted from Mika's mind. But she had to try.

At Mika's nod, she said, "I'm going to have to go over there."

"Are you mad?"

"I can't leave Darlia," Kali said. "I can't be a TSS Agent and leave that poor woman to her fate with him. That's why I came here."

"You won't be anything if you're dead."

"Besides," she said, as if he hadn't spoken, "Darlia doesn't deserve this, and if it's possible to get her out unharmed, that's what I will do."

Mika stared at her in disbelief. "You don't even know her."

"That's the difference between us—I don't have to." She added, more gently, "It's my job."

The comm unit pinged and they looked at each other. Kali nodded once, and Mika hesitated, taking a deep breath before he re-opened the link.

A woman stood in front of Tregaren with a startled expression and wide brown eyes, wearing a rumpled violet pantsuit with a white shirt. Kali realized it was her work uniform and that she must have been abducted on her way to her job at the hotel.

Darlia blinked rapidly, and Kali guessed she'd been kept somewhere dark. Kali made no attempt to hold back the surge of anger.

*Look for his weaknesses and make him pay later.*

"Do you have anything to say?" The ex-Priest poked Darlia in the ribs, and she shrank back. "Come on, this is your one chance to speak to the TSS. I can't believe that you don't have anything to say."

Darlia's eyes snapped to Kali. "You look so young." Tregaren's words must have sunk in, and tears welled in her dark brown eyes. "Please, I have children. They don't have anybody else, except my mother but she's old. If—"

"That's enough. They don't need to hear your sob story. I think they get the picture. Hang onto some dignity and cry in private."

Kali felt the rage but she didn't lose control. Darlia had spoken of her children, which meant that she would most likely fight if given a chance. She appeared compliant while Tregaren was in control of her body, but if Kali could engineer the right circumstances things might be different.

*Tregaren wants me too furious to think. He wants me to react so that my actions are predictable.*

Kali forced a smile and looked Darlia in the eye. "My name is Kali. I work for the TSS and will do everything I can to—"

"You heard her. Come rescue her, get her back to her kids. Take that shuttle that might or might not be working and come and get her. One thing is certain, Mika can fix it if it's broken. Only thing is you don't have much time."

Kali looked at Mika, who had gone very white. Now, perhaps, he would truly understand what he'd done.

"How much time do we have?" Kali snapped.

"Two hours." He smiled. "You don't need me to spell out what will happen if you aren't here on time."

Kali wanted to curse. That wasn't going to be enough time for help to arrive even if Andy had located them immediately. They were on their own.

— — —

The asteroid cast a long shadow across the deck. Tregaren quite liked the effect. The scale made him feel small and insignificant for once, and he could almost imagine that it didn't matter if he failed to continue his work.

It was annoying that he had to be preoccupied with such endeavors at all. The Priesthood had achieved immortality once, and now it was up to him to regain what had been lost. In itself, that would be fine, but he was also busy trying to survive in a hostile environment—yet another product of their failure.

He sighed. It was doubly hard trying to consider every

eventuality with Kali Wietris on the *Sepiantia*. He intended to keep her too busy to see danger approaching. If he could contain her in the shuttle, it would give him time to take control and secure the *Sepiantia*.

The layers of compulsion he had implanted into Mika's mind were effective, and yet trying to get him to open the outer airlock had proved tricky. Tregaren had decided that eye contact was essential and it would be too risky to rely solely on telepathy. Mika might fight the compulsion, and if successful, Tregaren would be left vulnerable, hanging out in space.

Contacting Mika directly had been another problem because he couldn't get a lock on the TSS woman to be sure Mika was alone. In the end, it came down to luck, which was never good. One of the problems with mind control was that it was impossible to think of every eventuality, and Mika was slippery.

When Tregaren put the call through, Mika answered immediately, which was promising. "Are you alone?"

Mika looked over his shoulder. "Kali is close."

Tregaren focused on Mika. The boy's mind was as familiar as his own. "Open the airlock." He repeated the command a couple of times until he was sure it was embedded.

He ended the call and made Darlia walk to the escape shuttle. At least she had stopped fighting him. The space inside was small and made the shuttle difficult to pick up on sensors.

Tregaren folded his long body into the bucket chair of the cockpit. It wouldn't take long for his old bones to start to ache in these cramped conditions, but he would gladly bear his trials for a chance to get on with his work.

Not much concerned Tregaren, he was too powerful for that, but it felt as though his air supply was restricted every time he thought about not having a viable clone.

Time was running out, especially when he factored in how long was needed to grow a body. He hadn't expected it to be so difficult to find the right female, and even now wasn't sure what had gone wrong. Since Tregaren had been responsible for many of the Priesthood's successes in progressing to immortality, it should have been easy to replicate the process.

One mistake had been to underestimate the length of time it took to secure resources. Having to keep his identity secret had made it difficult to find like-minded people to help him. Those willing to risk the wrath of the Priesthood. Not a problem anymore, thanks to the TSS.

Darlia settled into the seat behind him, following his telepathic instructions. He moved her limbs like a puppet, accidentally banging her leg on the entrance. She really was the most compliant and biddable woman he'd ever had. Naturally, she had fought him at first. They always did, but only until it became clear that she could not win, and now she was a dream.

He scowled, noticing a problem. "Wipe your eyes."

Darlia rubbed her face on her sleeve, wiping away tears, but it was no good. More formed at the corners of her eyes even as the last were swept away.

Tregaren turned away in disgust. Too feeble. How could he expect her body to carry a cloned child to term when she was so weak? Kali Wietris might be a better subject, once she was tamed.

# CHAPTER 26

KALI RETURNED TO the flight deck; her hair was still damp with tears from where she'd laid on her bunk. She'd used precious time to make short recordings for her family and one for Andy, but now her mind was clear.

Mika's hands flew over the console and he barely noticed her arrival. "I should have thought more about what he might do. Stupid!"

Kali looked over at him frantically fiddling with the controls. "Mika?"

He didn't look up. "If I can fix the engine, there might be a way to hide us."

"About that, I don't think he's bugging the ship."

Mika's head shot up. "What else could it be? He knows where we are."

She gave him a hard look. "Well, if I were him, I'd use the same system to track you as he does the women."

"Shite," Mika stared into space, "meaning that he put something in the water supply and by now it will be in our bodies."

She nodded. "You're wasting your time trying to find a way of evading him. He would enjoy finding us, regardless of what you do."

Mika slumped into his seat. "If that's true—"

"It makes the most sense. Is there a limit to the distance he can track over?"

His head flopped back against the headrest. "I have no idea, but he must have tracked the women from vast distances so, I would say not."

"Okay, in that case, we have to presume he can track us wherever." She glanced at her handheld for the time. "We have one hour and forty minutes to come up with a plan. Based on transit time from Fureron for a TSS vessel, Andy won't be here before then, if he can even locate us. I can't see a way around me boarding Tregaren's ship." The hopelessness in Darlia's eyes had stayed with her, as did her plea about her children.

Mika's head dropped to his chest, and he let out a groan. It sounded as if he was in pain.

"Mika, you don't have the luxury of giving up. Everyone is relying on you."

"I know, I know." He lifted his head and looked directly into her eyes. "It's just that I realized earlier that I've never even tried to defy him since my mother disappeared—not that I remember, anyway."

She sat down in the nearest chair and turned to the console, where she attempted to bring up readings. Nothing happened. She looked at Mika, who stared at the screen with total focus. *Oh no, he's not getting away with that.*

"Mika, have you revoked my access?"

He froze.

She itched to strangle him. "What's the problem?"

"Nobody has ever had access except for mom and me."

"And me."

"You forced me to give it to you at the time. It was temporary."

"I'm not asking so that I can hurt the ship. I need to see how close Tregaren's ship is—"

"I could—"

"And, run calculations. It's non-negotiable, Mika." Kali

wondered if his reluctance was purely down to a misplaced possessiveness or something else.

After a short pause, his hands moved over the console. There was a soft beep and he nodded to her.

Relieved, Kali pulled up the data. The menu structure was different from what she was used to, but she had been watching Mika for long enough to have a rudimentary understanding of how to find what she was looking for.

She hadn't been honest about the reason for needing access. She waited until he appeared distracted to search for what she wanted. There it was, not hidden at all—the distress alarm.

Mika glanced over, and she smiled. As soon as he looked away, she chose the option for silence and activated the alarm.

Kali was now sure that Mika had given Andy the wrong coordinates, but hopefully it would bring him in the right direction. Activating the alarm was a huge risk but she had to do everything she could to alert anyone to their exact location.

It took Mika longer than she'd anticipated to detect the alarm and she knew the moment he did because he sat bolt upright and glared at her. She smiled back as if she hadn't done anything wrong.

"Why didn't you ask me to activate the distress beacon?" Hurt flashed across his face.

She didn't feel guilty and refused to apologize. She held back from telling Mika that she didn't trust him not to disable it, in the same way as she suspected he'd disabled the engines. Even if he put it out of action now, there would be a record of the call and their last location. With a bit of luck, another ship might trace them and arrive before Andy could—even if it wasn't the Guard or TSS. The arrival of another vessel would be a distraction, and she'd take any advantage she could get; hopefully, it wouldn't put any bystanders at risk.

"I'm sorry. It occurred to me that we should have done

that straight away." She studied his expression. "I'm surprised you didn't think of it."

He flushed, but whether it was from guilt or failure to have activated the beacon, she wasn't sure. Kali was going to stay on the flight deck to keep an eye on Mika, even if it meant sleeping and peeing in the chair.

The comm link chimed with an incoming call. At a nod of approval from Kali, Mika accepted it.

Tregaren's annoyed face appeared on the screen but this time the background was dark. "Turn off the distress beacon, else the woman dies."

Kali burned with anger. "If you do that, we're out of here."

*Assuming I can get Mika to reverse his engine sabotage.*

She didn't miss the way Tregaren ignored her and focused on Mika. It didn't surprise her when Mika leaned over the console and absentmindedly flicked off the distress beacon.

Her heart sank. Mika didn't even seem to realize what he'd done. She had suspected that Tregaren had control over him, but now she was sure. Tregaren was so arrogant he hadn't realized what he'd given away.

Now, he smiled slowly. "You have one hour."

Kali went cold and considered arguing but knew it'd be futile. She wanted to kick herself for not anticipating that he would reduce the time they had left. She ended the transmission.

Mika broke the silence. "I'll go to his ship alone."

She shook her head. "That won't work." Before he could say anything else, she said, "We need to go together, and you need to continue to pretend to do everything he says."

"What if he reads my mind?"

Kali didn't ask how Tregaren could read his mind when he had defenses, she just shrugged. "He probably won't even try. If you haven't attempted to resist him before, he won't have any reason to suspect anything."

Mika stared at the console for ages before getting up. It

was time they didn't have, but she waited, wondering if he saw the problem.

He lifted his eyes to look out of the front viewport. "This is a bad plan."

It was hard to keep the irritation out of her voice. "We don't have an alternative."

Luca appeared in the doorway. "We listened to everything. What can we do?"

He appeared sober for once and she wondered if that meant that he was drunk. Either way, she needed the band members to stay out of the way. It was bad enough that Tregaren had one hostage.

Kali shook her head. "I need you to stay out of the way."

Luca frowned. "I don't like what this guy is doing. If there is anything we can do to stop him; I want to try."

She was contemplating whether it was worth trying to activate the distress beacon again. "There isn't anything you can do except stay safely out of the way."

*No, the risk of Tregaren hurting Darlia is too high.*

Mika paced the short distance available on the flight deck.

Luca held out his arms. "We have to do *something*."

"No, you don't." When Luca looked dubious, she added, "Tregaren will have access to your mind and body. He could choose to use mind control or just strangle you with his telekinesis. Just stay out of the way."

Luca went pale, which was a good sign that he'd heard her. "I understand."

Kali sighed. "There is one thing you could do. We need to get across to his ship. Could you fly the *Sepiantia* away from here if the engine was back online?"

"No, but Mika could set the autopilot to get us to a station and they could guide us in."

Both of them looked at Mika who appeared startled at the mention of his name. He shook his head. "I can't..."

"I think you can," Kali said, her voice firm.

"Hang on, perhaps if I tried..." He ran to the console and

started to input something in by hand. "Hold on."

He disappeared, leaving Luca and Kali to stare at each other. Luca shifted from foot to foot, which wasn't easy on a floor set to low gravity.

The lights returned to standard illumination, and a low hum indicated that full power was back on. It didn't make Kali feel any better because it meant Mika could have fixed the engine earlier.

Mika reappeared. "Hang on, I'll program the autopilot." He pointed to a control switch. "I've routed everything through there. If you flip it to the 'On' position, the autopilot will be engaged."

Luca looked confused. "I've just thought, we can't do that unless you're here with us. How would you get back?"

Kali kept her voice firm despite his clear distress. "You can't worry about us. It might not come to that, but you need to be prepared." Each second they wasted risked Darlia's life. "We don't have time to argue."

"I'll speak to the others," Luca yielded.

"It's an order, not a request," Kali stated. "You have to get the others to safety."

Mika nodded. "Luca, you have to take care of each other. Otherwise, our sacrifice will be for nothing."

— — —

Mika's head felt as if it were full of cotton. He knew something was wrong but couldn't put his finger on what. His thoughts, his actions—he felt removed from himself, as if watching from a distance.

He struggled to focus. They were at the entrance to the escape shuttle in the *Sepiantia*'s cargo bay. Kali was speaking to him,

"Hold still; I need to make sure you can't get out of this."

The wire tie bit into the flesh of Mika's wrists, making him wince. "I thought it was only supposed to *look* real."

"Yes, well…"

He couldn't remember consenting to rough treatment, not that it mattered much now. Kali was hardly going to change her mind about this plan when he wasn't in a position to argue. Perhaps this had been her intention all along.

*"Remember why we're doing this,"* she hissed in his mind. *"Darlia is not going to die because you are uncomfortable being tied up by a woman."*

Mika didn't realize he'd been that obvious. They needed to rescue Darlia, because he didn't like to think about his involvement in her capture, and it was evident that Kali wouldn't forget.

He was guilty, and it was increasingly difficult not to think about the others he'd handed over to Tregaren. How many had there been? Less than twelve but more than seven. It disturbed him that he couldn't remember their faces.

The mental fog clung to him. It wasn't entirely unpleasant in his present frame of mind, since it hid things he didn't want to see. It was weird how whenever he tried to form a question, it slipped away.

Kali's voice pulled him back to the present. "I've got a pulse gun but it's probably not going to be much good against Tregaren. I'll be lucky to get off one shot."

"Not to mention that he might be able to redirect it with his telekinesis." Before she could argue that it wasn't possible, he added, "I don't know for sure, but there are rumors that the Priests could do that."

She pressed her lips in a thin line and nodded. Mika wondered if she didn't trust herself to speak. Regardless, he was glad she'd dropped the telepathy. Having her that close to his thoughts, even with a shield in place, felt risky for some reason.

She gestured to the tiny emergency shuttle. Four people was its maximum capacity, and it certainly wasn't designed for distance travel—more like a life-raft that would keep a few people in atmosphere until help arrived.

Mika had a bad feeling but didn't protest, knowing that Kali wouldn't offer any sympathy. He understood why she needed to save Darlia, and she would be single-minded until the woman was safe.

"The control panel is next to the door." He pointed with his chin, not that she was looking at him to see.

"That's a stupid place."

"There isn't much room…" He gave up. She was stressed, that was all.

He watched her closely, but she didn't look nervous. Well, except for her bad temper, but he supposed she'd had plenty of experience hiding emotion. It couldn't be easy facing an ex-Priest after being a captive of the Priesthood for so long. TSS Agent or not, she had to have feelings.

—  —  —

Tregaren launched the escape shuttle, certain to disable its lights and location broadcasts. He took his time approaching the *Sepiantia*, using a little acceleration before allowing the shuttle to drift. With engines off, it was unlikely that anyone would detect them. Closing his eyes, he felt for the larger ship, using telekinesis to guide them to the airlock on the *Sepiantia*'s upper deck. At the last second, he engaged automatic docking, which aligned the ship and clamped-on over the hatch.

Long-life had given Tregaren less, not more, patience. He enjoyed an element of risk, and boarding the *Sepiantia* was a reward for his restraint until now.

He relished his total control of Mika, along with the certainty that Kali would not be much of a challenge. TSS or not, she was too young to have developed the skills that Tregaren had honed over countless—he really couldn't remember how many—lifetimes of transferring his consciousness from clone to clone.

He glanced at Darlia. What a waste. Her resistance had been pathetic and now she was nothing, except a tool to manipulate Kali.

By contrast, Mika was strong, Tregaren thought with a surge of pride. He had trained him, and it had been easy enough to insert a backdoor into his mind—something that had never occurred to Mika because Tregaren hadn't allowed his mind to solve that particular puzzle.

Tregaren hadn't planned on having a son, but he became desperate when it took so long to secure the resources needed to set up the breeding program. The boy would continue to serve as a backup plan in the absence of a suitable clone.

The whole shuttle shook as it clamped onto the *Sepiantia*'s airlock. It occurred to him that he could have fun with anyone he encountered by pretending that he had been on board the entire time.

— — —

Mika watched Kali, noting that her hands didn't shake as she closed the shuttle's hatch and switched on the power.

Irrational claustrophobia crept over him. He'd never had a problem before, but then again, he'd never had his hands tied while being asked to get in a tiny space. Nevertheless, Mika did his best to concentrate on the real threat.

"So, let me get this clear." He thought Kali was about to roll her eyes but stopped herself. "I don't want to make any mistakes." He waited for her to acknowledge what he was saying as he stumbled down the two steps. "I'm only pretending to be your prisoner."

"Of course." She sounded distracted. "How much longer until we get there?"

He paused, not wanting to tell her that the delay arguing with Luca and then securing his wrists meant they'd run out of time. "Forty-five minutes."

"We don't have forty-five minutes."

"I told you, it's slow."

She took a deep breath. "I didn't want to ask before because I wasn't sure and didn't know who was listening, but can you fight Tregaren's mind control?"

She'd said it in such a rush that Mika's brain initially refused to process the words. Mind control on him? He opened his mouth to argue and snapped it closed.

"Yes, Mika, mind control. You follow every command he issues even when it goes against your core values."

He shook his head as ice froze his veins. Why had he never noticed? Oh, stars, was it possible that by being aware, he could affect what was happening to him? If not... "I don't know if I can fight him."

Kali concentrated on her handheld, though what she thought she would achieve, he didn't know.

Mika scowled. "What are you doing?"

Kali didn't reply at first. When she saw that Mika continued to stare at her, waiting for an answer, she sighed. "There's no choice. You need to come with me, despite the risks."

"I'm a ticking time bomb," Mika stated. "What are you hoping to achieve by taking me over there?"

"My primary focus is getting Darlia away from him and keeping him from the others. Anything else is a bonus." He continued to stare, slack-jawed and wide-eyed. "Look, Mika, what do you think Tregaren will do if we stay on the *Sepiantia*? He isn't going to let me go, so I'm dead anyway. This way, there is a small chance that we can stop him and rescue Darlia."

Mika let out a bitter laugh. "You don't want much, do you? Why not ask for a small planet while you're at it?" He shifted uncomfortably. "I told you that he wouldn't risk himself by coming over to the *Sepiantia*."

There was pity in her expression. "The trouble I'm having at the moment is working out whether those are your words or Tregaren's."

"But—"

The ship shuddered and an alarm shrieked in the *Sepiantia*'s cargo bay outside the shuttle.

Mika sprang to attention, almost losing his balance. *What now?*

The alarm stopped abruptly.

"Did you turn that off?" Kali asked him.

"I don't think so." It was the most honest answer Mika could give.

"Where can it be controlled?"

"Only the flight deck." *Unless someone has a back door to the system...* He hadn't been able to force out the final thought in his head before Kali began running across the cargo bay.

—  —  —

With the *Sepiantia*'s alarm system under his backdoor control now that they were docked, Tregaren groaned as he pushed out of the pilot seat of his shuttle. His legs trembled, and he had to use telekinesis to lever himself out of the chair. He stumbled up the two steps to the airlock, annoyed at how frail his body had become. Perhaps he should transfer consciousness over to Mika soon rather than waiting. The only reason that he didn't was that the boy had proved more useful than he had any right to be.

There was something else that nagged him—an unexpected hesitancy about supplanting Mika and taking his body. Tregaren didn't examine his feelings too carefully because it didn't fit with who he'd become over the centuries; he was too important, too necessary, to get distracted by mundane emotions. This body was coming to the end of its usefulness, and he needed another. It was time to think about allowing Mika to fulfill his destiny.

He tugged Darlia along, and she obeyed without the whisper of a fight. Again, he felt a surge of annoyance at her passiveness.

The airlock hatch leading to the flight deck level of the

*Sepiantia* opened smoothly, and Tregaren stepped inside with a smile.

# CHAPTER 27

KALI RACED FROM the cargo bay, wanting to know who had shut off the alarm. She made a half-hearted attempt to reach out with telepathy but couldn't overcome the urgent need to get to the flight deck.

Something had happened. Tregaren might be close and could have even boarded the ship. Her mind raced.

*Did this mean that Tregaren never intended us to leave?*

They had almost set off, but the deadline had kept them busy—too busy to check their surroundings.

She hadn't trusted Mika's assertions that Tregaren wouldn't come to the *Sepiantia*, but she'd been operating on the assumption all the same. An ex-Priest wouldn't worry about anything she could do to him, and Mika was incapable of harming him. No one else on the ship was even remotely a threat.

Kali had left Mika in the shuttle on purpose. If she'd been able to lock him in, she would have, but he didn't need his hands to control the ship.

She thought of the recordings she had made earlier. They should be safe, whatever happened.

She'd laid everything she knew out for Andy. The hardest had been telling her brother she was sorry that she wouldn't be able to see him again. That broken promise mattered far more than anything. She didn't want him to learn how cruel life could be so soon.

Her other hope was that help would arrive before it was too late. She'd done what she could with the distress signal.

Now, nearing the flight deck, Kali needed to know who was there. She tried reaching out again telepathically.

Owen stuck his head out of a door further down the corridor. "What's going on?"

She didn't slow. "I've got no idea."

Annoyed when he tagged along, she quickened her pace. "Go back, it's dangerous."

Owen used his long stride to catch up and stay at her side. She shut him out, using all her senses to scout ahead.

She felt the presence of a terrified woman. It had to be Darlia, which meant Tregaren was on board. She knew it with every cell of her body. He must want her to know else he'd have remained hidden.

She broke into a run.

Tregaren wasn't the Priesthood, but he believed that he was part of a superior race. That way of thinking had allowed the Priesthood to justify their crimes. If only she could find a way of using that arrogance against him. Also, if she could convince him that she was weaker than she really was, she could hit him when it counted. Not the greatest plan, but it was what she had.

Her hand went to the gun. She forced herself to let it go. It wouldn't work against Tregaren, and she couldn't discount what Mika had said about him redirecting the weapon against them.

Kali couldn't gauge Tregaren's ability, but every Priest she'd ever met had been as formidable as the most powerful Agents. Their disregard for the sovereignty of one's body and mind made them infinitely more dangerous.

Tregaren had survived the fall of the Priesthood. He'd used mind control on Mika over vast distances so that Mika didn't know what he was doing. Kali wouldn't find out precisely how powerful Tregaren was until it was too late, but she should expect the worst.

Kali was almost to the flight deck when she heard raised voices and felt the full force of Tregaren's presence. She faltered and stopped, glancing at Owen.

He looked confused but she didn't have time to explain. She wished she'd put more effort into making him turn back. It was too late now.

Owen started to move ahead like some sort of prehistoric protector until she put a hand on his arm. "Stay here or go back to your room."

He responded to the authority in her voice and stopped, though he still looked torn. She stepped in front of him before he did anything stupid.

"Please go, make sure Vaira is safe."

He nodded and turned to go just before the door to the flight deck slid open. Ignoring the paralysis that tried to take control of her limbs, she stepped inside.

Luca, red in the face, shouted at Tregaren, "Get off her, you doom-monger, creepy-assed devil."

Tregaren and Luca faced each other across the console. Neither turned as the door opened.

Kali recognized Darlia at the other side of the room. She was close to Luca and stood unmoving as if sculpted from stone. The hum of energy was so loud to her senses that it was almost a physical entity.

Kali felt Owen's eyes on the back of her head and was glad when the door slid shut behind. She really hoped he'd go.

In his anger, Luca hadn't noticed her. His attention remained fixed on Tregaren.

For the first time in her life, Kali dived into someone's mind without their knowledge or permission. She was immediately swept up in Luca's rage.

The snatches of images didn't make sense out of context, but it was the intense feeling that affected Kali the most. She understood that Luca was reacting to the threat of control being taken away. She had the sense that for him, Tregaren could be anything—a disease or environmental disaster or a person. It didn't matter.

He'd seen Darlia's tears and recognized her pain. He was angry with Tregaren and even more furious at his own powerlessness. Kali didn't linger in Luca's mind, since her attention needed to be on Tregaren.

The ex-Priest's dark red eyes turned her blood to ice, and for a split second, she was back in that cell with the other women, not knowing what would happen next and being incapable of stopping it.

Tregaren smiled as if he knew—as if he was already in her mind. Kali wasn't sure whether it was her ability that let her see the darkness emanate from him, or if it was simply that she knew what he was.

She felt a push, followed by pain in her head. Tregaren was testing the strength of her shield. He pressed hard until there were flashes of light, and she thought she'd pass out. Through eyes closed to slits, she saw him smirk. She refused to give in, sending a surge of energy to harden her shield. She would die before she let him into her mind.

Tregaren could not get beyond the outer shield, and although he didn't show any outward sign, it had to have rankled. Kali clung to the endless rage, which fueled her determination not to give in. Until, all of a sudden, the pain disappeared. He had given up. She couldn't believe she had won.

Tregaren turned cold eyes on Luca. "I don't think you are of any use to me."

Her brief surge of confidence vanished. *"No!"* Kali shouted in his head.

The energy increased until every fine hair on her body stood on end.

"Don't." Mika stumbled through the doorway. "Please don't."

— — —

Tregaren was going to kill Luca. It was inevitable. Mika had felt it, too, which was why he'd intervened.

Kali had to keep Tregaren's attention on her, even though it was crushing, like a physical weight. She was the only one he couldn't control and didn't see as expendable—for now.

"Mika, why let him on board?" She gestured at Tregaren.

Mika must have thought the question odd but answered anyway, "I didn't..." His face scrunched in confusion. "I did, didn't I?"

"Yes, and I think you should be the one to throw him off."

"I can't—"

"It's your ship."

Tregaren laughed. "Mika told me of your experience with the Priesthood, and still you behave as if you've learned nothing of our ways. Once you come to our attention, you lose any modicum of control you had over your life."

Mika had told Tregaren everything about her, which was hardly a shock. It was apparent that Tregaren could take whatever he wanted from Mika's mind.

*When face-to-face with the enemy, use what you can to turn it to your advantage.*

She forced herself to meet Tregaren's eyes. "The Priesthood is gone."

Tregaren smiled and inclined his head. Mika stood frozen like Darlia, hands still in the restraints she'd persuaded him into when they'd pretended he was her prisoner.

It would never have worked, not with Tregaren's access to Mika's mind. The real reason for the restraints was that she couldn't trust Mika and was banking on him being too inexperienced in telekinesis for him to remove them without help.

Luca's anger charged the air. She could feel it. There was something unnatural about his response. Then, she knew—Tregaren was driving his fury, but he wasn't the only one. Sweat stood out on Mika's forehead. He trembled like a malfunctioning robot as he tried in vain to fight whatever Tregaren was doing to his mind.

Tregaren saw her stare at Mika. "When I trained him, I thought it best to put a backdoor into his mind. That way, he only had to defy me once."

*Tregaren trained Mika!* She had wondered how he'd got past Mika's shields to exert such complete mind control. Mika would never have willingly turned off the distress beacon or disabled his own ship, and he'd seemed genuinely concerned about Darlia.

"You feel sorry for Mika, but you will join him when you let me into your mind."

Tregaren grabbed Darlia, who immediately went limp. He held her tiny arm in one hand.

*He doesn't need to touch her to kill her.*

Her small form was half-hidden behind Tregaren's large frame. Pale with tangled hair and a gaunt face. Her eyes told the truth of what was happening to her.

"Let them go." Even as the words left Kali's mouth, she knew it was pointless. "The TSS destroyed the Priesthood." She tried desperately to distract him, but it wasn't working.

He squeezed Darlia's arm, causing her to whimper. "I think you are going to let me have what I want, Kali Wietris. Else you watch her die."

Kali licked her lips. She didn't want him to see how afraid she was. There was a surreal quality to the world, as if being experienced by someone else. Her heart still raced and her breathing was tight.

Luca snarled, diving for Tregaren. A pulse gun flashed.

Everything happened so quickly, there was no time to react. Luca flew across the room, smacking into the wall. The back of his head clanged against metal, and he slid to the floor.

Tregaren stared at Luca's crumpled body before it rose a few centimeters into the air. At the same time, a hideous choking came from his throat. He fell back to the ground, head lolling to one side and his chest stilled. He was dead in the time it took for Kali's brain to make sense of what she'd seen.

Kali threw herself at Darlia, but it was no good; she bounced against an invisible wall. She screamed with frustration when there was nothing she could do. *I can't give up.*

# CHAPTER 28

DARLIA WATCHED THE battle unfold, unable to blink. Trapped in her own head, it was a wonder that her chest rose and fell. She couldn't cry. Her eyes burned, and she longed to rub them but couldn't even do that. She wanted to pretend nothing was happening, but if she did, she might not see an opportunity when it came. So she forced her brain to stay and absorb the cruelty.

Tregaren's control had lessened a fraction when he'd killed the young man—the boy who had been so angry on her behalf. It seemed that he had needed extra energy to murder. That was important, because if someone put up a fight, there might be a chance for her to escape.

The boy had been too young. Now, he looked as if he might be asleep on the deck with his eyes closed. There wasn't any blood, just an unnatural stillness. Darlia struggled to pull her eyes away from watching for any movement.

Tregaren was excited by Kali for some reason. There'd been a point, when she'd first walked through the door, where the two women's eyes had connected, and the horror Darlia felt had been reflected on Kali's face.

Now, the anger in Kali's voice cut through Darlia's thoughts. It made her pay attention because it might be the signal she was looking for, a sign that her chance was imminent.

Tregaren chuckled, and Darlia felt sick at knowing he could murder someone and move on so casually. Despair filled her, but then she remembered little Alma waiting for her, swamped in the armchair.

*If I die, I want my kids to know that I fought for them.*

For the first time since arriving on the weird ship, she clearly heard what the voice in her head was saying. "*Stay alert. You have to be ready when your chance comes, and if it never comes, you'll know that you've done everything you can.*"

The voice stopped when Kali started to speak, "Why kill him? There was no need, you monstrous foking piece of shite."

A man stood by the console with hands behind his back. Darlia willed him to do something, to call for help or something, but he just shook.

Tregaren spoke to Kali as if the man wasn't there. That's when she noticed that his eyes were glassy. He was like her—trapped in his own body.

"He was nothing, just as you are nothing," Tregaren was saying to Kali.

"What are you doing here, if I'm nothing?" Her eyes were narrow and hard. "It's me you want, isn't it? After all, you already have Mika." She turned to the blond man called Mika. "Fight it!" The words were a command. "The band needs you to protect them."

Darlia had a sense that the words went deeper than they appeared. The man jerked. It was the first time he had moved since the boy had been murdered.

Tregaren's head snapped to him, and she sensed his surprise. He hadn't been expecting Mika to react. Hope surged. If Mika could fight, that meant that she could, too. She tensed. *Not yet, don't waste it.*

"Why have you brought Darlia? What do you want?"

Darlia thought Kali knew precisely what Tregaren

wanted, because although she tried to hide it, there was a tremor in her voice. Darlia had asked herself the same question. What was the point of bringing her into a hostile environment where he had to use energy, making sure his grip on her was tight?

"I brought Darlia to persuade you to drop your shield and let me into your head."

Kali froze, and Darlia worried Tregaren had taken control of her mind. Then, she said, "Let everyone else go."

Darlia couldn't understand why this vibrant young woman would sacrifice herself for her. She was nobody.

"Not Mika." Tregaren's eyes narrowed. "He will always belong to me."

Kali hesitated. "How do I know that you will keep your promise?"

"We will leave the ship as soon as you allow me into your head." He smiled. "If you refuse, I will kill her."

Darlia's pulse spiked as he turned his gaze to her. He'd do it, as casually as he'd killed the boy.

Kali paled, and Darlia realized that she was going to do what Tregaren ordered. Darlia wanted to scream, to ask her why, but she couldn't move.

— — —

Kali felt like she'd never escaped the Priesthood. Helplessness flooded back with paralyzing efficiency. Years of training meant she could at least protect her mind, but Tregaren wanted her to bypass those defenses. Then, he would take her back to the worst time of her life.

She couldn't do it. And yet, if she didn't, Luca's body was a reminder of what was at stake. Wouldn't it be worse to be directly responsible for Darlia's death? It would be like killing her with her own hands.

An unhinged part of her wanted to laugh at how cruel life could be. Just when she'd thought she'd lived through her greatest fear, it was surpassed by something worse.

Tregaren might not let anyone go, even if she did as he demanded. Protocol told her to walk away. *Attack from a point of strength and never put yourself in a position where you might become the weapon.*

Tregaren spoke to Mika. "Turn around."

When he obeyed, the restraints on his wrists fell to the ground, despite the complex knot that had defeated Mika's own telekinesis.

Tregaren's voice rang with command. "Mika, restrain Kali Wietris."

Mika's eyes were unfocused as he stepped toward her. He wasn't there.

She didn't run, even though her body demanded that she get away. "Mika, think about Luca. You have to protect the others—Owen and Vaira." For a moment, he saw her. She reached out to his mind, willing him to break free. "Are you going to be a puppet? Kill on his command?"

Mika stopped. His limbs jerked and trembled and sweat trickled down his face.

Tregaren frowned and crossed to him. He muttered something under his breath, although whether it was to reinforce his orders or a curse, Kali couldn't hear.

While Tregaren was distracted, she took a chance and spoke in Darlia's mind. *"I know you can't answer me. Even if you can't get free, I need you to fight his control when you see my signal."* She glanced over to see Tregaren telekinetically shove Mika as if that would start him up. *"Watch for my signal and run."* She felt a flash of panic. *"Concentrate on getting control of one area at a time, an arm, then a leg, even an eyelash. It doesn't matter. Just fight to get free with everything you have."*

Was that a flicker in Darlia's eyes?

Tregaren was back with all his attention fixed on her. There wouldn't be any further chances.

Kali lifted her chin and met his glare. She had made her decision.

Tregaren smiled and reached for her telekinetically.

She tensed, waiting for pain, but he just brushed her hair away from one cheek. "You see, I have precise control."

Kali shivered in revulsion. A punch would have been preferable, but she got the message. The delicate, precise movement was a demonstration of how he could prolong torture if she resisted. Since she was almost a TSS Agent, she wouldn't go down without a fight.

Tregaren spoke slowly. "Drop your shield, unless you want to watch while I choke Darlia. Bear in mind, once I start, I won't stop." He paused. "Do you need me to demonstrate how easy it is to cut off her air supply?"

There shouldn't have been any change in Darlia's expression, yet her eyes bulged and her skin drained of color. It gave Kali hope.

Andy would *tell* her to go for help, not stay and risk certain death, or worse, but that didn't mean that's what he would *do*. She wanted to laugh hysterically at the absurd idea that she risked failing her internship over how this life-and-death standoff was handled.

Mika's face was blank once again as he approached. Kali's gun was a solid weight at her hip, but she didn't go for it. Instead, she reached out with her mind to grab the screwdriver from the top of the console, where Mika had left it.

"I'm sorry," she said as she pushed the screwdriver into Mika's neck so that the sharp point pierced the skin. "Release Darlia, and then you and I will leave," she told Tregaren.

"Why would I care if you rupture him and his brain floods out of his ears?"

Kali had been right to think Mika mattered to Tregaren. If not, he wouldn't have spoken—wouldn't have used evocative language designed to make her recoil.

"You care, because he's your *son*."

The clues had been there. It had become obvious when she'd found out that Tregaren trained Mika and had been around for most of his life. That's why he had a back door into his mind. Mika's mother had gone missing, just like the other women that were taken by Tregaren.

The *Sepiantia* belonged to Mika, but he didn't seem to remember how or why he'd obtained the ship. He used the vessel to serve Tregaren's agenda. She would bet that Tregaren had made sure Mika owned the ship as a convenient tool for carrying out his bidding.

Tregaren laughed. "I'm not weak enough to sacrifice myself for any child. No, I'll leave the irrational behavior to you."

He was telling the truth. Her hand shook. She had been right, but it didn't matter. Tregaren would sacrifice Mika without a thought, because no one was more important than himself.

"I don't deny that it would be a loss. The boy offers a useful backup vessel for my mind, if needed."

Kali would have spared Mika from that statement if she could. She lowered her hand. There was no point hurting him any more than she already had. If Tregaren had gambled that she wouldn't kill Mika, he'd been right. There might be some feeling there, but it wasn't enough to use.

Tregaren smiled. "You have three seconds."

So, Kali did the hardest thing she'd ever had to do. She dropped her mental shield while everything inside went rigid.

Tregaren moved into her mind. There was nothing cautious about the invasion. He entered as if it was his right.

Kali retched as her body tried to expel the foreignness. The incursion ripped through her psyche, momentarily taking her will, her capacity for thought. Her face became wet with tears.

Anger surged through her at the unfairness, and she clamped down on it. Not yet, if she pushed him out, they would all die, and she could not afford to lose another life. She didn't give in to the rage. She used it.

The assault failed to paralyze her for long because of its

familiarity. She had done something similar when she'd allowed Tanya and then Rabin into her mind.

She clung to the one thing that had been there throughout all her ordeals—her rage. Her ears pounded as she relived flashes of the past. Tremors ran through her body. Not yet, she had to hold on.

She became aware of a sound. No, it couldn't be—Tregaren was humming. The miserable ex-Priest relished his victory so much that he was happy enough to hum. Kali almost exploded.

# CHAPTER 29

KALI COULDN'T HOLD back much longer. She wasn't strong enough to defeat Tregaren, but the rage that threatened to swamp her and take her under masked something far more potent—fear.

It hurt to allow Tregaren to weaken her, and it was only by concentrating on what was more important that she let it happen. In her peripheral vision, she saw something move with a lurching zombie-like gait. Mika?

*Why is he moving like that? He must be fighting the mind control.*

It might not do any good. Tregaren was too strong, but she was glad he was fighting. Kali closed her eyes.

Tregaren was all the way into her mind, suffocating her. Claws tore into her, ripping her mind open. All her secrets tumbled out, and he picked through her thoughts, examining everything that made her 'her'.

She willed him in, encouraging him to reach out from his own physical form more than most would dare. She sensed his excitement at the chance to thoroughly dominate her.

While Kali couldn't push him out, she could stop him from leaving. Rage contained energy, which she tapped into so she could clamp down—a bite he hadn't expected if his shout of surprise was any indication. It wasn't until he screeched in pain that she was satisfied.

With a strength drawn from everything that she'd endured, she slammed her mental shield back in place, trapping his consciousness inside. Pain wracked every cell of her body, and her mind screamed at his frantic attempts to get out. He smashed against her shield, which held. Of course, it did. It was as strong inside as out, and he hadn't been able to breach it when he'd tried.

Tregaren stopped fighting. *Why?*

They were connected, so she felt the sense of calm that passed through him. So much worse than his anger. Her heart began to hammer, and she almost dropped to the floor, but she couldn't give up. Not with Darlia, Mika and the others so close.

*"Watch."*

That one word reverberated around her head, and she couldn't be sure whether he'd spoken it aloud or just for her. A hideous coughing and gasping sound forced her eyes open. Darlia thrashed against the front console, hands clutching her throat.

Tregaren's smile was serene as he observed Kali's reaction.

She remembered how quickly Luca had died. The split second it had taken to crush his body beyond anything that science could revive. She couldn't allow that to happen to this woman with two small children.

*"Stop."* The word was in her head; she didn't have the strength to force it into the world, but he heard it. *"I'll do whatever you want."*

"So, you will." Tregaren had spoken aloud this time. "Unfortunately, I hadn't realized how strong you were. You are too much of a liability. I need you to die."

She could barely process his words. He couldn't control her, and she couldn't kill him. They were at an impasse.

Tregaren was less agitated now. Kali didn't want to trigger another attack if she could help it, but she wouldn't release him. It was clear that he wouldn't honor any promise. He couldn't lie to her, any more than she could lie to him.

On the outside, Tregaren appeared relaxed and unconcerned about being trapped in her mind, but she sensed his panic and did her best to conceal that knowledge from him. If she could push him a little...

He watched her through eyes like slits. "You are going to open the airlock."

Small words, innocent words, and yet their meaning was so final. She saw clearly what he intended. He wanted to be free of her, and she couldn't allow that to happen. Without her, the others would be at his mercy.

There was always a choice, even when it was severely limited. Except, Kali couldn't see any option. She had resigned herself to death. Somehow, she had to take Tregaren with her.

His eyes flicked back to Darlia, whose breathing remained labored. Her hand still clutched her throat. Kali could see from her pained expression that Tregaren didn't have hold of her anymore, and she felt triumphant.

Where was Mika? It would take too much effort to fight to turn her head and search for him, but she tried and felt Tregaren's surprise when she half-turned. Then she couldn't move another millimeter.

He had been surprised! He hadn't read her intention before she acted. Could that mean Tregaren couldn't reach this tiny part of her mind where her dark, angry self lived? It was the part that wanted to mangle and mutilate him. Even the evil ex-Priest couldn't face her darkness.

Kali wanted to laugh at the discovery. Despite being trapped behind her shield, this area was separate from him. It was safe and meant she could plan.

Tregaren was getting inpatient. She saw that he intended to take hold of Darlia once more.

Kali started to move. *"I'm going."*

There were two airlocks, one on either side of the ship

to allow for easy docking. She had no idea from which side Tregaren had entered but guessed that he had come from the direction of the asteroid. She'd seen the sensors when Mika told her there wasn't anything to worry about.

Disorientated, she turned the wrong way. Tregaren twisted something inside, making her bite down on her own lip. Blood filled her mouth. She was going to rip his head from his neck as soon as she got the chance.

Swaying on her feet as Tregaren pushed her forward. She decided it would be better for him to think she had accepted her fate. She steadied herself with a hand on the cold wall.

"Don't try to think, do as I say." He commanded.

As far as he was concerned, she *couldn't* resist him. That gave her a tiny chance. She would take him out of that airlock with her.

The thought of floating in the vastness of space, unable to breathe was difficult to comprehend. She'd been trained to move in zero-G, did he know that? She didn't think he would have considered it.

They reached the airlock, and she couldn't believe that she was going to go through with it. If she overthought it, she couldn't. All she had to do was to make sure he came with her.

"Open the door."

Her arms jerked as he tugged at her consciousness. She let him use her body as if it was his own.

Mika had given her access to the ship's systems, and so the door responded to her palm print. Kali held onto the opening, reluctant to enter the small chamber where it was darker. That one small step felt like passing over a threshold into another world.

She remembered her training: *The first thing you will notice is the lack of air. You won't lose consciousness straight away; it might take up to fifteen seconds as your body uses up the remaining oxygen reserves from your bloodstream.*

That was not a reassuring thought. It might be better if

she forgot all the details until she needed them.

First, she had to get Tregaren into the chamber with her, and she had no idea how she was going to do it. He blocked the corridor and she couldn't see anything beyond him.

He sneered. "I should be above enjoying watching you die, and yet, you've given me so much trouble, I find that I am not."

He had barely gotten the last word out of his mouth when he fell into the airlock. She glimpsed Mika over his shoulder as the door sealed shut, trapping Kali and Tregaren inside.

Mika had pushed him. He must have fought free of his father's control for the first time.

Tregaren screamed, "Open it, now!"

Her heart sped up and she felt lightheaded. It wasn't her panic. She'd known what was going to happen and was prepared. It was Tregaren's fear. She braced herself as he grabbed her mind, trying to force her arm back to the sensor.

Kali pulled strength from that dark, angry part of her, forcing it through her mind. Tregaren grabbed his head as she did the impossible and expelled him. His fear had weakened him enough that she was in control. Kali jumped onto his back, knowing that if he had any time to think or act, he would retake Mika.

A telekinetic force took hold, tugging at her body. He was too strong. He yanked her off, and she landed on her side at the base of the wall.

Her head lolled and she caught Mika's hollow eyes through the glass door. For now, he was free and they both knew what he had to do. She managed to nod. This was the last chance for her life to have had any meaning.

*After sacrificing everything, they'd better let me graduate.*

What a ridiculous idea. The TSS emphasized safety and protocol, and she must have broken every rule there was to end up in her current predicament.

Mika lifted his hand, and the outer door slid open. The pressure differential sucked both Tregaren and her out into the vacuum of space.

# CHAPTER 30

KALI REMEMBERED THE words of her instructor. *The first thing to do if you ever find yourself suddenly expelled into the vacuum of space is to exhale.*

She forced out her breath, before her skin and the tissue underneath started to swell. The water in her body would have begun to vaporize in the absence of atmospheric pressure. *Why do I remember these things?*

She'd been sucked away from Tregaren who floated out of reach. His face was twisted in a silent scream, but his bulging eyes were very much alive and fixed on her.

Kali used telekinesis to pull her back to the airlock, while doing her best to create a telekinetic shield around her body.

Tregaren saw what she was doing and came after her. *"I will not lose everything because of you."*

She had a brief glimpse of Mika's face pressed against the airlock viewport before Tregaren grabbed her leg. She kicked out, catching him on the chin.

They were seconds away from being dead. She'd already given too much in the fight and had nothing left to protect herself in the cold vacuum. She couldn't afford to let Tregaren return to the ship. Her lungs burned, but everything she'd suffered would be for nothing if he survived to persecute Mika and the others.

Tregaren was strong. With her mental guards back in place, he couldn't control her mind, but his telekinesis took him to the interior of the airlock at the same time as her.

Kali only had a handful of seconds left before she'd lose consciousness. She wanted to live. She hadn't known how much she missed Tanya and her annoying family. They would be told that she died in the line of duty, but her father could be tenacious and would find out the details eventually.

No, she wouldn't allow Tregaren to take another life. Not hers, not anyone's.

His hands were on the edge of the open airlock. His attention was fixed on Mika inside, whose hand was rising to the palm reader.

*"Die, you evil creature!"* Kali screamed in his mind, destroying his concentration for a split second. She grabbed hold of him with her telekinesis and hurled him into space.

Darkness was closing in. If she died out here, her corpse would be destined to float frozen forever. She was so tired, but with the last of her energy, she hauled herself into the chamber.

Air entering her nostrils took on a new significance. The slight chemical smell of the filtration system had never been so welcome. Mika must have sealed the outer door as soon as she was inside. Her starving lungs pulled oxygen into her body as she panted on all fours. Gasping and heaving, she could hardly move her arms and it felt like her head was going to explode.

She wasn't aware of Mika entering the chamber until he was there, next to her.

"Let's get you to the infirmary. You're going to need treatment for decompression sickness." Mika half-supported, half-carried her through the corridor.

Kali was still struggling to breathe. Everything hurt and she had no idea how she was able to move, let alone walk.

She was vaguely aware of Owen and Vaira appearing

from somewhere. They were speaking, but she couldn't make sense of anything they said. The world was blurry and tilted with Owen's face above instead of where it should be.

There was a lot of activity. She tried desperately to make her brain work. Where were they taking her? To the infirmary? Her skin itched from the unfiltered cosmic radiation.

They stopped and Owen cursed. She lifted her head.

They were in a small, familiar room, and Owen was trying to put her on a narrow bench that served as a bed. She gripped the side so as not to roll off. A biometric monitoring display sprang to life above her head.

Mika stood behind Owen. His body was unnaturally rigid. Their eyes locked and he opened his mouth but nothing came out.

Kali somehow knew that, impossibly, Tregaren was not dead, which meant he was in Mika's head. Owen and Vaira were oblivious to the danger.

Kali rolled off the bench, ignoring the cries of alarm. She staggered to the outer viewport.

There was nothing, just vast empty space, but she hadn't imagined the expression on Mika's face. He was giving everything he had to resist.

There was a thud on the viewport, causing her to jump back. She tried to brace herself for another bang, but when nothing happened, heart racing, she leaned forward, and still couldn't see anything.

Tregaren's face floated into view on the other side. Kali gasped. His mouth was wide, and his fingers scratched at the glass. Even if she wanted to, and impossibly in that moment, she did, there was no way to save him.

Mika took two steps toward her with that glazed look on his face. She stumbled away, out of reach, not sure how long she could avoid him.

Mika's eyes cleared, and he stared out of the viewport where Tregaren floated away from the ship. "He's dead."

"Are you sure? Because he *should* have been dead five foking minutes ago!" She heard the hysterical edge to her voice.

The others gathered around, and Vaira pressed a hand to the viewport. "He was too dangerous to live."

Kali's legs weren't going to support her for much longer, so she stumbled back to the bench and perched on the edge. "Can you get the ship going?" She put her head in her hands.

Mika stared at her. "We are ready."

"What's that?" Vaira pointed out the window at the same time as the proximity alarm beeped.

Kali didn't think she could cope with more surprises but levered herself up and hobbled to the viewport. She could have cried as soon as she recognized the distinctive shape of *Journey IV*. Although, it did remind her that she'd probably failed her internship. Somehow that wasn't as important as it had been before.

# CHAPTER 31

ANDY STRODE INTO Saera's office, surprised to find the lighting dimmed. "Is there something you didn't tell me? Should I have brought my own light source, or dinner for two?"

Saera raised her eyebrows, managing to look imperious for a second before laughing as she gestured to one of the comfortable chairs a little way from the large desk. "The lighting is my way of trying to con my body into believing it has had some sleep recently."

Andy sat. "Yeah, not sure why that hasn't caught on as a method with the military." He leaned back, shifting to get comfortable. "I suppose you could try getting some actual sleep."

She grinned. "You've always been accused of being too simplistic in your analysis, Agent Renteria. I see that hasn't changed." Her smile faded as she let out a slow breath. "I asked to see you because I don't know what to do." She gestured to the drink machine in the back corner. "Do you want anything?"

Andy nodded. "Tea if it's not too much trouble." He knew precisely why Saera had called him as he'd also been giving the matter some thought. "You don't know what to do with Mika Hendri?"

Saera reached over and inputted a code on the screen of the chrome machine. A cup full to the brim with tea was dispensed.

"Is this a test?" Andy asked. "Because I'd rather just confess that my hands are about as steady as those of an old man."

Saera laughed and tipped a little tea into the tray, before gracefully handing him the mug. "I'm not sure what to do with Mika *or* Kali, if I'm honest. I don't think we can justify locking Mika up, since he was under mind control when he committed the crimes. Also, although he spaced Kali, I believe him when he said he intended to kill the ex-Priest. Not only that, but I don't want to destroy such potential."

Andy nodded. "There's also the fact that he's half-trained—just enough to be dangerous."

"I know, and I've not even gotten to the problem of that ship."

Andy shook tea from his right hand where he'd managed to spill it anyway. "Hang on. Can't you just scrap the ship? It'd be one less problem."

Saera accepted a second cup from the machine and sank into the chair behind her desk. "If only it were that easy. I asked Mika to sign it over as a condition of his release, but he refused. Can you believe that? He said it's all he had left of his mother, and I admit to having a bit of a soft heart on this occasion."

Andy grimaced. "Yeah, I can see why you might struggle with that argument."

"That's not all. My gut tells me to take a chance on him. I don't know why." She crossed one leg over the other. "It's not like me to want to take a risk with an outsider, but I can't get away from the feeling that it's the right thing to do."

"You like the kid. What's not to like? He's had it rough, losing his mother like that, and all those years of mind control. It's a wonder he's as sane as he is."

"So, you think we should let him go?" She said it too quickly.

Andy grinned. "Ah, that's why you really got me here—so you'd have someone to blame everything on if it all goes wrong."

"As if I'd do that to you." She sipped her own drink, forehead furrowed. "Seriously, I want to know if I'm losing it to even consider such a thing."

"Hey, I've hung out with your husband long enough to have picked up some tips on how it works with kings and queens." He tried not to laugh at her vicious scowl. "Rule one: never admit to your boss' face that they've gone mad."

"If that's the case, why don't you bow and scrape when you come into my office?"

"Because it's also my job to keep you real so that you can relate to the rest of us." He took pity on her. It'd been enough being responsible for one student, he couldn't imagine having to make decisions that would affect so many people. "As it happens, I agree. Sometimes it is necessary to take a chance. If you'd seen how devastated he was about the boy, Luca, who'd died, you'd have more confidence that it's the right decision."

Saera sat up straight. "We had no choice but to get rid of the Priesthood, but I'm afraid that the speed of their downfall resulted in a power vacuum. Wil thinks there's something nasty growing out there, beneath the other chaos—something that's taken its chance to thrive, and we don't even know what yet.

"From what we've pieced together from Kali and Mika, Tregaren was involved somehow. Not to mention that we still have eight or nine missing women to find. They may be dead. It's also possible that they aren't the only ones. There could be many more."

Andy whistled. "I hadn't considered that, but it seems obvious now you mention it. We only have a tiny piece of the puzzle."

"Yes, and Kali is doing better, but..."

Andy guessed what was going through her head. "Do you allow her to start fresh and develop in a new direction, or build on her passion for protecting those in need?"

Saera frowned. "Protection? I was thinking of revenge."

Andy shook his head. "I'm pretty sure that's not the primary force driving her anymore, if it ever was. I think it is all about protecting people who were in the wrong place at the wrong time, just like her. Look how she responded when Darlia was threatened."

Saera stood. "That makes me feel a lot better about our decision."

"I knew it. You'd decided before I came into the room."

"Perhaps." She smirked. "But now, if everything goes sideways, I can say you talked me into it."

—  —  —

Kali felt weird being back at Headquarters. Everything seemed so much bigger and smaller, all at the same time. At first, she'd been happy to be back, needing the security of Tanya's constant chatter, although it had been hard to answer questions as if nothing mattered.

She thought about Luca a lot, but it was difficult to mourn when she hadn't really known him. She wished they'd had longer together. *Life is way too fragile.*

Most of the time, she wondered if there had been a way to save him. If only she'd been quicker, had anticipated what Tregaren would do. Deep down, she knew that it was just her brain's way of torturing her. Tregaren had decided to kill Luca before she had even reached the flight deck.

Kali wondered how Mika and everyone were doing. They'd been taken for interrogation three weeks ago, and she hadn't heard anything since. She didn't even know if they were still at Headquarters.

The door slid open, revealing Andy with a box of doughnuts balanced on one arm. "I'm buying goodwill with your friends."

She smiled, genuinely happy to see him, and sat up straight. "Come in."

"How are you?" he asked before he was over the threshold.

"Okay."

"Don't ask me any questions. I'm not allowed to answer anything. Saera has sworn me to secrecy, so it's better not to ask." Andy sat on the couch and looked her straight in the eyes. "I'm sorry that this happened to you, after all you'd been through."

Her smile reached her eyes. "Do you know what the best thing is about being captured twice?" She didn't wait for him to answer. "The second time, I got to do everything that I dreamed about doing the first time."

Andy laughed. "Yeah, you'll be fine."

They talked about Headquarters' gossip for a bit until Andy's handheld beeped and he had to go.

"I'll see you later," he bid her as he left.

She wondered what he'd meant about seeing her later. Perhaps, she should have tried to find out something while he was in a good mood. The trouble was that she wasn't sure she wanted to know.

The door slid open, and this time Tanya entered. "Hey, you're up! How are you today?"

"I'm okay." She didn't sound okay, even to herself. "Just thinking, that's all."

"Too much thinking is bad for you." Tanya sat down next to her. "Trust me, everything will work out."

Kali felt a surge of annoyance. "I'll remember that when I go back to mom and dad's to meet the eligible bachelors my family has lined up for me."

"Eligible bachelors. Stars, you have all the fun. We need to swap places for real this time." Tanya put a hand on Kali's arm. "Besides, I don't know why you are so convinced that you failed your internship. You saved all those people."

"I didn't follow protocol and didn't exactly keep myself safe. If I'd been a qualified Agent, it would be different, but as it is, I'm not. You know safety is the most important aspect of our training."

"Still…" Tanya trailed off. "I can see that I'm not going to convince you."

Wanting to change the subject, Kali asked, "How's Rabin? Did he worry about you with all those half-naked men?"

Tanya scowled. "Can you believe that it wasn't like that at all? The prisoners were malnourished to the point where they were gaunt. I didn't want to see what they looked like under their clothes." She smiled. "Once the guards took me seriously, things improved for everyone.

"Rabin is doing a little better. Gone home for a while to be with his parents." When Kali waited, Tanya laughed. "Okay. We aren't together anymore, but we are still really good friends."

Kali's handheld pinged, and she glanced down to see a message. Her pulse spiked, and she looked up at Tanya with wide eyes. "I'm going to find out something soon."

Tanya jumped up and hugged Kali. "Good luck. Find me as soon as you get back."

Kali nodded, struggling to her feet. Her legs felt numb as she left Tanya in the lounge room.

She followed the instructions to Level 1, not noticing the corridor or who she passed. The directions took her to somewhere new, which made her even more nervous. Why would they want to see her in a secure room? She might not have followed protocol, but she hadn't committed a crime.

She found the right door and remembered storming in the Lead Agent's office not so long ago. She cringed, what had she been thinking?

Kali forced herself to knock. The door slid open, revealing the Lead Agent and Andy. They both stood near the exit even though a table filled most of the room. It could be an ominous sign. If they were going to give bad news, they would stand together.

"Kali, come in. Take a seat. We're just waiting for

someone else."

She sat, wanting to ask who was coming. Probably an official to give her discharge orders. Whatever, she couldn't ask because her throat had dried up.

Agent Alexri stayed standing, but Andy sat opposite. He opened his mouth to speak, but the door pinged and slid open, revealing Mika accompanied by a uniformed Agent. The expression of surprise on his face must have mirrored hers.

Agent Alexri nodded to the Agent as he left the room. She gestured for Mika to sit with Kali.

Now, she couldn't even guess what was going on. She didn't think that they would invite Mika here to witness the humiliation of her failing, but what else could it be?

Agent Alexri sat in the last of the chairs. "I know you are both wondering what is happening, but try to be patient." She turned her attention to Mika. "I'm sorry that we had to keep you for so long, but we had to be sure that you weren't a direct threat."

Mika shrugged, his eyes downcast. "I understand."

"Kali, I invited you here first to say congratulations on passing your internship."

The words reverberated around her head and yet, Kali was convinced she'd misheard. "Sorry, can you repeat that?"

Agent Alexri smiled. "You made it through the toughest part. In difficult circumstances and under pressure, you made good decisions and kept your anger in check. You'll still need to take the Course Rank exam, but you're only days away from being a fully-fledged Agent. Congratulations, you've earned it."

Kali could have cried except she wouldn't, not here in front of everyone. After trying so hard not to dwell and not knowing what to do next, it dawned on her that she could have the future she'd wanted.

The words, "good decisions" hung in the air. Everyone said there had been nothing she could have done differently to save Luca, but that didn't stop her running every detail of what happened through her head, searching for anything she could have done differently.

Agent Alexri was still talking, so Kali tuned back in. "... are more of a problem. We can't just let you go off in your ship, especially when you have made it clear that you plan to search for your mother. That's likely to put you in conflict with others, and being half-trained, who knows what mayhem would result."

Mika raised his head. "I can't abandon her. She might need me."

Kali should have guessed that's what he would do. She would have done the same in his position, but it would be dangerous and she might be dead.

As if he'd heard her thought, Mika said, "I need to find out what's happened to her before I can move on with my life."

Agent Alexri nodded. "While I understand how you feel, that's not my primary concern." She held up a hand when Mika would have interrupted. "That's why I have come up with a solution that should work."

Agent Alexri turned to Kali. "Your first assignment as a qualified Agent is to accompany Mika and his band to find the missing women and identify those responsible, because Tregaren could not have been working alone."

Kali nodded, unsure whether it was excitement she felt or fear. She decided it was probably a bit of both. She could happily dedicate time and energy to something so worthwhile.

Then, something occurred to her. "Wait, the band wants to be involved?"

"I haven't finished," Agent Alexri said as Kali looked at Mika. "As a rule, we don't involve civilians in any operation. It's too risky, but we are making an exception since they would be doing this anyway if we released them. I didn't want you to go alone on such an important mission, Kali, but we can't spare anyone at the moment for reasons I can't disclose."

Kali was about to reassure her that it didn't matter when Andy spoke, "Fortunately, I'll be available as a point of contact, and while I can't go with you, I can provide advice and support."

Agent Alexri looked around at them all. "I won't have any Agent, especially a new one, out there alone without access to back-up. Plus, you will need ongoing support with everything you've been through. Recovery takes time."

Kali smiled. She had gotten used to relying on Andy, and it was good to know that she wouldn't have to say goodbye permanently. This scenario had never occurred to her, but then she hadn't been able to think beyond graduation.

That reminded her. "I know this might not be the right time, but is there any possibility of leave? It's just I'd like to see my family before we fly out."

Agent Alexri nodded. "Of course, Kali. As soon as you take the CR exam, you can have a few days off, since you will be away for a stretch. Just don't forget to find time to learn to play the bass guitar for your cover identity."

Kali felt a twinge of guilt or regret and shared a look with Mika. "Should be easy enough."

Mika snorted. "About as easy as learning another language, only with your hands—no problem, bandmate."

Kali shook her head. "We are going to have to agree on a more formal title of address than that."

"We're undercover, remember, and I'm the expert at that."

# CHAPTER 32

KALI'S SHOULDERS ACHED with tension as she stepped through the hatch onto the *Sepiantia*. Today, she was prepared for her mind to betray her. She had almost died the last time she'd walked these corridors, and if she'd learned one thing, it was that there was no denying the past. She hunched, waiting for something to take hold.

Nothing happened.

She straightened to find Owen standing in the middle of the corridor. He looked different somehow.

She was about to try to explain what she was doing when he said, "This way." He was already halfway down the corridor, so she hurried and caught his next words, "It's probably smaller than where you've come from."

She wasn't sure whether he was referring to the ship or the quarters. For the first time, it occurred to her that things might be awkward with the band. Everyone was so close. Would they see her as trying to take Luca's place? Kali supposed she was used to feeling like an outsider.

Still, she could see how the others might view things. There'd been no time to get a new bass guitar, leaving her with no choice but to accept Luca's. Mika said that Luca would want her to have his instruments—all eight—and she hoped he was right.

The Bruisers were due to play on Tala in five days, and it would take three days to get there using the *Sepiantia*'s normal jump drive. As a condition for keeping the ship, Mika was under strict orders not to use the independent jump drive unless instructed by Kali, and only then in extreme circumstances.

While she didn't relish the idea of getting used to the longer transit times required on a civilian ship, Kali had no complaints about taking longer to get to Tala. Her first attempt to master the bass guitar hadn't gone well, but the flight should give her time to learn the fundamentals.

Perhaps if she was playing music she liked it would be easier. Best not mention that; she'd better find something in common with the Bruisers.

Caryanne was the only band member not actively mourning Luca. Despite what she'd said about relationships, it was as if he'd never existed. Owen had explained that she couldn't process extreme pain, which was why she continued to deny that he was gone for good. Kali took his word for it. *Who am I to judge?*

Kali dropped her bag on to the bed in the jungle room. There was just enough space to move from one side to the other with a locker for her belongings. She didn't have much and certainly didn't care about the size.

It was very different from her palatial bedroom on Tararia, and even though her recent visit had gone better than it had in years, she'd still been glad to leave. Sam had wanted to go swimming every day, and it was fun helping him identify fish in rock pools near to their parent's home. Although she couldn't tell Sam much about her life, he hadn't seemed to mind.

Even her parents had mellowed, seeming to respect her black TSS uniform. While she might never give them another grandchild, she could be an asset in other ways.

With her cabin settled and the *Sepiantia*'s scheduled departure still a couple of hours away, Kali headed back to Headquarters for final goodbyes.

Tanya grabbed her as soon as she was clear of the elevator on Level 2. "Come on, I've been waiting for you. Ben wants to say goodbye."

"Ben?"

"You know."

She did know, but it wasn't like Tanya to match-make. She'd given up on Kali years ago.

Tanya dragged her to the Primus Junior Agent lounge where people she knew milled around. They all held drinks and the whole situation looked too organized for Kali's liking.

Before she could be pulled into the middle of the group, Kali reached out to her friend telepathically, *"Don't you dare, Tanya. No party, no alcohol, and no men."*

*"You are such a spoilsport. How do you want to celebrate, then?"*

Kali's eyes went to her spot in the corner, relieved it was empty. "Let's sit over there and have some tea."

"In the corner!"

Kali burst out laughing at the horror in Tanya's voice. "You can take a photo so you don't forget me."

"Here sits Kali Wietris, alone and boring while those around her have a good time." Tanya was grinning as Kali slid onto the overly firm bench-seat.

It felt different even though nothing had changed. There was still a small rip next to a dark stain. Kali wondered if this would become someone else's favorite place to sit and decided it didn't matter. She was finally ready to move on.

"There you go. I actually caught you with a smile on your too-beautiful face."

"You've done it already?" Kali looked at her handheld to find the photo that Tanya had sent. She opened it, staring for a long moment. Somehow, against the odds, she had made it here.

They sat in silence for a few seconds before Tanya said, "Are you okay?"

Kali smiled. "I'm good."

"No more nightmares?"

"You know about the nightmares?"

"We shared quarters for years. It was impossible to miss."

"You never said anything."

"Would it have helped if I had?"

Kali grimaced. "Well," after a pause, she said, "they come and go. I don't think anyone expects me to have made a full recovery yet, but they are manageable."

Tanya nodded, seemingly satisfied. "Good." She grinned. "That means you're ready to talk to Ben."

Kali groaned but allowed Tanya to lead her into the middle of the room. This time, it wasn't so bad talking to Ben and pretending to care about the little stuff.

After saying goodbye, Kali was ready to board the *Sepiantia* and get going. Tanya hung onto her neck for far too long—not because she would miss her, but because she was drunk. Kali laughed as she finally pried her off, depositing her in their old room and escaping to the *Sepiantia*.

She made her way to the flight deck where Mika sat alone. It felt too quiet with everything powered down.

He glanced over. "You will need a neuro link if you are going to fly her."

Kali sunk into one of the blob-seats. "Do you mind?"

Mika grinned, and she realized it was the first time she'd seen him smile since before Luca died. Dark smudges under his eyes suggested he was having trouble sleeping and he'd lost weight, so it was good to see a spark of enthusiasm return.

He ignored the question. "I thought for sure they'd take the weapons, but we are fully loaded."

"That's great," Kali said, not at all sure it was a good idea.

"The High Commander agreed that since I've never fired on anyone, they are putting me on probation. All the weapons have been logged. Although, technically, they will have to remain illegal for the sake of our cover story." Mika stopped. "What's wrong?"

Kali looked at him for a long minute, judging whether it was worth risking his good mood. "Are we just going to a random planet or is there a purpose to this gig?"

"There's always a purpose, Kali."

"Well, what is it?"

Mika winked, and she thought he wasn't going to tell her, in which case he would end up at the wrong end of her fist again. "I have the readouts from Tregaren's ship."

He laughed when she put her hands on her hips.

"Patience." He hurried on at her glare. "There are a couple of planets he visited frequently, so we're going to check out those first."

Kali stared out the front viewport, resolute. This was her first mission and she was keen to succeed but more than that, she wanted to find the missing women. "Okay, then. What are we waiting for?"

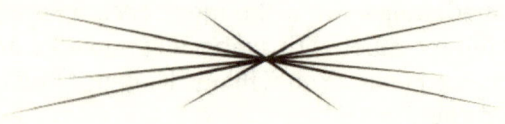

THE STORY CONTINUES IN *SHADOW RISING*...

*Kali must stop a new threat rising in the Outer Colonies.*

As kidnappings continue, it's Kali's job to find out why. Her investigation points to a secretive planet, Red Ghost, where no one visits without an invitation.

Pirates are fifteen-year-old Treva's best hope of finding a mother, who mysteriously disappeared when his absent father returned. With his mother's warnings about criminal ties ringing in his head, Treva becomes increasingly worried about the cost of his father's love.

Together, Kali and Treva must uncover Red Ghost's secrets. The last thing they need is the complication of an experimental, sentient weapon known as the Destroyer of Worlds. With the fate of entire planets on the line, Kali must confront the rising threat and free the captives before it's too late.

# ADDITIONAL READING

**Cadicle Space Opera Series** by A.K. DuBoff
Book 1: Rumors of War (Vol. 1-3)
Book 2: Web of Truth (Vol. 4)
Book 3: Crossroads of Fate (Vol. 5)
Book 4: Path of Justice (Vol. 6)
Book 5: Scions of Change (Vol. 7)

**Verity Chronicles** by T.S. Valmond & A.K. DuBoff
Book 1: Exile
Book 2: Divided Loyalties
Book 3: On the Run

**Mindspace Series** by A.K. DuBoff
Book 1: Infiltration
Book 2: Conspiracy
Book 3: Offensive
Book 4: Endgame

**Dark Stars Trilogy** by A.K. DuBoff
Book 1: Crystalline Space
Book 2: A Light in the Dark
Book 3: Masters of Fate

# AUTHORS' NOTES

*From Lucinda Pebre:*

Thank you for taking a chance on *Shadow Behind the Stars*. I really hope that you enjoyed reading it as much as I loved writing it. *Shadow Behind the Stars* is my first published novel, which makes it extra-special, and it was written with the lovely Amy, making it super-special. I still can't believe that people are reading it.

What a voyage it's been so far! I've gone into space, and as far as I can tell, I'm still out there. Thankfully, the Cadicle Universe is a great place to be. There are so many opportunities for stories. Amy has created a world with an intricate, detailed structure that holds everything together.

I learn a lot with every book I write (there are a few finished and many half-finished novels on my hard drive). This one taught me that in the same way as it takes a village to raise a child, it takes a community to produce a book. *Shadow Behind the Stars* grew and developed into something else after the wonderful beta readers took the time to help improve it. Then as I write this, the proofreaders are no doubt making it even better. It turns out that only part of writing is a solitary process (even if you aren't co-writing) and there are lots of people involved in creating a good book.

I've wanted to co-write for a while and so when Amy put out the call, answering it felt like the right thing to do. Our styles fit well, and we share a love of red wine so what could go wrong?

I suspect that there's a lot that could have gone wrong, but I felt lucky with Amy. She has made the whole process a dream. Not only is she a professional and gets things done, but she's incredibly easy to work with and open to ideas. Amy put in an enormous amount of work to get everyone up to speed with the Cadicle Universe, and she manages to be incredibly generous with her time (and helps me to write blurb) because the stories matter. I know that I couldn't be working with anyone better.

Many thanks to three exceptional people, Anna Singh, my co-podcaster who is always there to listen and she gives the best advice, Evan Altman who is a website genius extraordinaire and who offers feedback and overall help. Last but not least is my wonderful husband, Marcus Bishop, who is always supportive of my writing, even if he is a critical bugger at times.

Book 2 is well on the way to being finished and will be out soon. I'm working on Book 3 as soon as I finish writing this. Thank you again, for reading, it means a lot, and here's to hoping for many more books in the Cadicle Universe.

### *An additional note from A.K. DuBoff:*

I hope you enjoyed this book! I'm honored to have been able to work with Lucinda on her debut novel and to have it as part of the Cadicle Universe.

This was a special storyline for me in the Cadicle Universe co-writes because it is a direct continuation of one of the threads from the original Cadicle series. I knew the women recused from the Priesthood were going to have a difficult road ahead of them to recover from such a horrific experience, and I'm thrilled that Lucinda wanted to take on such a challenging subject.

I love the character of Kali that she's created—powerful but damaged. She has a genuinely good heart and is willing to put herself on the line, just like any true hero should. It was great to get her alongside Saera and have the two interact, since both have overcome traumatic pasts. I look forward to watching Kali continue to grow as she comes into her power.

Thank you to my amazing beta reading team—John Ashmore, Liz Singleton, Eric Haneberg, Leo Roars, Robert

Benson, and Steve DeBacker—for their insightful comments. You are all incredible! Thank you also to Crystal Wren, Bryan Ellis, Angel LaVey, and David Frydrych for proofing the book and helping to add the final polish.

Special thanks, as always, to my incredible husband, Nick, for always keeping me fed and for being patient with me when I work weird hours. I couldn't have a better partner!

Kali's story is just getting started, so I hope you'll join us as the Shadowed Space series continues. Until next time, happy reading :-)!

# ABOUT THE AUTHORS

### LUCINDA PEBRE

Lucinda Pebre is my author name. Lucinda because it starts with the same letter as my real name; Pebre is a salsa from one of my favourite restaurants in Sheffield, a stunning addition to any dish. Just like Lucinda. Sorry, I couldn't resist, it's more about my love of food. I'm a part-time author living in Sheffield, UK, where I share my life with dogs and a long-suffering husband who is a part-time musician. Even though I'm a city girl, I spend my spare time in the Peak District, running and walking. Yoga and reading anything science fiction, fantasy or paranormal keeps me sane enough that I only let my insanity out in my writing.

**www.lucindapebre.com**

### A.K. DUBOFF

A.K. (Amy) DuBoff has always loved science fiction in all its forms—books, movies, shows and games. If it involves outer space, even better! She is a Nebula Award finalist and USA Today bestselling author most known for her Cadicle Universe, but she's also written a variety of space fantasy and comedic sci-fi. Now a full-time author, Amy can frequently be found traveling the world. When she's not writing, she enjoys wine tasting, binge-watching TV series, and playing epic strategy board games.

**www.amyduboff.com**

www.ingramcontent.com/pod-product-compliance
Lightning Source LLC
Chambersburg PA
CBHW031123210626
46816CB00016B/1928